PRAISE FOR THE #LOVESTRUCK NOVELS

"Wilson has mastered the art of creating a romance that manages to be both sexy and sweet, and her novel's skillfully drawn characters, deliciously snarky sense of humor, and vividly evoked music-business settings add up to a supremely satisfying love story that will be music to romance readers' ears."

—*Booklist* (starred review) on *#Moonstruck*

"Making excellent use of sassy banter, hilarious texts, and a breezy style, Wilson's energetic story brims with sexual tension and takes readers on a musical road trip that will leave them smiling. Perfect as well for YA and new adult collections."

—*Library Journal* on *#Moonstruck*

"*#Starstruck* is oh so funny! Sariah Wilson created an entertaining story with great banter that I didn't want to put down. Ms. Wilson provided a diverse cast of characters in their friends and family. Fans of *Sweet Cheeks* by K. Bromberg and Ruthie Knox will enjoy *#Starstruck*."

—*Harlequin Junkie* (4.5 stars) on *#Starstruck*

THE
FriEND
ZONE

THE Fri♡END ZONE

SARIAH WILSON

Montlake
Romance

Published by Montlake Romance, Seattle

www.apub.com

Amazon, the Amazon logo, and Montlake Romance are trademarks of Amazon.com, Inc., or its affiliates.

ISBN-13: 9781542094290
ISBN-10: 1542094291

Cover design by Erin Dameron Hill

Cover photography by Wander Aguiar

Printed in the United States of America

For the real Stan Oakley, who is not a coach
but changed my family's lives in a profound way.

CHAPTER ONE

LOGAN

"Are you Logan Hunt?"

I'd climbed off the bus after a three-day ride from Texas wanting nothing more than a shower and a nap. Instead I got the woman standing in front of me. Young. Cute. Fresh-faced. She had dirty-blonde hair pulled up in a ponytail, zero makeup on, and dark-brown eyes. I also noticed her clothes. An oversize hoodie, big sweatpants. Almost like she had something to hide.

I briefly wondered if this was part of the college's pitch to get me to stay. It wouldn't have been the first school to offer me an unlimited stream of coeds if I accepted its offer to play football. It didn't seem like Coach Oakley's style, but when in Rome, right? I'd never pass up the opportunity to flirt with a cute girl.

"That's me," I told her with a wink. "And you are?"

"Jess."

"Just Jess?"

"Just Jess," she repeated. "I'm here to drive you to EOL."

By "EOL" she meant Edwin O'Leary College. It was a junior college. Unlike Texas F&T, the Division I school I'd played at before they threw me out.

One of my elementary school teachers had been very religious, and a phrase of hers flashed through my mind: *How the mighty have fallen.* From a full ride and a starting position at one of the best universities in the country to playing for a community college nobody had ever heard of.

Coach Stan Oakley was the reason I was here in Seattle. He had been the head coach at the University of Texas, Amarillo, which was one of the winningest teams in college football history. In fact, the only team that had won more national championships was Alabama. Back when I'd graduated from high school, I'd wanted nothing more than to play for Coach Oakley and Amarillo.

So when he'd shown up at my construction job site, offering me the chance to finally play for him, it had been like all my teenage dreams come true. I'd half expected a bikini-clad Miss Texas driving my new Camaro equipped with booming subwoofers to show up, too.

It had been very real, as had the bus ticket he'd offered me. "I have strict rules you'll have to follow. This won't be easy. But it will mean a scholarship and full tuition with room and board. EOL has both two-year and four-degrees, so you can earn your bachelor's."

Don't bother dreamin', Logan. People like us don't never get more than what we have now. My stepfather's voice crowded out my optimism. He had said that to me so many times, laughing at my hopes that football would give me a life that didn't involve working construction, living in a double-wide trailer, and being in and out of prison for drug abuse.

I wouldn't let the taunts of a dead man derail me. Getting my bachelor's degree was what I wanted more than anything. After F&T kicked me out due to my anger management issues—aka the bar fight that seemed to make the front page of the sports section in every

Texas newspaper—my hopes of graduating from college had vanished. Without my scholarship, I couldn't afford to stay in school. Any school.

Another thing my stepfather had ruined when he wrecked my credit by stealing my identity when I was seven. Leaving me to deal with the fallout.

Like always.

This was my chance to fix that. To get my degree, maybe become a teacher and a coach myself. All I had to do was go to the team orientation meeting, find out about these rules Coach Oakley had, and graduate. I'd arrived just in time for the meeting, and I was glad this Jess was offering me a ride to campus. It meant I wouldn't need to spend any of the cash I had left. I stuck my phone back in my pocket and swung my duffel bag up over my shoulder as I studied the girl in front of me. There was something about her that drew me in. Some kind of inner confidence, a type of strength, that made me want to talk to her and get to know her better. I hadn't dated anyone seriously in a long time. Hadn't really been interested. But now I was interested.

Funny thing was, I felt like I'd met her before.

"You look familiar," I told her.

She shrugged one shoulder. Like she couldn't have cared less if we'd met already. There was a big standoffish vibe to her that should have repelled me. Instead it only made me more curious.

"And?" she asked, challenging me.

That made me smile. She had no idea how charming I could be when I set my mind to it. I'd always liked a challenge. "Maybe it's because you were in my dreams last night. And maybe you'll be in my dreams tonight if you play your cards right."

She stayed quiet for a moment and then started to laugh. Really laugh, great big guffaws that drew the attention of nearly every person in the bus station. I shifted from one foot to the other. It hadn't been that funny.

"Oh, I'm sorry," she said when she caught her breath. She wiped tears from her eyes. "I'm so sorry for whatever impairment you have that makes you think that's sexy or appealing. Does that ever work for you?"

It had never *not* worked for me. And I'd never had a woman insult me before. It should have been a turnoff. Instead some twisted part of me just wanted her more.

Before I could respond, her phone beeped. "Whoops. Stay here, cowboy. I have to go grab somebody else before we can head over."

"Who?" I asked.

"Your roommate," she called over my shoulder, disappearing into the crowd.

I stayed put, like some recently trained puppy. Part of me wanted to irritate her and move somewhere else, but I was willing to be a good boy.

I was willing to do just about anything to be here. I'd even sold my stepfather's tools, basically ensuring that I couldn't go back to my construction job even if I wanted to. Like Hernán Cortés, the Spanish conquistador who burned his ships before he went to fight the Aztecs. He'd given himself and his men no option but to win. There was no going back.

I'd done the same thing. Now I had to succeed. I had nothing else to fall back on. I'd force my way forward, no matter how hard it was.

I had my eye on the prize, and I wasn't going to lose it.

A couple of vending machines stood nearby, and I selected a Snickers bar from one and a Coke from another. I wasn't actually hungry, but lifelong habits like that died hard. I stuck the candy bar in my bag, just in case. It felt comforting to have extra food on hand. I grabbed the soda out of the vending machine and then opened the tab quickly. Probably too quickly considering that I showered myself with brown liquid.

I had just let out a groan of disbelief when Jess returned, followed by a very tall dude; I was six foot four myself, and he easily had two or three inches on me. She raised a single eyebrow at me, eyeing my mess. So much for seeming cool and suave.

"Problems?" she asked in a sarcastic but sweet tone.

"I'm fine," I muttered.

"In that case, Logan Hunt, I'd like you to meet Ian Sebastian."

"Everybody calls me Bash," he said, holding out his fist for me to bump. "I'm an inside linebacker."

"Good to meet you," I told him, flinging the excess liquid off my hand and returning his gesture. "I'm QB."

"Bash? Is that because you're so bashful and sweet?" Jess asked, motioning for us to follow her.

"No." He looked confused. "It's because I like to bash people and tackle them. Hard. It's my favorite thing in the whole world."

The teasing look in Jess's eyes was small, her smile slightly bent at the ends. That smile was directed at me, like we were sharing an inside joke. I liked that more than I probably should have.

"Where are you from?" I asked him, watching as people got out of his way. They were probably afraid of getting trampled on. It was hard to imagine that someone so big was fast enough to chase down running backs and wide receivers, but he wouldn't be here if he weren't good at it.

"I used to go to a school in Pennsylvania, but they kicked me out when I failed my third drug test," he said in a slightly apologetic tone. "My antidepressants made me feel all weird and thick, and I couldn't concentrate. In school or on the field. I missed plays that I shouldn't have. So I took marijuana instead of my medication, and they kicked me off the team because I kept using. A few months ago my doctor and I switched up my meds and found something that works. Which I probably should have done in the first place. Anyways, I'm hoping to play at End of the Line for a year or two and then move back to another Division I school."

"'End of the Line'?" I repeated.

"Yeah. That's what everybody calls EOL. End of the Line. You don't get your act together here, there's nowhere else for you to go."

End of the Line. That seemed about right. Only I wasn't willing to let it be the end for me. It would be a new beginning.

It was a new beginning for a lot of players. The NCAA required transfer students to sit out a year before playing. But by going to a junior college, they bypassed that rule and had the chance to get their lives back on track. It allowed them to start playing ball immediately and gave them the opportunity to be recruited by a Division I school again.

Or by the NFL.

We arrived at Jess's car, which was a small red sedan. She opened up her trunk to let me and Bash throw our stuff inside. I claimed the front seat and Bash sat directly behind me, neither one of us really fitting all that comfortably.

"Thanks for the ride," I said to Jess as she pulled out of the parking lot.

"No worries," she responded. "I'm sure I'll be giving you another one soon."

"Is that right?" I asked her, admiring her profile as she surveyed the traffic around her. "So what I'm hearing is that we'll be going out soon and you're going to drive."

"Time to get your ears checked, cowboy. Trust me when I say we will never, ever date. Ever. I meant I'll be your ride when you go back to the bus station."

"Why would I go back to the bus station? I just got here."

"Right. But you haven't heard the rules yet. And you are not going to like them."

"You're basing this off what, the three minutes that we've known each other?"

She pulled up to a stoplight and turned toward me to give me her full attention. "There's not much more to know, cowboy. Three minutes is all it takes to know that you are really not going to like the rules."

The coach had briefly mentioned his rules in our initial conversation, but I hadn't paid any attention to them. I was much more focused on the chance to play football again with a scholarship.

But now . . . should I have been worried? Should I have asked about those rules before getting on the bus and setting fire to my life in Texas?

Jess still wore that teasing look. Was she trying to scare me away?

I was reading way too much into this and being ridiculous. I mean, how bad could Coach Oakley's rules actually be?

CHAPTER TWO

LOGAN

Given that Jess seemed to be enjoying some kind of private joke in her own little world, I mostly talked to Bash the rest of the way. We talked about how our soon-to-be nearest NFL team, the Seattle Seahawks, would do this upcoming season. We also chatted about the Portland Lumberjacks, my all-time favorite football team. Since I'd grown up on the outskirts of Dallas I probably should have been a Cowboys fan, but they were my stepfather's favorite, and I couldn't bring myself to root for anyone that he liked. So I chose to support one of their rivals, knowing just how much it would piss him off.

Bash also told me a little about his college career. "I averaged eight point five tackles per game last season," he boasted. It was a high number and I was impressed.

"Eight point eight," Jess corrected.

"What?"

"You averaged eight point eight tackles per game."

There was a pause before he responded. "That's not what the team statistician told me."

"Well, then he or she was wrong."

"What about me?" I asked. "Do you know the intimate details of my playing time? How many touchdowns scored? How many passes successfully completed? Total yardage gained?"

Even though I could only see one side of her face, I did note with amusement that she rolled her eyes. "You don't need me to tell you anything about your time at F&T. I'm sure you've memorized your stats backward and forward. I'm personally surprised you don't have them tattooed on the inside of your thigh."

I couldn't help but laugh. In our entire interaction she had been so different from every other woman I'd ever met that I wasn't sure how to respond.

About twenty minutes later, we arrived at EOL. I got out of the car and realized that it smelled like rain. Unlike the bright sun of Texas, the sky here was filled with clouds that looked like they were on the verge of busting open and pouring down rain.

"Is it always like this?" I asked Jess, pointing up.

"Usually."

Well, I'd never been a big fan of rain, but it would probably make the training camp and practices a lot easier to deal with. I grabbed my bag from her trunk and took a good look around. The campus was much smaller than I'd imagined. I was used to F&T, which was probably ten times the size of this place. I could see some construction happening on the edge of campus, but most of the buildings looked like they were refugees from the 1960s. Jess took us to one of the oldest buildings, which turned out to be the dorms, and showed us our room. I made a note of where the bathrooms were so that I could shower as soon as the meeting ended. Our dorm room was basic, a couple of beds and desks. We dropped off our bags and took the keys she offered us.

"You two are the last ones to arrive. The team meeting is going to start in a few minutes, so let's hurry over to the athletic building. I wouldn't want you to miss a single word of it."

That private smile was back, and I couldn't find it in me to give her a hard time about it. For some reason I got the feeling that she didn't smile very often.

Jess took us to the athletic building, my soon-to-be second home. I intended to spend a lot of time lifting weights here. We followed her down a flight of stairs and through a hallway that smelled like itch cream, mildewy towels, and dirty feet. I breathed it in deeply. It was the smell of football.

The smell of home.

We stopped at a desk that was being manned by an attractive woman. She had black hair and dark eyes.

"Logan, Bash, this is Keilani, and she has a last name I butcher every time I try to say it so I'm not going to attempt it. Anyway, she's the academic adviser for the team."

Keilani stood and gave us a big grin as she enthusiastically shook our hands. "I'm so glad you're here. And we're going to get to know each other really well this year. I'm here to help you out with all your academic needs. I'll be following up with your professors to make sure you're getting your work done and that you're showing up to class. I'll be giving more details to the team as a whole, but please know that I am here for you and will do whatever I can to help!"

A guy who looked to be about my age and was wearing a polo shirt with the football team's logo on it walked past us. "Coach isn't going to be too happy if you keep his players out here, Keilani."

The infectious enthusiasm melted off her face, and she glared at the man. "Don't worry about me, Ford. I know how to handle my business."

This Ford guy glared at her long and hard before heading inside a room. Keilani muttered under her breath for a few seconds before her bright smile returned. "Here are your name tags." They already had our names handwritten on them. "Follow the douchebag for your meeting."

She pointed us to the doors that Ford had just walked through.

I turned back to look at Jess. "You coming?"

"Nope. I know what happens next. Good luck, cowboy."

I watched her go, wondering how long I'd have to wait to see her again.

"Come on, dude," Bash whispered, urging me inside. We took two seats in the back near the door. Multiple conversations were taking place, giving the room a dull roar. The walls were made of cement blocks that had been painted white, and there were inspirational football-themed posters hanging everywhere. As I looked around, I realized that I recognized some of the players. There were record-breaking athletes in this room. I wondered what they'd done to screw up and land here at EOL.

Coach Oakley entered the room then, followed by about seven other men, including Ford, who were presumably his coaching staff. They stood in a line off to the right, giving the floor to the coach.

He didn't even have to say anything. He stood there, his arms folded, waiting for us to be quiet. Most coaches I'd grown up with would have yelled at us and told us to shut up. I was not used to a coach who had so much authority that his presence was enough to make a rowdy group of football players fall silent.

"Welcome. To those of you that I haven't met personally, my name is Stan Oakley, and I'm the head coach of EOL's Owls."

A couple of the players made hooting noises in response.

"I thank you all for being here, for taking time out of your lives to hear what I have to say. Either one of the members of my staff has spoken to you or I have, and we have mentioned that this team has some serious rules. I'd like to talk to you about that now and what exactly those rules are."

Here it was. I straightened in my seat and wondered what he could possibly throw at us that would be bad enough that Jess thought she'd be taking me right back to the bus station.

Coach nodded at Ford, who walked over to the white board and picked up a marker.

"First, punctuality. You will be on time. To class, to practice, to tutoring, to everything in your life that you need to show up for, you will respect the time of everyone around you and be there when you're supposed to be."

Ford wrote "#1 Be on time" on the board.

"There will be no drinking at all, ever. No drugs of any kind. You will be randomly drug tested on a regular basis. First time you fail, you're out. There will be no second or third chances here."

I felt Bash sinking down in his seat next to me as several of the guys murmured. "How are we supposed to let off steam?" someone asked behind me.

Coach kept talking. "There will be no swearing or cussing."

"That's not even realistic!" a guy in the front row protested.

"It is realistic. And you will do it because you represent me and you represent this team and you can do it without swearing. Next, in accordance with NCAA standard, you will maintain a minimum of a 2.5 GPA. I may give more playing time to guys with a higher GPA. The more playing time you get, the more likely you'll be seen by a scout or a recruiter. Especially in the playoffs and the national championship game. Take your academics seriously. Keilani Kahananui will be talking to you about your options later and how we can help."

There was more dissent among the ranks, more guys murmuring and complaining about the rules. None of them seemed that bad to me.

But I had the feeling the worst was yet to come.

"Next rule—no fighting. On or off the field."

Now it was my turn to slouch down in my seat. As if that one had been directed specifically at me.

The marker squeaked against the whiteboard as Ford continued writing down Coach's rules.

"In addition to being punctual, you will treat authority figures with respect. You respect your teachers by showing up to class. By not talking back. By turning in your assignments. You respect your coaches by showing up to practice ready to give a hundred percent every time. By listening and doing as you're told."

Off to my left somebody shouted out, "Yo, Coach! Respect has to be earned."

"It absolutely does not," Coach Oakley quickly countered. "Respect will be given without reservation. If you think that it must be earned, there's the door. Because there's no way you're going to be playing on my team."

The coach fell silent, waiting to see if anybody would leave.

No one did.

"I won't get to coach most of you for four years. My goal is not to build a program that keeps you all here. My job is to get you to the next stage of your life. To turn you into men." There were some more sounds of discontent, and the coach held up his hand. "I know a lot of you think you're already men. But you're not. Not yet. I expect you all to start behaving like real men. Like gentlemen. For your entire lives, because you had some talent to play football, nobody cared how you behaved off the field. I care. I'm holding you to a higher standard. Better today than you were yesterday. Especially when it comes to women."

My spidey sense started tingling. Whatever he was going to say next, I knew I wouldn't like it.

"And our final rule for the evening: no women. No girlfriends, no dating, no one-night stands."

That led to a loud and physical reaction in the room. Which I got, because I felt like I'd been sucker punched. It was one thing to be asked to give up most of the things you did to entertain yourself and relax.

But women? How were we supposed to go an entire season without girls? I didn't know if I could do it.

"How will you know?" somebody asked. It was a legitimate question. Short of installing hidden cameras in our dorms, which at that moment I wasn't putting past him, there was no way for Coach to know if we were messing around.

"I'm expecting you to behave like gentlemen, with honor and integrity. I'd like to be able to take you at your word."

"No way! That's it! I'm out!" one guy declared.

"That's fine," Coach said, shrugging one shoulder in the same way Jess had earlier. "Some of you may think that because once upon a time you were recruited by a Division I school, you're better than this place. You're not. I don't have to play any of you. I don't have to keep any of you on scholarship. And for anyone who thinks this team will fall apart without you, you couldn't be more wrong. This team will be just fine."

That one word, *scholarship*, made my decision easy. I didn't necessarily need women in my life. It would probably help to have one less distraction as I went about dedicating all of my time to school and football.

"You really expect us to live like monks? Will we at least get to hang out with girls in the off-season?" another guy asked.

Coach Oakley was silent, again giving off that commanding vibe that made people sit back down and be quiet. "You all know why you're here and what's at stake. For most of you, this is the end of the line. There is no somewhere else. But if you feel like you can't live with my rules, again, there's the door. You all have round-trip tickets to take you back home." He turned and faced the dude who had asked the last question. "There is no off-season at EOL. You are my players until I say you're not. I am holding you to a higher standard. But I know every person in this room is capable of rising up to do what I ask of you. Of being better. Prove me right."

He walked out of the door at the front of the classroom without another word.

There was a heavy silence after Coach left. His rules seemed arbitrary and unrealistic. But I would find a way to be fine with them. I wouldn't lose this chance.

And hey, at least he hadn't made us give up video games.

Not everyone felt the way I did. Two guys left. The rest of us stayed put. They might not have been happy about it, but as Coach said, we knew what was at stake. We could make sacrifices.

Ford stepped up to the front of the room. "My name is Coach Ford Blackwell. Since I'm not much older than most of you, you can call me Ford. I will be working specifically with the quarterbacks this season. Right now we're going to go over the team's practice schedule for the next few weeks, until the season starts, and then what practices will look like once school begins."

Jess stuck her head in the door, and it was like a rabbit wandering into a fox den. We'd just been told all girls were off-limits, and this was our first encounter with one since we'd heard the rule.

She really was cute. And appealing.

Once he realized that he'd lost our attention, Ford turned and noticed her. "He's not here, Jess. He's probably in his office."

"Oh. Thanks." The door closed quietly behind her.

"As long as we're talking about rules," Ford said, "Coach said no girls, but the ultimate rule to rule all other rules is never, ever that girl."

He went back to talking about schedules and I raised both of my eyebrows at Bash, who was nodding.

"She's probably the reason the rule exists in the first place," he murmured.

Jess? Why? "You know something I don't?" I asked.

A look of shock and confusion crossed his face. "She's the reason Coach Oakley got kicked out of Amarillo three years ago. Jess is Coach's daughter."

How were those two things connected? Now it was my turn to look confused. Although it did clear up one thing: why Jess seemed familiar. It was because of the resemblance to her dad. "How did she get him kicked out?"

"Don't you pay attention to the news? She went to some football party as a freshman, somebody there spiked her drink, and she figured it out right after it happened. She texted Coach and he arrived just as half of his starting lineup was dragging her off to one of the bedrooms. He beat most of them up and said he'd kick them off the team. The

15

university decided it would rather lose one coach than its offensive line, which is how he ended up here."

"That is fu—messed up," I said. Might as well start following the rules now.

"Something you two want to share?" Ford interrupted Bash's response, and we both shook our heads no. But it had the intended effect, and we fell quiet.

I was trying to process this. Part of me wanted to run after her and apologize for what had happened to her. Even though I instinctively knew that if I did, it would piss her off. I felt terrible. Nobody deserved to be treated like that. Nobody. Those Amarillo a—jerks should be sitting in prison right now.

It must have been so hard to walk around like nothing was wrong and have everyone know this horrible thing that had happened to you. My past secrets were just that—secrets. Nobody knew how I was abused. Starved. Tormented. My demons were my own.

Jess's demons were out where everyone could judge them and make stupid remarks.

I wouldn't be one of those people. I wanted her to be my friend. My very attractive and intriguing friend, but pals only. Because it would stay platonic. It had to.

No more flirting for me. It made me wonder if her past experiences with football players was the reason why she was standoffish and not interested in my attempts at flirting. Or was I giving myself too much credit? Maybe she knew it couldn't happen because of her dad's rules. Or she wasn't attracted to me.

Jess is off-limits. Untouchable, I told myself.

But I'd never been very good at resisting forbidden fruit.

CHAPTER THREE

JESS

"Really?" I asked Keilani. "You assigned Logan Hunt to me?"

She batted her eyes innocently. "He came to me, and while he's doing well in his other classes, he's having some issues with math. Is that a problem?"

I loved this woman, but I was seriously going to kill her. Yes, it was obviously a problem. Logan Hunt was hot. He'd un-convert a nun. Which made him dangerous and not somebody I wanted to spend time with.

Especially because he was a football player. One of my dad's players.

When I'd seen him in that bus station, tall, muscular, with light-brown hair and honey-colored eyes, that dusting of five o'clock shadow on his strong jaw, I'd nearly swallowed my own tongue. I'd seen pictures of him before, helped my dad by studying Logan's stats and recommending him as a good risk. But those online photos were nothing compared to the real thing. It was like he'd just walked out of the pages of a Greek mythology book.

Yep. Logan Hunt was definitely dangerous. Not just to me, but to all womankind.

And when he'd been flirty with me? More swallowing of my own tongue. It was all I could do to put up a facade that said I didn't care and wasn't interested. His barely noticeable Texan twang prompted me to call him "cowboy" in hopes that it would make me think of the other cowboys who'd tried to hurt me. That I could put him in that category.

It hadn't worked.

I hadn't been attracted to anyone for a long time. And it was Ben, one of the other math TAs, who I'd had a crush on. Still had a crush on. But it was almost like recognizing those feelings for him had opened the floodgates so that suddenly I found lots of boys appealing.

Including stupid Logan Hunt.

And now Keilani was assigning me to be his tutor? It was probably payback for my suggesting that all of her hostility with Ford was just masking a deep-seated longing that they obviously had for one another. I don't think she's ever quite forgiven me for that.

"He needs the help," she told me. "And you're the best math tutor we have."

"I wish Professor Gardiner saw that." Professor Rupert Gardiner headed up the math department at the University of Washington, and I wanted to get my master's there with him as my adviser. He had the best connections, and the students he mentored went on to accomplish amazing things.

He was also a big advocate of volunteer work. Which was one of the reasons why I spent so much time in the EOL math lab.

Professor Gardiner only took on one student to mentor each year. The competition was fierce. And I wasn't the only one spending this much time volunteering. Danielle Chatsworth was here, too, trying to take the one opening. She'd been competing with me for the last three years.

Somehow she'd even picked up on the fact that I had a crush on Ben, and through some combination of voodoo magic and her extensive plastic surgery, it seemed like they'd gone out a few times.

I'd have liked to say that the idea that they might fall in love wasn't keeping me up nights, but that would have been a lie.

So if Keilani wanted me to tutor Logan Hunt, I would. I wouldn't be happy about it, but I hadn't really been happy in a long time. Why should this be any different?

"Okay, fine," I grumbled, and she grinned at me.

"Fantastic!" she said, handing me a packet from Logan's math teacher. "Here's what they're working on now. And by the way, Logan seemed pretty excited when I told him you'd be his tutor."

I wanted to destroy that knowing smirk she was giving me. "How is Ford?"

It worked. The look disappeared. "Ha ha."

"You know I love you, Keilani!" I said, taking the packet and settling in at my favorite table. I didn't want to make her too angry, as she was in charge of the assignments at the math lab and could make my life miserable. Well, more miserable than it would be from tutoring hot Logan Hunt.

I had just started going through his math packet when I smelled a sausage-and-pepperoni pizza from my favorite restaurant, Gino's. My stomach growled in appreciation.

"Hey, Jess. Long time no see."

It was Logan. And he was right about not having seen me in a while. I'd purposely steered clear during football camp and their practices. Not only because of my dad's rules, which most women on campus seemed to view as some kind of personal challenge, flirting and seducing until they got the players to forget about the no-dating thing.

I also stayed away because I didn't need to have a crush on two guys. That was a little too nighttime-soap-opera for me. Triangles were already my least favorite shape, and I had no intention of being part of one. Even an imaginary one, since neither guy had actually expressed any interest in me. I was a one-fantasy-crush-at-a-time kind of girl.

I got to feel justified about that decision when I ran my eyes over the length of him. He really was stupid good-looking. I wondered why he'd never tried to be an actor or a model. My tongue tried to jump down my throat again in order to stop my breathing.

I cleared my throat, not knowing what to say. Then my mind went blank for a few seconds when he smiled at me.

"How have you been?" he asked.

I couldn't very well say, *Oh, I've been counting down the minutes until I got to see you again.* One, because it was humiliating, and two, because I hadn't realized until that very moment that it was true.

"There's no food or drink allowed in the math lab" was what I actually said, watching hungrily as he slid the pizza box onto the table in front of me.

"They can't make an exception?" He said it teasingly, but I got the impression that, just like every other college football player's, his entire life had been about people making exceptions for him.

"No, they can't."

He leaned over conspiratorially, and whatever cologne or soap he used hit me full in the face, overwhelming and tantalizing. Even better than the pizza, and I would have never thought such a thing possible. "Do you think I could bribe somebody in charge with a slice? Get them to look the other way?"

Ha. Just as I'd suspected. Logan Hunt thought he was above the rules. Rules he had agreed to follow. Another reason not to let myself get too attached. My dad would never tolerate that kind of behavior and Logan wouldn't last for very long.

"We're all about the rules here," I said to remind both him and myself, leaning back to get out of scent range. And I'd thought he was dangerous before. Obviously, I'd had no idea just how attractive he really was. Even his pheromones were bewitching me.

Against all my instincts, I pushed the pizza away, too. I really, really wanted to eat.

"You seem hungry," he observed. "Sure I can't tempt you?"

If he only knew. "I am hungry. I forgot to eat breakfast this morning. And lunch."

Logan shook his head. "I've never understood that. I don't ever forget to eat. Usually I forget that I've already eaten and then eat again."

I couldn't help it, a giggle bubbled up inside me. I kept it inside, but I couldn't stop my lips from twisting into a smile.

"Okay, after tutoring is over we'll go outside and find somewhere that isn't wet from the rain and eat it."

I nodded, two different parts of me warring over whether I should have pizza with him. It seemed harmless enough, but I got the feeling that nothing was harmless when it came to Logan. He was the kind of guy a girl could fall hard for, and fast.

Unfortunately, I knew all about guys like that.

"How about we start on the packet?" That seemed safe. Ish.

Until he leaned in, looking over my shoulder as I began to explain the first problem to him. I prayed for strength.

Logan seemed to catch on pretty quickly as I went over each equation with him. He had already figured out the answer to some of them before I told him. "It seems like you know what you're doing."

"I understand some of it, but not everything. I'm probably getting a C in the class right now, but I'd really like to get an A."

"Why? You only need a two point five."

He shrugged. "I want to get a four point oh. I know it doesn't matter at this point what my GPA is, only that I graduate, but I want to prove to myself that I can do it. The only time I've ever been close to a four point oh before was my blood alcohol level."

I admired his conviction and his self-deprecation as I returned his smile. Geez. He was funny and clever. Now I was in need of even more strength and willpower.

And I seemed to be managing myself okay until Ben walked into the room. I always knew when he arrived, like every molecule in the room loved him the way that I did and got excited by his presence. I felt him in the actual air.

Without thinking, I put my hand over my thundering heart.

I couldn't help but stare.

Which did not escape Logan's notice.

"You like that guy?" he asked incredulously.

"What? No." I was such a terrible liar. I hoped he couldn't tell.

He could. "You do. You like him. Why?"

I pushed my shoulders back. I knew Ben wasn't conventionally handsome. *Like Logan*, some traitorous part of my brain whispered with glee. I told it to be quiet. "Why wouldn't I? Ben is very cute. And nice."

His smile let me know a second too late that I'd fallen into his trap and had basically admitted that I liked Ben. "I'll give you this, Jess. It's certainly a creative way to annoy your father." He folded his arms and observed Ben. "Why is he wearing all black? Did no one tell him there are other colors? And his hair doesn't move. Like a Lego guy."

"He's . . . unconventional."

"You mean weird."

"I don't mean weird. He's talented and sensitive and feels things deeply and—"

Logan cut me off before I could finish. "You forgot weird."

"No, I didn't."

"I'm pretty sure you were coming to it."

I let out a sigh of exasperation that only made Logan's grin intensify. "You don't even know him. You can't say he's weird."

"Just my probably totally correct assumption. But putting that aside, why are you sitting here? Why not go over and tell him nicely that you'd like to spend clothes-free time with him? I'm sure he won't object."

"That's why." I pointed at Danielle as she came into the room, all blonde extensions, fake boobs, and spray tan.

"They're dating?" Logan sounded as incredulous as I felt whenever I saw Danielle and Ben together.

"*Dating* may be a strong word. They've been out a couple of times. I don't know if it's serious." I hoped it wasn't serious.

"Huh." He leaned back in his chair to consider this information. "Two dates do not a relationship make, trust me. Especially for a couple so . . . mismatched. It's kind of like seeing a peacock and a bat date. I mean, I can see why he's into it. Her body's a ten. Face, too."

"Yeah, and so's her IQ." I immediately felt bad. "Okay, she's not dumb. Just evil and mean. Like if Ebola were a person."

"Why do either one of you like this guy? You're both totally out of his league."

It made my heart glow a little that Logan thought I was out of Ben's league. I usually felt like the opposite was true. "At the risk of sounding totally self-centered, I'm pretty sure that Danielle is only hanging around him to torture me. As for why I like him, I don't know. He's different. Not like other guys."

"That's for sure," Logan agreed. "He looks like he'd blow away in a strong wind."

Yes, Ben was lanky and skinny. He didn't look like he'd gone shopping in the muscle store like Logan had. Sometimes I wondered if that was part of Ben's appeal. That he didn't resemble a football player at all.

I again felt like I had to defend Ben. "There's just . . . something about him. Something that makes my heart skip a beat." And it had been so long since I'd felt that way that I often thought I could stay happily in this limbo state, never progressing and just crushing on him from afar.

"I learned in biology class that when your heart skips a beat, that's called an arrhythmia. You can die from that."

I elbowed Logan as he cracked himself up. I again felt that urge to laugh along with him.

His laughter stopped suddenly. "Now, that's interesting. Here, let me try something." He put his arm around the back of my chair and moved in closer.

"What do you think you're doing?"

"I'm doing an experiment. Just wait."

His nearness was making my breath go a little wonky. "Wait for what?"

"This."

I'd been so wrapped up in Logan's closeness that I hadn't noticed Ben approaching our table.

"Hey, Jess." Ben waved and smiled at me.

I straightened up at his gesture and couldn't help my giddy grin back at him. "Hi, Ben!"

Argh. I was super pathetic.

"So I don't know if you have plans tomorrow night, but I'm doing a performance over at the Corner and I'd love for you to come by." Ben handed me a bright-blue flyer that had the words "Poetry Slam" at the top.

My heartbeat sped up. "That sounds great."

"We'll see if we can make it," Logan interjected, sounding for all the world like a jealous boyfriend. I wanted to turn and glare at him, but Ben had invited me (me!) to watch him do one of his live poetry performances. Obviously I'd seen him do them before because I'd discovered I had slight stalker tendencies, but this was the first time he'd ever invited me to go!

"Oh." Ben sounded like he wasn't sure what to do with Logan's statement. "Well, I hope you can. See you later, I hope!"

"Bye!"

Ben walked back to his table, where a fuming Danielle waited for him. They had an angry, harsh whispered conversation, and I derived an incredible amount of satisfaction from knowing that I'd played some part in their fight.

"That guy's a poet? He said he hoped you'd come to see him twice. That doesn't really suggest a wide vocabulary."

I ignored Logan's gibe and held up Ben's flyer. If I'd been alone, I probably would have smelled it to see if his cologne was on it. But there was no way I was doing that in front of Logan.

And I liked the fact that Ben said he'd hoped to see me, not once but twice.

"He's never done that before." What was it about this entire situation that was making me open up to Logan like we were two twelve-year-old girls at a sleepover? I was so used to hiding things about myself that this should have felt foreign and unnatural, but it didn't. Which was foreign and unnatural in and of itself. Maybe it was the pizza offering.

Whatever. I didn't want to think about why I felt so comfortable with Logan; I just wanted to discuss the miraculous event that had occurred with Ben. "He's never come over and invited me to one of his performances."

"Yeah, you should probably be thankful for that."

I glared at him, but Logan just kept talking.

"And you should be thankful to me, because I'm the reason he did it."

"What?" That made no sense.

"This guy knows you have a crush on him. He started watching you the second he stepped into the room. He kissed that Danielle chick and then immediately turned to see your reaction. He likes that you have feelings for him. Some guys collect crushes the way other guys collect comic books. And someone was putting their fingers all over his Action Comics number one. Which, in case you didn't know, is the one where Superman made his first appearance."

Was he saying Ben was jealous of him? That I was a Superman comic book? "What are you trying to say?"

"I theorized that he would be threatened by me because he and I are total opposites and I'm, forgive my arrogance here, much more appealing to women than he is. So, worried about you possibly defecting to a much better specimen of manhood, he would try to win you back to his side. A theory that I proved when he came running over here just because I sat close to you."

As excited as I was to think that Ben might have felt jealous of Logan, it didn't matter. "Danielle, if you'll forgive my insecurity here, is much more appealing to men than I am. Even if Ben was threatened by you, he has her to hang out with."

"And Bash has a test in psychology tomorrow that he hasn't studied for."

"What?" I was so lost.

"Sorry. I thought we were naming things that were about to get cheated on."

"Ben would never—"

"Oh, he would. But no cheating will be involved. Because I can see just from looking at them that they're not serious." Logan sat up and gave me an intense look that did funny things to the backs of my knees. I was glad I was sitting down. "You and I are going to be friends."

"I don't need any new friends." Especially handsome ones.

"Who doesn't want to have a new friend?"

"Uh, me? As I just explicitly expressed? Besides, I already have plenty of friends."

"Do you?" Logan sounded like he didn't believe me.

I didn't, but that was beside the point. "Why do you need to be my friend?"

"Because, as your new best friend, I'm going to help you get that guy. I don't know why you want him, but when we're done, he'll be all yours."

CHAPTER FOUR

JESS

Logan stood up and grabbed the pizza box. "Come on. Let's go eat this and discuss battle strategy."

"What about your packet?" I asked. I knew I should be responsible even if I wanted to follow him and indulge in the pizza that had been torturing me with its cheesy, tomatoey, and spicy smell.

"Another time."

So instead of doing the smart thing, I decided to follow him. I tried really hard to eavesdrop on Ben and Danielle as we walked by, but they stopped whisper-arguing when we got close. So I said, "See you tomorrow, Ben!"

Ben didn't respond. I hadn't expected him to.

Yes, it was an obnoxious thing for me to do, but the look on Danielle's face made it all worth it. Serious or not, she was still possessive of him, and my goodbye bothered her.

Logan led me to an alcove with a couple of stuffed armchairs not far from the math lab. When we sat, he opened the pizza box and offered it to me. "Ladies first. I didn't know what you liked, so I got a couple of options."

"I've found you can't really go wrong when it comes to pizza toppings." Half the pizza was sausage, ham, and black olives, the other half just pepperoni. Both made my mouth water and I didn't know which side to pick. So I took one slice of each. Then my dilemma became which one to eat first. I settled for going back and forth between them with each bite, which made him laugh. But each bite was a crispy, gluten-filled piece of heaven, and my eyes might have rolled back in my head.

"What?" I asked when I realized he was studying me. My mouth might have been full of food at the time.

"Nothing." Logan managed to eat half his slice with one bite, which I found highly impressive. "It's always nice to see a girl who doesn't mind eating carbs."

"I love carbs. I would marry carbs tomorrow and start popping out carb babies if I could."

He laughed again. After we'd demolished most of the pizza, he offered me the last slice, but I shook my head.

"Do you want it?" I asked, just in case he was only being polite.

"I'm stuffed."

I took the box and stood up. He'd brought dinner; the least I could do was help clean up.

But he put his hand on my wrist and it caused an electric charge so strong I felt it zinging around my body. It made me come to an abrupt stop.

"What?" I asked, my voice sounding too breathy.

"What are you doing?"

"I was going to throw this away."

"Don't do that. I'll take it back to Bash. He'll be sad that he missed out."

There was a weird tone to his voice, but despite his offer to be my new friend, I didn't actually know very much about him. I wondered what was going on, but I gave the box back to him and he released my wrist to take it. My arm suddenly felt cold, as if he'd sucked some vital part of me away with his hand. So strange. He put the box on the floor next to his backpack. Away from me.

I sat back down in my chair, thoroughly confused. And thinking way too much about what had happened the moment he touched me.

As if he realized that he'd acted a bit strange, he said with a weak smile, "I can't stand waste, I guess."

There was something else there. Something that I didn't understand. Something that made me think Logan Hunt was a lot deeper than I'd given him credit for.

I realized that I wanted to help him. To gloss over this situation and make both of us feel comfortable again. "What is this plan of yours? For Ben?"

"It's not really a plan." That conspiratorial tone was back in Logan's voice. Like he couldn't wait to make Ben my conquest. "It's more like one of those run-of-the-mill genius ideas."

I let out a snort. "The last time someone said they had a genius idea I ended up in mall jail."

"This one won't get you arrested. At least, I don't think it will get you arrested."

"Good. Because we can't end up in prison since neither one of us wants me to have to call my dad. But this isn't going to be one of those let's-pretend-to-date situations that only happen in movies, is it?" Because I didn't know if I could fake-date Logan.

"Nope. I'm not allowed to date at all, real or otherwise."

A familiar rush of guilt washed over me. "Yeah, sorry about that. I think my dad made up that rule for my sake."

The words were both an admission and a test. To see if Logan knew what I was talking about. I tested everyone I met in the same way, and so far, without exception, everyone knew who I was before we'd ever spoken.

I hated that I was famous for this horrible thing that happened to me. And that everybody knew about it because of my father. Otherwise, it would have just gone away. But every time anybody on ESPN or ISEN talked about Coach Stan Oakley, former head coach of Amarillo, they brought this story up and it was like the cycle of people knowing everything about my private business started all over again.

Which was so incredibly wrong. It should have been my decision who knew about it and who didn't. It felt really unfair that I had no control whatsoever over that part of my life, that it was offered up as some sort of entertainment tidbit for sports fans.

So I was let down by the understanding in Logan's gaze. Part of me had hoped that he wasn't aware of my situation, the thing people used to define me even when I'd long moved past it. It would have been nice to have a fresh start with someone.

But instead of telling him that, I jokingly said, "Yeah. He couldn't prevent his team from trying to hurt me, so he's going to prevent every future team from hurting another girl. Not really the thing you want to be the poster child for."

He put his hand on top of mine, and despite my body's response to it, the touch wasn't meant to be romantic. It was meant to comfort. I wasn't very comforted, though. More on the thrilled and excited end of the spectrum. "I know what it's like to feel a little broken. And to want to cover it up with humor."

That sent a shock through me so deep, so intense that I actually gasped. It was like he'd peered into my soul and, without even really knowing me, had understood me in a way that no one else ever had. He took his hand away, ignoring my reaction.

Logan cleared his throat. "So, we've established that it's not a good idea to fake-date you."

"What about Danielle?" Was that his genius idea? Get Danielle to go after him to let me have Ben to myself? "Are you going to try and date her?"

"No dating of any kind with anyone. I am really committed to your father's rules. I want to be on this team. I have to graduate and get my degree. If I don't do it now, I never will. No girl is worth walking away from football. No girl is worth walking away from graduating." I heard the determination in his voice, and I believed him. "But I may be . . . a little hard to get when it comes to Danielle. Which will most likely grab her attention and clear your path to the Dork Knight."

I bristled at his Ben insult. "My guess is you've never played hard to get in your entire life."

He shot me a mischievous smile. "'Hard to get' for me used to mean I sat through the entire movie."

I shook my head. "Consider my jaw dropped at the idea that you used to be a player. So very unsurprising."

"Maybe, but it means I know what I'm talking about. You and I need to hang out at places where Ben will be. Like this stupid poetry thing. And you need to ignore him, like he doesn't matter, until I tell you otherwise."

I blinked a couple of times, not sure I'd heard him correctly. "That's your genius idea? We neg Ben and just show up wherever he is?"

"Trust me, it will work. I'm telling you, he's threatened by me. Just my being at your side will be enough to get him interested in you. Now the trick is being where he is. My guess is he's not really a partygoer?"

"Neither am I."

Understanding dawned in Logan's eyes. "Right. Sorry." He paused, as if unsure of what to say next. "If you need to talk about what happened or anything, I'd be happy to listen."

When people found out what had happened to me, usually one of two things occurred. Either they ignored it and never brought it up again, or they went too far in the other direction and wanted all the salacious details, forcing me to relive it, which made me . . . uncomfortable. Logan had somehow found a happy medium, and I was touched by his effort. "That's actually . . . sweet. But I'm good. I did a lot of work on myself, I've dealt with it, and I've talked at length to a very well-trained and well-paid professional who helped me get through it."

"I just wanted to be, I don't know, sensitive about it or whatever." As if he'd let the moment get too deep, he teasingly added, "Because I know how much you love sensitive men."

"You're hilarious."

"Is Ben funny? I mean, on purpose?"

"No more ripping on Ben. We'll see him at the math lab all the time. He volunteers there, too."

Logan nodded. "Right. But we need more social settings. Like that stupid poetry reading. Against my better judgment, I think we have to go to that. Maybe while we're there we can find out what else he does in his free time. Besides Danielle."

I groaned. "You are gross."

He looked offended. "What? I only meant that he spends some of his free time with Danielle. If you thought I meant something else, that's on you and your obviously unclean mind."

Logan started to laugh and I leaned across the chair to smack him on the forearm. His very sculpted, manly, muscular forearm.

I was seriously so shallow.

But not so shallow that I could believe he was doing this out of the goodness of his heart. When his laughter died down I said, "I guess I don't understand why you want to help me."

He hesitated before answering. "Isn't that what friends are for?"

There was a world of hidden meaning in that hesitation. "Seriously. Why are you doing this?"

More hesitation. More studying me, like he was trying to figure out whether or not he could trust me. "You're going to help me get an A in math. I feel like I owe you, and I don't like owing people favors. I don't like charity."

"It's not—" It wasn't charity. I wanted to help him. Part of me needed to, as I'd discovered that volunteering, serving others, helped me to reclaim my power over myself and my life.

"It is."

"You don't mind the scholarship my dad gave you," I reminded him.

"That's different. Both Coach and I are getting something out of that arrangement. He pays for my room and board and for me to get a degree; I win games for him and his school. It's equal. But this, this isn't equal."

"You brought me pizza from my favorite restaurant."

He let out a short bark of laughter. "Not quite the same. The pizza was only a thank-you."

This was obviously important to him. I could tell that he needed it. And if the end result was that I got to date Ben . . . well, was I really going to turn that chance down? "Okay. You help me win over Ben, and we'll consider ourselves square."

"Perfect." I heard the relief in Logan's voice. He held out his hand, offering to shake mine to seal our deal.

Had what had happened earlier been a fluke? I'd never felt that sort of charge from touching a guy before. It had to be a mistake. Or an abnormal burst of static electricity caused by a rogue solar flare or something.

As I shook his hand, I lifted my feet up off the floor just to be sure.

Still there. A current so strong and powerful that I could see how easy it would be to get swept away by it. I tried sucking all the oxygen in the hallway into my lungs so that I could keep breathing.

I pulled my hand away quickly, wondering if he'd felt the same thing or if it was some kind of personal hormonal rebellion because I'd stayed away from men for so long.

Which was probably also the reason why I wanted Logan's help with Ben. I'd told myself that I was happy in my limbo state, but even

I knew an actual relationship would be better than hoping and waiting. I'd been so busy trying to figure out why Logan would want to help me that I hadn't stopped to think about why I was willing to go along with it.

Because I was desperately out of practice and I needed whatever help I could get.

Math lab let out, and students started filing into the hallway. Ben and Danielle walked out together and she spotted me. Then she stood up on her tippy-toes and pulled Ben into the world's grossest and most public display of affection ever.

Which caused me to roll my eyes so hard I nearly went blind.

And, of course, Logan didn't miss a thing. After Danielle had finally finished examining the inside of Ben's mouth and they'd left, Logan said, "I get the feeling you don't like her."

I wondered what had given it away. My calling her evil earlier? "Yeah, in the same sense that you'd call a hurricane a light breeze. I more than just don't like her. I despise her with the fiery, burning intensity of a thousand urinary tract infections."

That made him laugh. "That was . . . descriptive. But why all the animosity? Is it because she's hanging out with Ben?"

"Give me a little credit, would you? I'd never hate on another woman for dating a guy I had a crush on. I was serious when I said she was evil. Like I'm pretty sure she was voted most likely to commit war crimes in high school."

"I've never met anyone described as evil before. What makes you say that?"

I probably should have told Logan that it was none of his business. I'd never even told my dad or my friends about what Danielle had done.

As if he could sense my concern, he said, "Trust me."

"Two words that get people into a lot of trouble." I said it as a way to end this particular conversation. But I realized that I didn't mean it.

There was something about Logan, like his soul could communicate telepathically with my soul, and I instinctively knew I could trust him.

So I told him. "Right after my dad and I moved here, I wanted to go on like nothing had happened to me. I wanted to live my life the same way I had at Amarillo. I was able to transfer to the EOL branch of my sorority. It happened just as the new pledges were finishing up rushing, and Danielle's best friend didn't make it into the sorority and Danielle blamed me for it."

"Wait, you were in a sorority?"

Logan would have been shocked by what I used to look like. I'd been such the stereotypical sorority girl. I'd sported the bright-blonde hair with perfect beach waves, the always on-point outfit, the matching mani-pedis. Back when everyone called me Jessica.

"Yes, but not really the point. Anyway, I decided to ignore her little barbs and passive-aggressive comments about how I didn't really belong. Then I found out that she'd given me a nickname. RV."

The bitter anger I'd felt at the time bubbled up inside me before I continued. "And I thought it was a 'she's a whore' type of reference, like I was a recreational vehicle that gave everyone a ride or something. Turns out that wasn't it at all." It would have been easier if she'd just been slut-shaming me. "Someone finally confessed that RV was short for 'rape victim.' Which some of the sorority sisters apparently found hilarious. I quit that day." And I'd changed my clothes and my fake appearance and started insisting people call me Jess. It was like it had given me permission to finally be my real self. The self I'd always hidden behind clothes and makeup in an attempt to fit in.

"That is . . . horrible."

"Yep. And then, as if that wasn't enough, it was like she made it her personal mission to try and ruin my life. She changed her major from fashion design to math. Which she somehow managed to be good at, but I wasn't interested in being the villain in her own personal reenactment of *Legally Blonde*. She competes with me for grades in classes, with Ben, and now with the graduate program I hope to get into." Problem was, she had been beating me for the last three years. And I was worried she would beat me again when it came to working with Professor Gardiner. "And so far she always wins."

I blinked back the hot tears that had sprung up on my last couple of words.

Logan sat straight up in his armchair and proclaimed, "Key words being *so far*. And I'm known for winning myself. She's finally going to know what it's like to lose."

I nodded. I would not allow myself to cry over evil Danielle.

"Well, I've got a class, so I should get going." He stood, slinging a backpack over his shoulder and picking up the pizza box. "This will all work out. I think this is going to be the beginning of a beautiful friendship."

"Really?" Could he have said anything more clichéd?

"Okay, maybe not beautiful. Attractive." At my look, he corrected himself again. "Slightly attractive? Like a four?"

That made me laugh, and he grinned at the sound.

"For this poetry thing, should we meet up at six thirty or so?" Logan asked. "Do you want me to come to your place?"

"No!" I practically shrieked it. "I mean, a normal-voice no. I live with my dad."

"Oh. I get it. Bad idea then."

"I'll come pick you up at your dorm."

"Let me have your phone for a second and I'll give you my number. Text me when you're in the parking lot."

I handed him my phone, and after punching in his digits, he gave it back. If someone had told me that a few weeks after picking up Logan Hunt at the bus station I'd have his phone number and we'd be going somewhere together on purpose, I would have laughed and laughed and laughed and might have risked being involuntarily committed given my reaction.

"I'll see you tomorrow night at six thirty," I confirmed.

"Yep. Bye!"

I waved to him and realized that I was really looking forward to our not-a-date. Why was I excited?

Because I was going to win over Ben.

Not because of Logan.

Right?

CHAPTER FIVE

LOGAN

There was a knock at my dorm-room door at 6:28. I was a little surprised to find Jess standing there. I was even more surprised to see that she had dressed up. Instead of her usual comfy, baggy clothes, she wore a pair of tight black jeans and a red top that, as a man, I couldn't help but appreciate. I cleared my throat. "I thought you were going to text me."

"That wouldn't have been very gentlemanly of me, would it?" she said with a slight smile. "Digitally honking at you from your driveway?"

I stepped aside with a short laugh, letting her into the room. Bash was sitting on his bed, wearing headphones while he studied. He took them off and smiled at our guest.

"Hey, Jess. How are you doing?"

"I'm good. How did your psychology test go?"

Bash shot me a confused look, probably wondering how she knew about his test, and I flashed back to my joke about his cheating on it. I would need to clear that up with her. I hoped she didn't think Bash would cheat. Or that she'd tell her father as much.

"It went okay. I probably should have studied more, but I've never actually been very good at studying."

"Let Keilani know, and she can get you set up with some tutors. And if you need any math help, I'm available."

"Thanks."

While she'd been talking, Jess's eyes had darted around the room. It was then that I realized that the reason she'd come inside was not to be polite but because she was curious. When she'd dropped us off on that first day, our room had been empty. Now we'd lived in it for a few weeks. In the past I'd noticed some girls treating a room inspection like a test, but Jess wasn't acting that way. She just seemed genuinely interested in the posters we had hanging on the walls and the type of bedding we used.

"You guys are a lot cleaner than I thought you'd be."

"That's Logan's fault," Bash said. "He's kind of obsessive about the room."

I shrugged my shoulders. There was nothing I could say. Bash was right. I was compulsive about it. But growing up with lice, roaches, and bedbugs did that to a person.

"Then you probably shouldn't ever come to my house," Jess said. "I typically only clean when I'm mad. So if you stop by and the house looks nice, you'll probably want to reconsider your visit."

Bash and I laughed at her joke, and I wondered if there was any truth to it. Her being a slob should help remind me to keep her at arm's length. I could never be serious about someone who would leave our shared space a mess.

But this was not the time to dwell on things that would never be. "We should probably get going," I reminded her.

She said her goodbyes to Bash and we headed out to her car. Since there was no one sitting behind me this time, I was able to adjust the passenger seat to a much more comfortable position.

Jess started up the car, and the radio blared a country song at an extremely high volume. She quickly turned the station off, looking embarrassed.

"I wouldn't have pegged you for a country-music girl."

"We lived in Texas for a long time. All my friends listened to it, and, I don't know. I just started liking it."

Her reminder about where she'd grown up made me think about the online search I'd conducted last night. Her talking about her sorority had intrigued me. That lifestyle seemed so the opposite of Jess's personality that I'd had to know more.

I'd tried looking up her name, but she had no social media accounts. There were, however, plenty of pictures from her time at Amarillo as a freshman. She'd been tagged in photos from what looked like frat parties, suggesting that she'd had Facebook and Instagram accounts at some point but had shut them down.

She'd looked so different. Like the Barbie version of the Jess sitting next to me now. Although I preferred current Jess over the woman in the pictures.

I did think that the tags were interesting—all of them listed "Jessica Oakley."

As we crawled to a stop at a yellow light, I asked, "So, is 'Jess' short for 'Jessica'?"

The car suddenly screeched to a halt, as if she'd slammed her foot down on the brake. It took her a second to respond.

"Yes."

I'd hoped she would explain, but it became obvious that she wasn't going to say more unless I asked. "Do you ever go by 'Jessica'?"

"No. I'm not that girl anymore."

Why did every cryptic thing she said make me want to get to know her better? Why couldn't I just leave well enough alone? Help her land Emo Zorro and move on with my life?

She is so very off-limits, I reminded myself yet again. Not just because of Coach, not just because of his rule, but because she liked someone else.

The Friend Zone

"It's not that abnormal to go by a nickname," she continued. "Like 'Bash' being short for 'Sebastian.'" As if that explained her choice away.

I got the distinct feeling there might be more to her story, although I sensed now was not the time to press her on it. But her mention of Bash did remind me of the cheating thing and how I needed to clear his name. "There's something I said to you yesterday that I feel bad about."

"Just one thing?" she teased.

"I don't feel bad about anything I said about Ben. All true. But I did joke about Bash cheating on his test. He wouldn't do that. He didn't do it. I was just trying to be funny."

She paused and then said, "I know that. Why are you telling me this? Are you afraid I'm going to run off and tattle to my daddy?"

Yes. "It's not that. Bash is a good guy. We're both trying really hard to live up to your dad's expectations."

"Yeah, I know how that goes," she said, releasing a deep sigh. It was hard enough being Coach Oakley's quarterback. I could only imagine how difficult it would be to be his daughter. "I think it's impressive that you're trying so hard to do what my dad has asked. It says a lot about the kind of person you are."

Jess turned to look at me. The moment felt charged and heavy between us, and I had the strongest urge to lean over and kiss her. Which I couldn't do. Shouldn't want to do. So I covered it up. "Your dad's honor-and-integrity thing must really be getting through to me."

She smiled and then returned her gaze to the road.

What was that? Yes, Jess was cute; yes, I'd wanted to kiss her since I'd met her; but that wasn't unusual. Especially now that all girls were forbidden. It would make sense that I'd want to kiss the one closest to me.

But it was more than that.

And it was something I had no intention of examining closely.

She seemed determined to thwart my efforts, though. "In case I didn't say it earlier, you clean up nice, cowboy."

41

"Thanks." Now anything I said to her would probably sound suspect, like I was only paying her a compliment because she'd paid me one. I could keep it neutral while still letting her know that I'd noticed her efforts. "You look really nice."

Nice was good. *Nice* was safe. *Nice* wasn't *pretty* or *hot* or *I'd like to kiss you now, thanks.*

"Thank you! I have to admit, I was kind of surprised you didn't instruct me to dress up for this evening. Do my hair, put on a ton of makeup. Like in some kind of rom-com makeover montage."

"You should dress how you want, and no guy should tell you differently. Ben sees you all the time like this, right? He knows what you look like."

"Gee, thanks."

I could hear the hurt in her voice. "I didn't mean that as an insult. You're adorable."

Too adorable.

This seemed to mollify her a little. "Just FYI, girls don't want to be adorable. That term should be reserved for golden retriever puppies and baby sloths."

"What? It's a good thing."

"How do you figure?"

Then I said something I definitely shouldn't have. Even though I tried to make it theoretical, it was absolutely a step too far. "When I'm dating a girl and I tell her she's adorable, I'm not comparing her to a baby dog and/or a slow-moving animal. It means I want to adore her, worship her, in every way imaginable."

If that moment earlier had felt heavy, it was nothing compared to what was going on right now. I was screwing everything up and had to attempt to get this friendship back on track.

"But that's someone I'm dating. And obviously we're not dating and never, ever will if I remember your words correctly, and while some of the intent is the same, in conclusion it wasn't a bad thing."

I didn't say I did a great job of getting it back on track. Just that I attempted it. So I took the lamest cop-out ever. I asked, "Why are you majoring in math?"

Jess gave me a look, as if she knew exactly what I was doing, but she played along. "Lots of different reasons. I don't know if there's anything quite as satisfying as working through a problem and finding the answer. And when something is true in math, it's always true."

"It's never really been a strength of mine."

"Me either, actually. That's one of the reasons why I was drawn to it. It's harder for me than for some of the other students, but that just makes it more worthwhile. And it makes me feel like if I can figure out this thing that's hard for me, life seems less intimidating. Like as long as I work at it, I can solve any problem."

Now it felt like it was about more than just math. "When you talk that way, you make me want to find some Amarillo football players and kick their a—butts."

I immediately regretted my statement, even though it had been true. Was it okay for me to bring it up? To say what I thought? It was her story. I probably shouldn't have been stomping around near it.

But Jess didn't seem to mind and even made a joke about it. "My dad already took care of that, thanks."

I smiled, but I still felt like I was pretending as if I hadn't been just totally awkward. So I said something even dumber, just to make things worse. "I'm the opposite. I like history, I'm good at history, so that's what I'll get my degree in."

She nodded. "History is a little like math. Dates and events don't change, even if our perceptions of historical figures might. But I've never been into my English classes because so much of that is subjective interpretation. I like that math is always straightforward. Logical. Cold. Dispassionate."

"Like a Vulcan."

Now Jess laughed as she pulled into the parking lot of the Corner. I'd thought it would be a dedicated bar, but when we got inside I realized that it was a coffeehouse that apparently served alcohol in the evening. There was a large counter where people gathered, along with booths and tables. Christmas lights were strung back and forth across the industrial ceiling, which had exposed ductwork. A small stage was set up in one corner, and a woman with large glasses and curly hair stood in the spotlight holding a violin above her head, not speaking and not making any sounds with the instrument.

I tried not to groan. I'd never liked performance art.

We grabbed a couple of barstools at the counter and the . . . barista? bartender? came over to take our order. "I'll have a glass of milk."

The barista-tender looked at me funny. "Milk?"

"Yeah. Like the stuff that comes from cows. Milk."

"And I'll have a club soda," Jess said, and the barista-tender left to get our drinks.

"You sure?" I asked her. "Liquid courage might help."

"In addition to avoiding parties, I typically stay away from alcohol. You kind of lose your taste for it when somebody drugs your drink. What about you? Milk?"

"Haven't you heard? Milk does a body good." I slapped my hand against my abs.

I'd meant for it to be a joke, but Jess's gaze traveled up and down my body, as if assessing what I'd said. When she realized that I'd caught her checking me out, she flushed.

Interesting. She might have been in like with Ben, but obviously I wasn't the only one feeling an attraction.

I didn't tease her about her lingering stare and instead said, "I can't drink coffee past one in the afternoon or I'm up half the night. And I can't drink alcohol, even if I wanted to. Coach's rules. So I make sure that nobody can accuse me of anything when I come to a place like this.

Milk can't be mistaken for something else. Avoiding the appearance of evil and all that."

"Speaking of evil, there's Danielle."

I glanced over and saw Jess's nemesis sitting in a booth near the stage. She was accompanied by three girls who could have been her clones. They wore so much pink and glitter it was like a group of strippers had sneezed on them. All four women were on their phones, texting. I wondered if they were texting each other.

"Why do they travel in packs like that?" I wondered out loud.

"It takes them less time to tear the flesh off their victims if they have help."

"Wow. You just made them even scarier than I'd initially imagined."

"Really?" she asked, both eyebrows raised. "I would think that's the kind of girl you'd normally go for. Long of leg, big of breast, short of brain."

"Shows what you know. I like a girl with a brain."

"Only zombies like girls for their brains."

"Pretty only gets you so far. You need to be able to have conversations at some point. I bet even your precious Ben wants a girl who can speak more than one syllable at a time."

Jess frowned. "Speaking of girls Ben wants, isn't part of your genius plan to get Danielle's attention? Because you know she has no idea we're here."

"How do you know that?"

"Duh. Because she hasn't released her flying monkeys to get us."

Before I could respond, the barista-tender handed us our drinks. "Here's your club soda, and here is your *milk*." She gave me a weird look as she handed me the glass. Which was okay. My whole life had become weird. I was getting used to it.

I took a gulp of my drink, wiping away any potential milk mustache with the back of my sleeve. Jess wasn't looking for Ben, which seemed strange, considering he was the whole reason we were here. "Where is your knight in dull black denim? Your future boyfriend?"

"He likes to meditate backstage before his performance."

Deciding not to mock the meditation part, I said, "This place has a backstage?"

"It's just the manager's office, but he needs to get centered before he goes on stage."

Must . . . not . . . make . . . fun.

As if sensing my internal struggle not to mercilessly mock Ben, Jess offered me an out. "The team has been doing really well."

That was sort of an understatement. We'd been crushing the competition. Like a kid with an anthill. Everyone crumpled under our feet and offered no resistance. "Yeah."

"You, in particular, have been fantastic."

I took another drink. "Thanks, but we have some great coaches. Your dad and his staff are excellent, and the guys are all working so hard."

"You're not going to take credit for the wins?" She sounded surprised.

"It's a team effort. We win together, we lose together."

Jess recognized her dad's words. "Only in this instance it's 'We win together and we win together.'"

"We're definitely on a nice winning streak." And privately I would admit that some small part of me hoped that an NFL scout was out there noticing me. That professional football might not be totally out of my reach. No matter how long that shot was, no matter how much I told myself to forget about it, I still wanted it.

Someone stepped up to the microphone. "That was Shiraz and her magic violin. Thank you, Shiraz! Next up we have Ben Edwards performing his new original piece."

Ben walked out on the stage, all darkness and solemnity. Holy sh—crap. Was he actually wearing a black fedora?

"This is called 'Ben, I Am.'"

Oh no.

Then he made it worse.

"Ben, I am. I am Ben. Ben, Ben, Ben. Ben is me. Me is Ben. Ben, Ben, Ben. Ben, I am."

Was he serious with this sh—crap? He went on for another ten minutes with variations of those sentences. Like some kind of maniacal Dr. Seuss who was trying to create a "poem" with as few words as possible.

Ben I Am was sucking my will to live. I wanted to do a double Van Gogh and cut off my ears. Maybe that's why Van Gogh did it in the first place. Somebody made him listen to really bad poetry.

Me Is Ben finally brought his particular form of torture to an end, bowing deeply when he finished.

There was a smattering of applause. Danielle didn't look up from her phone, while Jess clapped loudly, drawing people's attention. I put my hand over hers. "Not so enthusiastic. We have to play it cool, remember?"

This should have been no big deal. I only touched her for a second. But it was like someone had scorched my hand. As if I'd held it over an open campfire. I'd never experienced a physical response so immediate or so overwhelming with any woman before. Something about Jess made my nerves go haywire.

Even more reason to make sure we stayed deep in the friend zone.

"Right. Play it cool. Sorry." She sounded out of breath, and it made my stomach muscles tighten. "Wasn't that so good?"

The hazy, wanting gleam in her eyes made my chest feel too small for my lungs. "That's not quite the word I would have chosen."

"He's planning on getting his doctorate in poetry."

I couldn't keep it in any longer. "That sucks for poems."

"Logan!"

Ben walked off the stage and over to Danielle and her friends like he was expecting some validation, but none of them acknowledged his existence. It was kind of pathetic the way he was hanging around the outskirts of Danielle's group. I figured it was probably an apt metaphor for his entire life.

But the pack had left their wide receiver open with no coverage by ignoring him.

"This is it," I told Jess. "Time to grab Dork Vader's attention. I want you to go to the bathroom, making sure you walk in his eyeline. If he says something to you, don't respond. Say nothing. Smile, so he knows you heard him, but walk on by. Stay in the bathroom for a few minutes and when you come back out, do the same thing. Head straight back here. We need to make him come to you."

"When he does, what do I do?"

"I'll make myself scarce and you flirt with him."

The barista-tender asked if I wanted another glass of milk, and I told her to hit me again. She returned with it about a minute later.

Jess waited until we were alone again before speaking. I saw her cheeks reddening in that all-too-appealing way. "I don't know if I remember how to flirt."

"What are you talking about? You flirt with me all the time."

"Um, no." She shook her head a little too hard. "And I don't think you're clear on our dynamic, but I appreciate the effort."

"You flirt. Sometimes it's kind of mean flirting, but I know you can do it. Now go get him, tiger!"

Jess stood up from her barstool. "Right. I can do this. Do I have anything in my teeth?"

I wondered what kind of bizarre female ritual this was as she flashed her pearly whites at me. And it should have been off-putting, but instead I again found myself weirdly wanting to kiss her.

I had to stop the madness.

She likes I Am Ben, I reminded my hormones.

"Nope. All clear. Go. And don't fumble the ball."

"There's the emotional support I was looking for." And despite her assertion that she didn't flirt with me, she shot me the most flirtatious smile ever. I realized that I was currently in need of some emotional support. I needed to make this Ben thing happen, and soon.

I took a big swig of the only kind of drink I was allowed to have. I'd always considered myself strong, but this situation with Jess was quickly turning crazy.

It was a good thing I had a lot of willpower.

And lots and lots of emotional-support milk.

CHAPTER SIX

JESS

I totally meant to do just what Logan said. I walked across the room like I owned it, faking confidence with every single step. Ben had moved away from Danielle and was checking his phone near the jukebox. I pretended to ignore him right up until the moment when he said, "Jess! Hi!"

What could I do? He was just so . . . there and talking to me.

"Hey!" I came to a stop and could almost feel Logan's eyes boring into me as I was in the middle of doing the opposite of what he'd said to do.

"I'm glad you made it. What did you think?"

I could see that he was eager for praise, and I was eager for him to like me, so . . . "You did so great."

He nodded, like he totally agreed. But he didn't say anything back, so I had to keep talking. "It was just . . . brilliant?" I hadn't meant for it to sound like a question, but I felt pressured, and not knowing what else to say, I settled on *brilliant*.

"That's exactly the word I would have chosen. You totally got it."

Ben looked so proud of himself. So . . . vain. And kind of cocky. It was a turnoff. Especially compared to Logan's humble reaction when I'd complimented him on being such an incredible quarterback. Because Logan was beyond gifted. I'd never seen that much natural talent in a football player before. He should win every athletic award known to mankind.

And Ben? Ben had said his name a bunch of times on stage.

Man. Even that was kind of arrogant and self-centered.

Okay, so I didn't think his performance was brilliant. I thought it was . . . average. But I probably just didn't understand poetry or performance art well enough to get it.

I wanted Ben to be artistic and deep and insightful because my entire life had been filtered by a football bro zone, where everything was about sweaty dudes and the sports they played and how well they played them.

Was that expectation my fault, or was this on Ben? I wasn't sure who to blame for how badly things were going right now.

Logan would probably blame me for not listening to him.

"Well, I'll see you around," I said. Not because I was doing as Logan had instructed, but because I suddenly didn't want to talk to Ben. He looked different. Like his star had dimmed.

And his hat was stupid.

I didn't wait for his reply and instead headed straight to the bathroom.

Where I immediately ran into Keilani, who was finishing up washing her hands.

"Hello!" I said, giving her a big hug. "What are you doing here?"

"Blind date," she said with a sigh, throwing away the paper towel she'd used. "And I don't think he's going to be happy about how this night will end: with me sending him on his way and telling him not to call me again."

I pulled out my lipstick from my jeans pocket and started applying it. "Huh. I thought maybe you were here with Ford. I know how much you love him."

And even though I was obviously joking, Keilani pounced. "I the opposite of love him. I hate him."

"Hate isn't the opposite of love. Indifference is. Hate means you feel something for him."

"Yes. Hatred."

It was not nice of me to torment Keilani about Ford, but I really did think that they liked each other but were both hiding it. She was owed some payback because she'd given me a hard time for years about getting back out there and dating someone.

Other than Ben. She was strangely not on the Ben train.

"What about you?" Her question interrupted my thoughts. "Did I see you with Logan? Is there something I should know?"

Was she asking as my friend or as my dad's academic adviser, dedicated to keeping the football players in line with his rules? "Nothing is going on. He's helping me figure out how to, um, encourage Ben to fall for me. Logan thinks he owes me for helping him with tutoring."

"Oh." She pursed her lips, looking a little concerned. "Did you tell him that's not how it works?"

"Yes. But he's insisting. And he's kind of stubborn."

"I've witnessed that stubbornness firsthand. Okay, wish me luck before I head into the breach once more."

"Good luck!" I said, putting my lipstick away. "Text me if I need to punch somebody for you."

Keilani paused at the bathroom door. "Jess? Be careful. Don't let things with Logan get serious. For both of your sakes."

Ha. There was little chance of that happening. Even if Ben and my dad's rules didn't exist, someone like me would never stand a chance with a demigod like Logan. He was out of my league, and well I knew it.

I blotted my lipstick and then headed back to Logan. I ignored Ben on the way out, not even making eye contact.

When I got to my barstool and sat down, Logan let out a heavy sigh.

"What?" I demanded. Even though I knew exactly what he was going to say.

"Seriously, Jess? I gave you a really simple set of instructions to follow and you didn't do it. Now I know how all my high school teachers felt."

"I'm sorry. You were right. I think I messed things up. Or he messed things up."

I only got a moment to wonder just how many glasses of milk Logan had downed this evening as he finished his current one off and then asked, "How so?"

"He asked what I thought of his performance, and when I said I thought it was brilliant, he agreed with me. In a really cocky way."

Logan loudly sighed again. "You can't tell him stuff like that. A guy like Ben I Am needs to earn his compliments and favors or else he thinks they're not worthwhile. He doesn't want a fan club. He wants a woman he has to work for. Otherwise he wouldn't be hanging around Danielle. Because, trust me, she hasn't told him he did a good job."

"Isn't that what men like? A woman who will stroke their ego?"

He pressed his lips into a thin line. For a second I thought he was angry, until I realized he was holding in laughter.

"What's so funny?"

"Sorry, I'm just trying really hard to refrain from making an inappropriate joke."

That made both of us laugh. It had been a long time since I'd hung out with a guy who made me want to laugh this much.

Logan ordered another glass of milk.

"How many of those are you going to have?" I asked.

"Hey, don't knock my emotional-support milk."

"Emotional-support milk?" I repeated.

"I really like milk. At the moment it's the only thing getting me through this evening of people who think they're poets. I'm hoping my lit professor will give me extra credit for showing up to this because it's the only way I can think of to salvage tonight." He paused. "Did you really tell him he was brilliant? I'm sorry, but are you on crack?"

"Yes," I giggled. And yes, I thought my giggling was obnoxious, too.

Logan was on a roll. "You know, I was doing this to level the playing field. Make us even. Now I feel like I should be given a prize for sitting through all these readings. Maybe even a medal."

"Your self-pity is not helping my situation. How do we regroup after I failed to follow instructions?"

"Ben's a guy," Logan said with a dismissive wave. "He'll forget all about it."

"Do you . . ." I looked down at my club soda. "Do you think it's weird that he agreed with me? Didn't even pretend to be humble?"

He didn't speak at first, as if giving my questions serious consideration. "I guess that depends on you and what you like in the guys you date. But to be fair, after a game I'm all hyped up on adrenaline and have been known to say and do stupid things. Maybe this was the same. He was just all pumped up and acted like an idiot. Maybe even to impress you."

I knew Logan thought Ben was pathetic, and what did impress me was his trying to be fair instead of making another dig at Ben.

"Maybe," I agreed with him, not sure what to think. "Or maybe we should just quit while we're behind."

"Look, we're at first and ten here. We have plenty of time and four downs to move this ball. Maybe we've lost tonight's battle, but I plan on winning the war."

"This isn't the Roman Empire. We're not actually at war with anyone."

"Don't you listen to pop songs? Love is a battlefield. All's fair in love and war," he said.

"I think that last one's from an old poem, not a pop song."

"Whatever. The point is, pop songs are like modern-day poetry and infinitely better than anything we heard here tonight, so I win the argument."

"What?" I said with a laugh. "That makes no kind of sense. And by the way, you don't win any arguments right now because you still haven't launched your genius plan yet. We were supposed to use tonight to find out what Ben does in his free time."

"I got this. I have a unique and subtle way to find out exactly what he does. Watch me work since your goth Jedi has started staring at us. Excuse me while I . . ." Logan scooted his barstool closer. For one heart-stopping moment I thought he was going to put his arm around my shoulders or touch me and make me spontaneously combust, but he just sat really close to me again.

Close enough to pique Ben's interest, but not enough to get Logan in trouble.

Problem was, Logan's magnetic warmth spilled across the slight opening between us, beckoning me to move closer. To get enveloped by him and all his manly manliness.

"Hi! I don't think we've been formerly introduced. I'm Ben Edwards."

The sound of Ben's voice startled me so badly I nearly fell backward off my barstool. Logan's lightning-fast reflexes put his arm behind my back, helping me to regain my equilibrium. Then he turned to Ben and offered him his hand. "Logan Hunt. Nice to meet you."

"You too. So . . . you and Jess are dating?"

"What?" Logan asked as I said, "Oh no. Just friends."

"I thought you two were—" Ben replied, but Logan cut him off.

"No. Just friends." Then Logan gave me a look that said he wanted to be anything but just friends.

And I felt it in my toes.

He was a much better actor than I would have given him credit for.

"She's just tutoring me in math, and we hang out from time to time. How do you know my Jess?" Logan asked, and neither Ben nor I missed his use of the word *my*. I'd give him this, Logan definitely knew what he was doing, because an unmistakably jealous look crossed Ben's face.

"We've had some classes together, volunteer at the math lab together. Things like that."

Logan said, "So I'm new in town, Ben. What do you do in your downtime?"

This was his master plan? To just ask Ben? There was no subtlety there at all.

"I'm not sure you and I are into the same kinds of things," Ben said with a hint of laughter in his voice.

"Oh, I don't know." Logan's smoldering gaze flickered over to me and I couldn't help myself. I gasped as liquid heat pooled in my stomach. I was not equipped to handle Logan's full-frontal sexiness. "We might have more in common than you think. Try me."

"Well, I study a lot. I perform my art when I can. I work at that restaurant, Madison and Main, a couple of nights a week. I've also been doing the football games–parties-and-dances thing lately."

Was that due to Danielle?

"Really?" Was Logan actually surprised, or was this just more of his Academy Award–worthy acting? "You don't seem like the joiner type."

Ben shrugged one shoulder while he glanced at Danielle, seeming to confirm my suspicion. She was still on her phone. "The things we do to get a girl's attention, am I right?"

"Definitely," Logan agreed. "And thanks for the info, Ben. I'll have to check some of that stuff out."

There was a tone of dismissal in Logan's voice, which Ben warily responded to.

"Uh, okay. No problem. I'm on my way out, but I'm sure I'll see you guys around. Thanks for coming to see me!"

Wanting to let Logan work his magic and not mess things up again, I'd stayed quiet for the entire exchange. But now I finally spoke. "Bye! See ya! Soon! Like at school!"

Ugh, I was all desperate enthusiasm and patheticness.

Yeah, I definitely knew how to bring all the boys to my yard.

Maybe if I'd had some time to talk to Ben alone it would have gone differently. Logan had failed in that department. "Weren't you supposed to make yourself scarce so that I could flirt with Ben?"

"Last-minute lane adjustment. I sensed we'd do better if I stayed. And trust me, that went well. We got tons of info and Ben left more intrigued than when he started. We're going to win all the battles and the war at this rate."

"If you say so. You didn't get Danielle's attention at all."

Somehow Logan's grin got even wider and his face even more attractive. It was so unfair. "She's been aware of us since we sat down. Which makes sense if she's as competitive with you as you say. She didn't miss how Ben has sought you out twice now, and there's no way she's going to let you have a new boy toy. In fact, she's planning on getting her revenge by flirting with me in three . . . two . . . one . . ."

"Did you see where *Ben* went?" Danielle asked in her unmistakable, high-pitched voice. The emphasis on his name was clearly meant for me. It was possessive sounding.

But I did notice that she didn't call him her boyfriend. Which I expected, just to let me know that he was off-limits.

"Out that door," Logan said, jerking his thumb toward the exit. "You just missed him. And you are?"

"The devil incarnate?" I whispered under my breath.

Or I might have said it loud enough for everyone to hear me.

Danielle glared at me. "I'm Danielle."

"I like your name." That flirtatious look was back in Logan's eyes, only this time he was directing it at the she-devil. And it made me feel stabby.

"You do? Then just wait until you hear my phone number," she flirted back, practically purring at him.

"Wait, didn't we just establish that you're looking for Ben?" Logan teased, as if this were all fun and games and not valid defenses for a justifiable murder. "By the way, I'm Logan. And I think you already know my friend Jess."

She deigned to look down her nose at me. "Jessica."

"Homicidal Barbie" was how I returned her greeting.

Danielle then wedged her way in between us, focusing all of her attention on Logan. "You say Ben just left?"

"Yep. We saw him go. Do you need a ride somewhere?"

Did Logan want to add himself to my people-to-off-tonight list? I wasn't going anywhere with her.

"No, thank you. I have my car here. But you are so very sweet." She glared at me while she said it.

Was that her worst dig? That I wasn't sweet? Pretty much everybody knew that, including me.

Then she kissed Logan on his cheek, and I'd never wanted to strangle somebody so badly in my entire life. How dare she touch him with her collagen-filled lips?

And why did that bother me more than Ben full-on making out with her?

Her kiss lingered far longer than what anyone would consider normal, and I was about to pull out her fake hair by its fake roots when she finally pulled away.

"I'll see you around, Logan."

She was then joined by her fellow fembots and was definitely swaying her hips for Logan's benefit as she strutted away.

The outline of her hot-pink kiss was still on his cheek. I handed him a napkin. "Here. She marked you."

"Again, this is a good thing," Logan said as he took the napkin and scrubbed where I indicated. Seeing that it wasn't coming off easily, I took another napkin and dipped it into my club soda. He took it from me, and that seemed to work better. "They left separately. Danielle obviously thinks we're together and went out of her way to try to annoy you. Just as I predicted."

"Maybe you should have majored in psychology. You seem to be excellent at predicting human behavior."

"These humans' behavior, at least."

"Or you just dated a lot before you got to EOL."

He smiled. "Or I dated a lot before I got to EOL."

Why did that bother me? Not wanting to think about it too much, I asked our bartender for our check. Logan was here helping me out, so I could pay for our drinks.

Or, more accurately, my dad would be paying the check since he didn't want me to have a job while I was in college and still basically gave me an allowance. Hopefully my account wasn't overdrawn.

Logan said, "Thanks for getting that."

"You got me pizza, I can pay for your emotional-support milk."

"We can't keep track of who owes who what or else we'll drive ourselves crazy. We'll be indebted to each other for forever."

I took my wallet out of my purse and handed my credit card to the bartender. "Or we could try to keep one-upping each other. And someday when you're playing for the NFL I'll very nicely let you have the last gift. I like muscle cars, FYI."

The bartender handed me back my card and my receipt, along with a pen.

"I'm not going to play in the NFL." He said the words quickly, almost spitting them out, as if they tasted bad in his mouth.

"What are you talking about?" I asked as I filled in the tip and signed the receipt. "You are so talented. There's no way you're not getting recruited by somebody. And my dad has a ton of connections."

Logan stood up and I did the same. He gestured toward the door, indicating that he wanted to go. I wondered why he was so touchy about the NFL. If anyone on the planet deserved to be playing professional football, it was him.

I wanted to ask him why he was behaving strangely, but I got the impression now was not the right time.

Just before we reached the exit, our way was blocked by a man. He was probably ten years older than us and had that look about him where you could tell he used to be an athlete, but years of drinking and junk food had filled his frame with fat instead of muscle. He held a mug of beer in his left hand. The end of his nose was faintly red, and he swayed as he stood there, obviously wasted.

Like a drunk Rudolph the Red-Nosed Drunk Guy.

"Excuse me," I said.

But the man ignored me. "You Logan Hunt? Quarterback for the Owls?"

Logan stepped in front of me, shielding me from the drunk. "I am. If you don't mind, we were on our way out. Have a good night."

Rudolph didn't move. Instead, he jabbed Logan in his shoulder with his free hand. "You think you're so great? You think you're better than me?"

"I don't even know you, man."

"Oh? You want to take this outside?" Rudolph's words were slurred and slow but definitely angry.

Logan didn't seem far behind in the anger department. "Bad idea. You couldn't take me and I'm not going to fight you." And then, as if he couldn't leave well enough alone, he added, "I get hit every day of the week. You look like the last thing you tackled was a bag of Doritos."

Rudolph went from being rude and angry to downright belligerent and furious. "I played rugby at EOL. That's like football, only without all the pansy safety pads you . . ."

My dad's no-swearing rule had been instituted in my home and on his team for so long that it actually shocked me whenever I heard a really vulgar curse. Like the one this drunk rando had just used to describe Logan. I gasped out loud.

Given what I knew of Logan's past temper—that it was the reason he'd been kicked off the team at F&T—I half expected him to take a swing at the guy.

"Real classy, man. Why don't you go sleep this off somewhere?" Then Logan looked over his shoulder at me. "You okay?"

"I'm fine. Let's just get out of here."

Logan took my hand, enveloping it with his own. The same fiery response roared to life, but it was tempered with the real fear I felt in this situation. Who knew what this guy would do?

As if to answer my question, he continued jabbing Logan's shoulder. "You think you can just walk away from me? You think you can just leave?"

"I am leaving."

Then Rudolph threw his beer on Logan, covering him in liquid and yelling, "Whatcha gonna do now? Huh? Now what?"

Oh no. Logan was going to beat the crap out of this idiot and get kicked off the team. I had to get him out of there.

CHAPTER SEVEN

JESS

At this point other people started to intervene. Rudolph's equally drunk friends were telling him to chill, restraining him, while a bouncer came over to tell Rudolph and his reindeer friends that it was time to leave.

I tugged on Logan's hand. I could feel his rage in every corded muscle in his arm and hand, the tension that engulfed his body. I wouldn't let him do this.

"Come on, cowboy. I want to go."

He followed me, his steely gaze trained on Rudolph. I knew it would take very little to push Logan over the edge. I led him over to the passenger side of my car, unlocking the door and practically shoving him inside. There was still yelling happening at the doorway of the Corner, so I closed the door and ran around to the driver's side, got in, and started the car up before Logan could get out and do something he shouldn't.

I turned on the radio because I could feel Logan seething beside me, like a raging bull, and I hoped music might soothe the savage beast.

"I'm kind of hungry," I said. "Do you mind if I stop by Gino's and pick up some pizza?"

"Fine."

His one-word answer was terse, and while I understood that he wasn't angry with me, it still made me a bit anxious.

Neither one of us said anything until I reached Gino's. I said, "Stay here. I'll go grab something and be right back."

Logan just nodded, his arms folded across his chest. I ran inside and asked the cashier if they had anything ready to go. Thankfully, somebody had canceled an order that the restaurant had already made up. It was a large supreme pizza. I paid for it and took it back to my car.

"Doesn't that smell great?" I asked him, wondering if he could detect my faux enthusiasm. I handed him the pizza so that I could drive.

"I can't really smell anything but this beer. Sorry about making your car smell like the inside of a brewery."

"That is not your fault. And it also wouldn't be the first time." At Logan's raised, questioning eyebrows, I went on. "Let's just say it involved a hijacked keg and two overeager frat boys who thought they knew how to tap it."

A smile. Faint, but there. I felt a small sense of relief. I drove back to his dorm and pulled into the parking lot. It was then that I realized my mistake. We probably should have gone inside Gino's to eat, but it had been full of people. There was a park nearby, but, as always, the weather was drizzly and cold. And it was late enough that I couldn't go into his dorm without getting both of us in trouble.

As if he could read my mind, Logan said, "Do you want to eat it here?"

"Sure." I opened the box and grabbed a slice. I noticed that the windows were getting fogged up from our breathing and the heat from the pizza. "Are you worried about anyone seeing us together and jumping to the wrong conclusion?"

"We aren't doing anything wrong. And at this moment, I kind of don't care." I again experienced that twinge of relief when he started eating and seemed to be calming down.

I was in the middle of trying to decide the best course of action moving forward. Did I sit here quietly and say nothing? Just eat and then say good night? Did I pretend like nothing had happened and maybe talk more about Ben? Or did I bring up the almost-fight and let him talk it out? I didn't know what the right move would be.

Logan solved my dilemma for me by saying, "I really, really wanted to punch that guy."

He'd chosen door number four, talking it out! I let out a small sigh of relief before agreeing. "I really, really wanted to punch that guy, too. I think we should both be commended for our restraint." I took a bite of pizza and swallowed it down. "Why didn't you hit him?"

Logan chewed slowly and pulled some deep breaths into his lungs, which seemed to help. "I told you. There's nothing and no one worth losing my scholarship over. I'm not going to spend my entire life living in poverty. This is my way out."

I'd always assumed that Logan had grown up in one of those suburban neighborhoods where everyone in town went to the Friday night football games and he was the local hero. That he'd been adored and his life had been easy because he was so talented. But poverty? A way out? Those things were totally at odds with the idyllic childhood I'd imagined for him. "What do you mean?"

He was quiet for so long that I thought he wasn't going to answer. And when he finally did, I felt like I couldn't catch my breath. "My earliest memory is being hungry. Going through the kitchen cabinets, trying to find something to eat. I think I was about three years old."

When I was three years old, I was finger painting and singing songs. Logan had been starving.

"My mother was a drug addict and had a series of boyfriends in and out of the house. She married my stepdad when I was five. He was terrible, like the others, only he took things a step further. He liked to hit her. And me. And if he wasn't hitting us, he was verbally abusing us. I think my mom put up with it because he kept her supplied with a steady stream of her favorites. They didn't care much about me. I was like some plant that they occasionally watered when they remembered that I was there."

My stomach churned and my mouth got a sour taste. Suddenly not able to eat anything else, I set my pizza back in the box. Was that why he felt so strongly about wasting food?

"At least when I got to first grade it meant I finally got at least one meal a day. As I got older, I spent a lot of time at my friends' houses so that I could have snacks and dinners there."

An image of a six-year-old Logan, desperately hungry, made hot tears spring to my eyes. "Did you tell anyone?"

"No. I never told anybody. That trailer was the only home I'd ever known. I didn't know we weren't normal until I was older. I just thought that's how families were. I didn't realize that most homes weren't as filthy as mine, overrun with vermin and insects. That other kids were fed multiple times a day. Then my mom got arrested for several drug-related charges, and given that it was her third strike, she got twenty years. I was eleven. I went home with my stepfather and it seemed easier to stay. The devil I knew was better than the one I didn't."

"Oh, Logan." I put my hand on his forearm. I wanted to show him how sorry I was. I couldn't even begin to comprehend what his life had been like.

He looked at my hand and then put his own on top of it. The warmth and heat of him slammed into me, quickly turning this tender moment into something potentially much bigger. I reluctantly drew back.

Logan continued his story. "It did come to an end. He was a mean drunk and I was his punching bag until one day, when I was fourteen, I hit him back. He never touched me again. And I promised myself that I would never end up like him. I didn't want to do really hard manual labor into my old age, sell and use drugs, live in some tiny trailer with no prospects. I thought football would be my way out. But now I realize that's too unrealistic. It's my education. I'm going to graduate, earn my teaching certificate, and no one can ever take that away from me. Least of all some drunk a—idiot in a bar."

"Teachers don't make very much," I said as both an honest statement and a weak attempt to make him laugh.

"There's a future there. I can build a career. I know they don't make a lot, but it's better than the alternative." He again took in a deep breath and let it back out, slowly, carefully. "They taught me these breathing exercises when I went to anger management classes. F&T insisted. They didn't help as much as my coach was hoping. I think I had a lot more pent-up rage than people realized."

"I think you had good reason for it."

He shrugged. "Punching people made me feel better. It used to be like a release for me. It gave me a sense of control. Power. Until I figured out it was going to turn me into my stepdad. I tried to focus all my energy and anger into football, but I hadn't quite worked it out. And my temper made me lose everything I'd worked for. Never again. So now it's exaggerated breathing and keeping my hands to myself. Especially since your dad took away all of my other outlets."

I was glad he had enough willpower to keep himself out of trouble. "I guess you'll have to let it all go on the field."

Logan turned to me with his signature grin, and the sight of it made me feel better. "That's what all of us have had to do. Why do you think we've been winning so much?" He drummed his fingers against his leg. "Jess. I came so close tonight to losing control. I don't want to lose control."

Unfortunately, I knew exactly how he felt. "It's a terrible thing when you don't feel like you're in control of yourself or what's happening to you. I know how hard that is."

Logan shook his head. "I didn't see that guy coming, you know? I was so focused on you and this Ben thing that I wasn't prepared for it."

I shifted in my seat so that I could face him. "How could you have prepared for that?"

"Do you remember earlier when you said I should have majored in psychology because I was good at predicting what people will do? It was a skill I had to learn to survive in my house growing up. When you live with an abuser, you get really good at reading people and what they'll do next. It's what makes me so good at executing plays on the field. I know how the other team is going to react to my plays. I can sense it. It's almost like having a superpower."

A superpower that he'd had to develop since he was being beaten. I let out a shaky breath. I had no experience at all with stuff like this. "I don't know what to say." I wished there were some perfect phrase I could utter. Something that would take away his pain. But I knew better than anyone how impossible that was. How you had to work through your pain one minute at a time. Then you had to be able to exist with that pain for an hour, knowing you were strong enough to overcome it. Until you could cobble together twenty-four hours where you didn't live in that pain every minute. And with each day that passed, each week that passed, it somehow got easier. It never went completely away, but human beings were built to survive and overcome. "I wish I could help."

"It's enough that you're willing to listen." Another one of his cleansing breaths. "In fact, you're the only person I've ever told about this."

"I think it's the pizza," I told him. "Because you're the only person I've told about Ben besides Keilani. I think Gino might be putting some kind of truth serum in the sauce that's making us confess our deepest, darkest secrets."

"That's not it." That intense gaze, the one that made my spine so light that I partly feared it was about to float away out of my body, was back. "You're so easy to talk to, Jess."

"So are you." It was a big admission for me. A movement toward trusting a man I'd only known for a couple of days.

Another one of those charged moments when it felt like our bodies were trying to communicate, to get closer to one another, but our brains were interfering.

Which was a good thing. Our brains should be interfering, keeping us from doing something truly stupid.

Something that would ruin Logan's life. I was not going to be responsible for killing his hopes and dreams.

"Well, as you can imagine from my past, I don't much like being dirty." Logan gestured at his beer-soaked clothes. "I'm going to go in and take a shower. I'll see you at the math lab in a couple of days and we'll figure out our next move, okay?"

"Sounds good!" His admission had made so many things fall into place. Like why he was a neat freak. I felt like I understood him at a scarily intimate level. "Have a good night!" Like we were just good buddies and there was no physical attraction between us whatsoever. At all.

He got out of the car, holding the pizza box above his head as a shield. We'd been so caught up in our conversation that I hadn't even noticed the massive raindrops that were slamming fast and furiously onto my car. I had to wipe the inside of the windshield to see him run into his dorm.

Once he was inside, I started up my car. Then I drove slowly out of the parking lot and headed home to my dad's townhouse. It seemed like the rain was keeping everyone else indoors, and I was the only person in the world out in this quasi-monsoon.

Which was good, because as much as I wanted to turn off my brain and just drive, there were things to consider.

Like Logan's and my confessing that we found each other easy to talk to. My realization that I was finding him easy to trust. I thought of how he wholeheartedly threw himself into helping me with Ben, even though he thought Ben was weird. How tonight at the Corner, when that Rudolph guy seemed threatening, Logan had stepped between us, ready to keep me safe. How he so carefully followed all of my dad's stupid rules when I knew the majority of the football team did whatever they wanted and just hoped my father never found out.

And how he'd confided in me? Told me things he'd never told another person? How could I not be moved by that?

Here I'd been thinking about the physical attraction between us, but there was starting to be an emotional attraction. It wasn't just that he was pretty. Okay, it wasn't just that he was Greek-god gorgeous.

There was something else there. Some kind of heartstring that linked us together. I worried that the more time we spent together, the more heartstrings would develop. Until I was completely caught in his net.

I had to make sure that didn't happen.

Logan Hunt would graduate if it was the last thing I did.

When I got home, I petted our dog, Suzette, who danced around the foyer excitedly. She was a white labradoodle and was most likely bipolar. Some days she needed more attention than any other living creature I'd ever met; other days she seemed to barely tolerate having to share a home with us. I patted her and told her what a good girl she was while I kicked off my shoes.

"Dad?" I called out, wondering why Suzette wasn't lying across his lap. I heard him laugh. But it sounded almost like a man giggle.

I went into the living room, and he was sitting on his hideous favorite recliner in front of the TV. He had earbuds in and his cell phone out. When he noticed me, he went "Oh!" and put his phone in between the armrest and the chair cushion while yanking out his earbuds. He was acting so strangely.

"Hi. What are you doing?" As soon I asked, I wanted to retract the question. There were several possible explanations for what my father had been doing and why he had hidden his phone, and I was grossed out by every one.

"N-n-nothing. Just . . . watching the game." He pointed at the TV, which was very off.

I'd never heard him stutter before. Ew. It had to be really disgusting. Time to change the subject.

"Did you eat?" I asked and went into the kitchen to wash my hands. I'd lost my appetite earlier, but it had returned with a vengeance and brought along some very hungry friends.

"Yes. I'm fine."

I pulled some meat, lettuce, tomatoes, cheese, ketchup, and mayonnaise from the fridge to make myself a sandwich. My dad wandered into the kitchen with an expression I recognized all too well.

Now that his embarrassment over whatever weird thing he'd been doing on his phone had passed, it was interrogation time.

"Where were you tonight?"

My dad was always urging me to go out and enjoy myself. It was probably because he remembered how I was Before. How nothing had made me happier than being out with my friends.

Now I spent most of my time at home.

But I saw his expression and realized my dad knew. It wasn't my father standing in the kitchen, it was Coach Oakley. Somehow he knew I'd been out with Logan. Who told him? Had Keilani done it? I couldn't imagine her calling or texting my father without telling me first. It wasn't like her.

There was no way for me to know who saw what. Who else was there? One of the coaching staff? Maybe a third-string quarterback hoping to get Logan's position? Danielle, trying to get me in trouble?

Or maybe somebody had taken out their cell phone and filmed that confrontation with Rudolph? For all I knew something like that could have gone viral and had Logan's name attached to it.

The best defense with my dad was an excellent offense. Better to get out ahead of him before he jumped to majorly wrong conclusions. "I was with Logan Hunt at the Corner. We are not dating. We are barely even friends. I am his math tutor and helping him with his schoolwork.

Nobody drank, nobody fought, nobody swore, and nobody got kissed. Especially not me."

"Even if I let the team date, Logan Hunt is the last guy I'd want dating my daughter."

I stopped spreading mayonnaise on my bread to stare at him. "How can you say that? Logan's a really good guy, Dad."

"He's an angry kid. It's why I didn't recruit him after high school. He was a hothead both on and off the field. I did my research on him. He has a lot of trauma in his past."

"So do I," I reminded him, unnecessarily. "Does that mean I'm undatable?"

"What? No! That's not what I meant." His expression shifted from coach back to my father, and I could see that he hadn't meant anything toward me by his statement. He looked contrite.

But it really bugged me. Logan was amazing and any girl would be lucky to have him. No, not just lucky, the freaking Mega Millions winner of dating. Instead of letting it go, I dug my heels in further. Like Suzette with her favorite toy bone. "Don't you believe in the power of redemption? Isn't that why we're here at this school? So you can take these messed-up boys and put them back together again? Make them better than they were?"

"Yes, of course I believe that, and I wasn't trying to—"

I didn't know what had gotten into me. Why I was so protective of Logan. Maybe it was all he'd shared with me that night. But no way was I letting my dad paint Logan as the bad guy. "Some idiot verbally attacked Logan at the Corner. Then he threw his drink on him, and Logan did nothing in response! He just walked away. Two years ago, would he have done that? He's come such a long way."

"You seem awfully defensive of him," my dad commented.

"Because you're not being fair." I jabbed my butter knife toward him to punctuate my words. "You should be proud of him and instead you're telling me all the ways he'd make a terrible boyfriend. People can change. And don't you trust me? Don't you think I know your rules better than anyone? I'm his math tutor. I tutor him. In math. That's it."

"I know that." He held both of his hands out in a placating gesture. "And I'm sorry. You're right. I know Logan's a good guy, and of course I trust you. I just don't want something irreparable to happen here."

Neither did I, but my father did not need to know that. I so rarely won arguments that I was going to take this one. I finished up my sandwich and put all the ingredients back in the fridge. "Thank you. I need to go study and then I'm going to bed. Good night."

He kissed me on the top of my head as I went out of the kitchen with my sandwich, head held high.

My bedroom felt little girlish. I'd gone through a phase when I was sixteen where I'd been totally obsessed with Paris. I'd had pink-and-white pinstripe wallpaper with black-and-white photos of the Eiffel Tower hanging all over my room. It was a phase I'd quickly gotten over, but I'd been too lazy to change it. Then we moved from Texas to Oregon and my dad had painstakingly re-created my room to be exactly the way it had been. I couldn't tell him I'd outgrown it, not after he went to so much effort. So I'd left it alone.

He'd even installed the same bookshelves I'd had all my life—and they were crowded with little fairy houses and gardens. My mother had made them, baking the ceramics in her molds, then painting them. It had been her favorite hobby, and when I was little, I'd truly believed that fairies came into our home and lived inside the fantastical little buildings and yards she'd created. I'd thought magic was real.

I had tried to create my own houses, but I lacked her talent. So I just displayed the ones she'd made and focused on the thing I loved best—coloring.

Sitting down at my desk, instead of grabbing my stats book to study, I pulled out the adult coloring book I'd been working on. I had my sandwich in one hand and my colored pencil in the other. The first time I'd heard about coloring, I'd thought it was some short-lived hipster fad that would quickly fade away.

But after one of my sisters at the sorority house lent me one of her books, I discovered that I loved it. Coloring in intricate designs was the one thing in my life that would clear out my brain and totally soothe me. I had to do it each night before I went to sleep as a way of emptying out my pitcher at the end of the day.

For some reason, tonight it wasn't working as well as it usually did. Instead of making it so that I didn't think of Logan, it made it so he was all I could think about.

I should have started getting ready to go to sleep. Instead I sat in my chair, staring at my bed.

I thought of how Logan had looked at me. The heated expression in his eyes when he'd said, "You're so easy to talk to, Jess."

It hadn't meant anything.

How I was feeling right now? None of it mattered.

I couldn't quite convince myself to believe it.

CHAPTER EIGHT

LOGAN

I went to practice the day after Jess and I hung out at the coffee bar/place that offered the opportunity for people to spout off bad poetry. I was trying not to think about how close I'd come to breaking Coach's rules, not once but twice—by nearly getting in a fight with that drunk and by still wanting to kiss Jess every time I was around her. It put me in a foul mood, and I wasn't alone. Tensions were high on the field. It was our last practice before playing EOL's long-term rival, Sequoia Tech. Even Coach Oakley seemed a bit stressed out. I undid my chinstrap and raised my helmet up slightly so that the some of the light drizzle could get on my face.

"Did you see that? Did you see how Frederickson missed his block?" Bash was pacing back and forth, yelling. One of the defensive coaches was trying to calm him down but Bash wasn't having it. "Hit your man, Frederickson! I can't do everybody's job! This is sugar, man! Total sugar! Bullsugar!"

You knew things were bad when even Bash was repeatedly faux-swearing. The coach got his arm around Bash and took him off the field.

Sequoia Tech was 4–0, just like us. And neither team dominated the other at these rival games—sometimes EOL won, sometimes Sequoia Tech did. But we all knew we were being watched and evaluated in order to be ranked against other junior colleges. Not only did we need to beat Sequoia Tech, but we needed to beat them by a decent margin.

Coach Oakley seemed to realize how much everyone was stressing out. He called the team in to gather in a circle around him. "You've all been doing a fine job today." I heard Bash snorting somewhere off to my left, but Coach ignored him. "And I think maybe it's time we have a little fun. So I'd like to introduce you to one of my former players. You may also know him as the starting quarterback for the Portland Jacks. Everybody, please welcome Evan Dawson!"

What? Evan "Awesome" Dawson was here? That dude was my hero.

The entire team started to hoot and holler as Evan ran onto the field, waving at us. My jaw was hanging open and I couldn't quite get it to shut.

"Now I hope you all appreciate this," Coach said when he got us to quiet down. "Evan flew up here for a game and agreed to visit with us for a few hours, leaving his wife and young son at home. How old is your little boy?"

"Bailey is eighteen months old," Evan said proudly, taking out his phone to show the coach a picture. "He gets into everything and does not listen to anything we say. He's got his mom's red hair and her stubborn personality."

Evan sounded like the world's proudest dad and probably would have gone on, but none of us really cared. The fatherhood thing was fine or whatever, but we wanted to hear about what it was like to play professional football.

Coach seemed to realize this. "Looks like you've got a future linebacker on your hands. But for now, how about we have Evan throw some balls?"

There was an enthusiastic and resounding yes from everyone, including me. Until I realized that it meant I'd have to sit on the sidelines and watch my hero play with my teammates.

And it was as miserable as I'd feared. I watched the guys celebrate as they caught his passes, cheering for each throw and handoff.

While I sat and quietly observed.

Well, you better get used to it, I told myself. *This is how the rest of your life will go. Watching from the sidelines while everyone else gets to play.*

"Hey! Hunt!"

I actually looked around to see if anyone else had the last name of Hunt, even though I knew no one did. It was hard to believe that not only did Evan "Awesome" Dawson know who I was, but he was calling my name in front of the entire team.

"Come out here!"

I put my helmet back on and rushed over to him, not sure what to say.

"I'm Evan."

"Logan. Hunt." Which he already knew, considering that he'd yelled it across the field. I felt so stupid.

We shook hands.

"Would you mind throwing a few?" Evan asked. "My arm's not quite as young as it used to be."

"Yeah, absolutely." I caught the football that he tossed to me. I wondered if I could get him to sign it later. I'd buy the team a replacement.

I called out the play and watched as my guys lined up. Evan stood off to my right, just out of the way, watching us.

Part of me was afraid I'd screw up. That I wanted so badly to impress my idol that I'd make a total fool of myself. Trip over my own feet. Fumble the ball on the handoff. Run the wrong play.

But instead, it was like the gods of football were shining down on me. The drizzle actually stopped; the clouds parted and let the sunlight through. I reared back and threw a thirty-yard spiral that was breathtaking perfection, which my wide receiver caught with no problem.

It was fantastic.

Evan came over to clap me on the shoulder and said, "Beautiful pass."

I decided this was one of the greatest moments of my entire life. "Thanks."

"Do you mind chatting with me for a second?" he asked.

Did I mind? DID I MIND?? "Sure. Hey, Pete! Take over for me!" I threw the ball to the second-string QB.

I walked off the field with Evan, wishing that I had my cell phone with me so that I could record every moment of whatever was about to happen. For all I knew he was going to try to sell me on some multilevel marketing scheme. I would still want to memorialize everything he said.

Evan spoke first. "I've been watching your games. You've quite an arm and an ability to read the field."

"Wow. Thanks." What did you even say to that?

He let out a laugh at my wide-eyed wonder routine. "To be honest, it makes me feel a little nervous about keeping my job."

"I would happily play backup for you any day of the week." I legitimately sounded like a tween girl meeting her favorite boy-bander.

"Coach Oakley has told me how great you are, and if you don't mind, I'd like to pass along some of your game tapes to our scout, Rick."

Again with him worrying about me minding. "That would be fantastic. Thank you."

He took out a couple of business cards and a pen from his back pocket. He handed everything to me. "Here's my card. Keep it in case you need it. And why don't you write down your info for me on the back of that one so that I have it."

Without hesitation, I wrote down my phone number. And my email. And my Instagram and Twitter accounts. Just in case.

I gave him back the card and the pen.

Evan put his hand on my shoulder. "You've probably heard this kind of stuff a lot, but I'm serious about this. I am going to help you in any way that I can. Coach Oakley did so much for me, and I'm always happy to pay it forward. He says you've worked hard, improved on the field, and I've heard you've overcome a lot in your past. You're just the kind of kid I like to help out."

I held tightly on to the card Evan said I should keep. "I feel like I keep thanking you, but seriously, thank you."

"You're welcome. See you on the field. And protect that arm!"

With a quick smile and a wave, Evan left me alone on the sidelines. The whole experience felt like a dream, as if it had happened to someone else and I'd just watched. Had Evan Dawson really just offered to connect me with his team's scout? Saying I was good? That he was worried about his job?

He was right about one thing. This wasn't the first time a recruiter or scout had gotten my hopes up. I'd heard the whole thing before. How huge I would be. How they would help me get there. How every football fan in the country would know my name.

And then . . . nothing. Poof. Gone. Just like that.

I supposed the difference was that I'd never had an NFL star say it to me before, which somehow made it more believable.

It had always been fun to dream and imagine, but past experience had taught me to hold on to what was real.

The thing that felt most substantial, the realest thing in my life at the moment, was Jess.

That was a sobering thought.

Then her father yelled out, "You planning on joining us sometime today, Hunt?"

Absolutely. I had an NFL recruiter to impress.

When I arrived at the math lab later that afternoon, Jess was at the same table we'd used last time. She kept looking around like she was waiting for someone. I quickly realized that someone wasn't me when she put her head down as I approached.

"What are you up to?" I asked, sliding into the seat next to hers. "Looking for your Prince Boring?"

"Shh. I'm working."

"Obviously. And I wouldn't want to interrupt you while you're pretending to do your homework. Your book's upside down, by the way."

Jess flushed and I again found that soft pink in her cheeks way too appealing. She turned her book the right direction. "Okay, fine," she hissed. "I've been looking for Ben. He's never late, and he's not the type to just not show up."

I pulled my math book out of my backpack. "Maybe he's serving the less fortunate by feeding them his poems and making them the even less fortunate."

She twisted her mouth to one side, as if trying not to laugh. "His poems are not that bad. Why are you so sparkly and glittery today?"

"Sparkly and glittery?" I repeated, insulted. "Don't you mean manly and . . . manly?"

She arched one eyebrow at me, silently questioning why I was so happy.

"Okay, you've beaten it out of me. I got to play football with Evan Dawson today."

Most of the women I'd known wouldn't have had the first clue about who Evan was. Not so with Jess. She hit my shoulders with both of her hands.

"Get *out*. Are you kidding me? Are you kidding me? Evan Dawson?"

I nodded, glad that she was amping up my own enthusiasm. That she seemed so excited. It let me live in the moment even longer.

"Evan Dawson," she repeated, just shaking her head. "I was a little girl when my dad coached him, and I completely failed to grasp the significance of how important he was when he read me *The Very Hungry Caterpillar* one night. He's so talented. I am so jealous of you right now!"

"He's been on my fantasy football team for years," I said.

"He's been on my fantasy team for years," she said with a teasing grin. "Although I should probably take him off, considering that he's been married for a few years. But anyway, tell me everything!"

I told her every detail, everything he'd said and everything I'd said, although I may have done some internal editing so that I didn't sound like quite so much of a tool.

I finished up my story and she let out a little squeal. "This is so great! Now you totally have an in with the NFL. Maybe it's not such a pipe dream after all?"

"That would be great, but I'm not pinning any of my hopes on it. Honestly, it was just fun to even have him offer to help me out."

She shook her head, like she couldn't believe it. Which I totally understood. "The only thing that could make this day better would be if Ben decided to ignore Danielle completely, and then Danielle spontaneously combusted from a lethal combination of spray tan and silicone."

"That girl will never catch a break with you, will she?"

Jess grimaced. "I've kind of dedicated my life to hating her."

"Well, at least you have a cause you believe in."

Picking up on my sarcasm, she retreated into little-kid logic. "Danielle started it."

That was probably true, but I knew better than anyone how hating somebody could eat you up inside. "Personally, I don't think she's worth the effort. She's one of those people who are better to leave in the dust behind you as you move on."

Jess tapped her forefinger against the table as if considering my advice. "You're probably right. But literally everything about her bothers me. Like, I support women having whatever work done they want to feel better about themselves. But I look at her and I can't figure out what kind of pictures she brought in to her plastic surgeon. Did she print out an image of the prow of a ship and say, 'Make me look like this'?"

"Seriously?"

There was no mistaking Danielle's voice. We both turned slowly around in our seats to face her.

I had to salvage this for Jess. If Danielle told Ben that Jess was being catty . . .

But before I could do anything, Danielle kept going. "This is how you talk about other women when it comes to their appearance? Someone who spent our freshman year spouting body acceptance? I can't believe my ears."

"I don't believe your boobs, hair, skin tone, or nose, either. And to think I was about to apologize for being mean, but then you had to go and speak and mess it all up. Where do you get off condemning me? The entire time I was in the sorority you bad-mouthed my appearance every chance you got."

Danielle crossed her arms. "You're exaggerating."

"You printed out pictures of me and hung them on the bulletin board, circling everything that was wrong with me!"

"Is it my fault you don't know your angles, how to apply bronzer, or how to hide a muffin top? I mean, your thighs touch. I don't know how anyone could choose to live that way. I was trying to be helpful. Point out your problem areas. Because it's all about lifestyle choices, Jessica."

I could almost see the steam coming out of Jess's ears. "Oh, right. Lifestyle choices. Like cutting out everything that tastes good, running three miles every day, and having a daddy who will pay for every plastic surgery procedure you want."

"Oh, Jessica. You're so predictable. So pathetic and so utterly pre-dictable," Danielle said with an evil grin that made even me shudder.

"What are you smiling about?" Jess asked. "Did your huntsman bring you your stepdaughter's heart?"

"Okay!" I said with an enthusiasm I was far from feeling. Time to put a stop to this girl-on-girl crime. "Danielle, do you know where a water fountain is? Can you show me?"

"Yeah. Follow me."

I wished I had some kind of secret signal or code word to tell Jess not to worry, I had this handled. Instead, I had to walk behind Danielle, fighting off the urge to smile every time the words "prow of a ship" ran through my head.

Danielle pointed out the drinking fountain and I leaned down to get some water. I needed the chance to clear my head. I was having a hard time shifting gears—I was trying to be nice to this girl, but all I wanted to do was stick up for Jess and take her side.

When I straightened up, Danielle was leaning against the wall, studying her nails. "What's wrong with Jessica? Did she wake up on the wrong side of the web this morning?"

"I'm not out here to talk about Jess," I said, coming over to lean against the wall right next to her.

That seemed to get her attention. "Oh? What did you want to talk about? Math techniques?"

How did she make that sound dirty? "Right now my math techniques consist of the guess-and-hope method."

She moved closer, her prowlike attributes bumping into me. "I get the feeling you're the kind of guy who knows. No guessing or hoping necessary." She ran her fingers up my arm, and it made my skin crawl.

My reaction surprised me. Danielle was the kind of girl most guys would describe as hot, but I kept thinking about her calling Jess "RV" and circling "problem" areas on Jess's pictures. Which made zero sense to me because Jess had a fantastic body. All of that was beside the point, said point being me realizing there was no way I could ever be attracted to Danielle.

I backed up slightly.

Danielle seemed to notice, the corners of her mouth turning down. "Haven't we already established that you're seeing someone else?"

"Seeing someone?" she asked in a teasing voice. "I'm not serious with anyone. Ben and I hang out, but we're not exclusive. Which means . . ."

"Which means?" I repeated.

"It means that we can talk about whatever it is you want to talk about."

Her invitation was obvious. I knew I only had to say the word and she'd do whatever I wanted. "What is it you think I want to talk about?" I asked.

"I think you want to talk about whatever is happening between us." Again she moved closer, and I forced myself to stay put. "Which is something I think your poor little math tutor isn't going to like."

My poor little math tutor would probably like it just fine if Danielle fell for me. Instead, I said, "What?"

"Oh, don't play dumb. You may tell everyone you're just friends, but I've seen the way she looks at you. She's into you."

Suddenly my throat felt too thick and my chest constricted at her words. It was hard to breathe. Jess didn't have feelings for me. She couldn't. I knew it wasn't true, but obviously some part of me wanted it to be.

I needed to change the subject, only I didn't end up changing it very much. "What is your issue with Jess?"

"My issue with Miss Jessica Oakley is that she acts like she's the only person in the world who's had something bad happen to her."

There was a note of pain in her voice, on her face, but it quickly went away.

Danielle plastered on a smile. "Are you going to the game?"

Was I going to the . . . I was the quarterback. Along with the coach, I'd be running the game. "Uh, yeah."

"Good. Maybe I'll see you there. Or at a celebration party afterward." She tapped me lightly on the chest and gave me a smile that looked like she was going for sultry.

She missed.

Danielle slid my phone out of my jeans pocket and tapped on it, presumably putting her phone number in.

After she finished, she put the phone back in my pocket and I again had to will myself to stand still and not move away from her.

"Now you have my number. Text me and let me know what your plans are for tomorrow night. And be sure to tell me if you ever realize that you're in desperate need of a real tutor," she offered as she walked away, blowing me a kiss.

I realized how forced everything felt. Maybe it was because Danielle wasn't really feeling something between us, either. Her vendetta against Jess, dumb as it seemed to me, was so serious that she was only pretending to like me.

And what if she was only acting interested in Ben for the same reason?

These thoughts ran around in my brain as I headed back into the math lab.

Where I ran into Jess. Hard.

Immediately I realized that we'd both been walking too fast, had too much momentum. There was no way to straighten up and regain our balance.

We were going down.

So I wrapped my arms around her waist, turning and twisting so that I could catch her and take the brunt of the fall.

We landed with a loud thud, and I had the wind knocked out of me for a second.

When I raised my head, I was looking directly into Jess's dark-brown eyes. We were both breathing hard, and it was difficult to tell if it was because of the shock from falling, or something else. I could feel her heart racing against my ribs.

I tried to make light of the situation. "Usually when people tackle me, it's because I have a football in my hands."

Jess didn't respond to my joke, and I became aware of the delicious sensation of having her against me, from our chests to our feet. I wanted to hold her tighter. Her lush curves pressed into me and I felt a little light-headed.

Maybe I'd cracked my skull on the way down and hadn't realized it.

Especially since I wanted to stay like this and never move.

I found myself wondering what she would do if I lifted my head slightly and pressed my lips against hers. Her lips looked so soft and inviting. Kissable.

That was also when I remembered the entire math lab was watching us. Along with Keilani. Who had direct access to Coach.

I moved Jess to one side and stood up, my legs feeling weirdly shaky underneath me. I offered her my hand to help her up, but she wisely declined and got up next to me.

"Clumsy me!" she declared, following my lead from earlier and turning this into some lighthearted situation when it felt like the opposite. Wherever she'd been going, she seemed to forget all about it as she headed back over to our table. I followed behind reluctantly because at the moment I was torn between putting as much distance between us as possible and grabbing her, pulling her back into my arms, and letting desire take over.

Even if I knew what a mistake that would be.

"What did the she-devil want?"

What? My brain and my senses were so scrambled that it took me a second to realize who she was talking about. "Danielle? Nothing much. She did talk about you a couple of times, though."

Like when she'd said that Jess had feelings for me.

Instead of bringing up that potentially touchy subject, I kept talking. "Part of me wants to tell you to lay off the attacks."

"They're not attacks. I like to think of it as verbal release therapy."

There was nothing therapeutic about it for either one of them. Just a bunch of animosity. "I think your fighting is helping our situation. But for your sake, I hate to see you so angry." I knew anger better than almost anyone. It had been my constant companion for years.

It was no way to live.

Now was not the time to tell Jess that, though. I noticed that she hadn't made eye contact with me since we'd sat back down at the table.

"Should we get back to your math packet?"

Right. The packet. The entire reason for us being here. "Sure."

But I didn't pay attention as she went through a problem on the fifth page. I could still feel a phantom imprint of her pressed against me, and I wondered what my issue was.

Why did I want this? Want her? Was it because they told me I couldn't have her? Convenience?

That couldn't be it. Danielle was also off-limits and she'd made herself as open and convenient as a 7-Eleven. I could snap my fingers and have her if I wanted to.

But I didn't. Danielle's touch had turned me off, while Jess's had made me want to forget about everything else in the world.

It meant this was something more.

That there was something special about Jess.

Which basically screwed up everything in my life. Because I didn't know how to keep being friends with her and keep her at arm's length.

I let out a deep sigh. I had to do it. I had to figure out a way.

Even if it killed me.

86

CHAPTER NINE

JESS

I'd always been a huge bookworm, and the summer I turned twelve I ran out of age-appropriate books to read. I went through our bookshelves in the living room and found a thin book that was a category romance. I'd never read a romance before, and sensing my mother wouldn't be pleased to find me reading one of her books, I hid in my closet to check it out.

I couldn't devour it fast enough. It was the tale of a Greek shipping tycoon who planned to marry his rival's daughter in order to gain control of the rival's company, but their marriage of convenience quickly turned into real love. I was hooked.

About a year later they turned that book into a movie. I must have watched it at least sixty times, and it sank deeply into my tween psyche.

Which led to the Dream.

I'd had the Dream off and on my entire life. It was the climax of the novel/movie, and while I was always the heroine, my hero would change. Sometimes he was faceless, sometimes a famous actor, but usually my current crush would play that starring role. It was always the same.

Distraught and thinking that Stavros couldn't possibly love me, I escaped to my family's estate. I ran to the top of a cliff to stand in our large gazebo in my gauzy white sundress while feeling deep emotions and angstily crying.

I heard the rush of footsteps behind me and turned.

Stavros! Here! My heart leapt with excitement.

"Alexandra, I love you. I've always loved you. Nothing in this world matters to me as much as you."

Even though it was summer and we were in Greece, at this point the sky would suddenly open, sending down a torrential rain. And apparently Alexandra's family hadn't sprung for a good roof on the gazebo, because the rain poured through easily, drenching us both.

"Oh, Stavros. I love you, too."

Stavros rushed to me, pulling me into his arms. He kissed me wildly and passionately, our bodies slick with rain and sliding against one another as we struggled to get closer. Stavros stopped the kiss suddenly and pulled back to cup my face and declare, *"Latria mou."* My adored.

It was then that I realized that Stavros had morphed into Logan.

Not Ben, as he'd been the last two times I'd had the dream, but Logan.

I woke up with a start, my breathing shallow and labored.

Logan? Where had that come from?

Suzette yawned at me as I got out of bed, laying her head back down to resume sleeping. I absentmindedly petted her on the head a few times.

That dream . . . it had been different. The kiss that time felt so . . . vivid. Real. I'd had a visceral reaction to it that I'd never experienced before.

And the Stavros/Logan kiss had been exploding-volcano hot. I went into my bathroom and splashed some cold water on my heated face.

As I got ready for school, I figured this all had to be some residual weirdness from lying on top of Logan in the middle of the math lab. Because it hadn't just been two people accidentally running into each other and falling down. No, Logan had cradled me so that I wouldn't hit the floor. Obviously he was used to taking a hit and knew how to fall, but his reaction had still stunned me. In less than a second he'd made me feel protected. Cared for.

No guy had made me feel that way for a long time.

He'd also set my heart to racing and made my mouth go dry. There was no denying the connection I felt with Logan.

Even if I couldn't deny it, I didn't have to act on it.

We were adults. I just had to make sure that no more touching happened. Ever. Even in my dreams.

I didn't know how to tell my subconscious mind to shut up, but I'd do my best.

None of my resolve was helped by seeing Logan down the hallway after my Calculus with Theory class.

What should I do?

My instinct was to turn and run. For a long time and an even longer distance.

But I was going to have to see him again sometime. Might as well be now; might as well deal with whatever strangeness my brain wanted to conjure up. I got tangled up in my own feet as I tried to make a decision.

"Jess!"

Logan made the decision for me. He hurried down the hall, and for a second I pictured him as Stavros, running up the hill in his flowy, white button-down shirt, coming to claim me.

I shook my head. Hard.

"Hey!" he said, all friendly grins and tempting muscles.

Something was seriously wrong with me.

"Hi. Where are you off to?"

"Just got done with my Native American History class and now I'm heading to the dorm cafeteria to get lunch. What about you?"

I let out a sigh of relief. I wouldn't be able to join him. I had a legitimate excuse! "I have another class in about fifteen minutes. So I should just . . ."

"I'll walk with you. There's something we should discuss."

OMG, if he brought up yesterday's fall or if he was a psychic and somehow knew that I'd dreamed about him, I. WOULD. DIE.

"W-what?" I hated myself for stuttering and my heart for beating so hard in my chest that it was bruising my ribs.

"Tomorrow night's the game against Sequoia Tech. Are you planning on coming?"

"Yes." I always went to the games. Sometimes I even sat in the box to feed my dad statistical information and the mathematical probabilities of certain plays against specific teams. Other times I just sat in the stands and enjoyed myself, not wanting to overanalyze everything.

Tomorrow would need to be a sit-and-enjoy-myself kind of night, because I didn't know if I was in the right headspace to do some math.

"I have it on good authority that Ben will be at the game. So you need to be there and be cheering for me."

I moved to one side as a guy came running by, obviously in a hurry. His backpack swung into my arm and I absentmindedly rubbed the spot where it had made contact. What kind of good authority? It would be bad if I asked.

"Are you cold?"

Logan had noticed me rubbing my arm and had started taking off his jacket.

"What? No! I'm fine. Just . . . not cold."

He needed to knock off this chivalry crap immediately. I was a total sucker for it. What was it he was saying about the game? Oh, right. Cheering. "I always cheer for you and the Owls."

"No, I mean for me specifically. Loudly. Where Ben can hear you."

"Aw, do you need your ego stroked?" I realized how that sounded a second too late.

Logan grinned at me suggestively. "You should ask me that again later. When we're alone."

I sighed. I had walked right into that one. I deserved the goose bumps breaking out on the back of my neck, the liquid heat running through my veins.

"Ha ha. You're so funny" was my very weak response.

"Somebody's got to do it."

We arrived at my classroom and I pointed at it. "This is me."

"Enjoy your class. I'll see you tomorrow night."

I watched him go and realized that every woman within twenty feet was doing the same thing. Because he looked so very nice in his jeans.

Crap. We needed to get this Ben situation worked out soon.

~

Football games embodied everything I loved about the fall. The leaves on the trees were red, orange, and yellow; there was a cold nip in the air that made it necessary to put on scarves and jackets and flannel shirts; there was the faintest hint of woodsmoke in the air; the snack bar was selling hot chocolate, apple cider, and pumpkin cookies. Not to mention the excitement all around me as everyone expected our team to crush the Sequoia Tech Titans.

I took my hot chocolate and started scanning the crowd for Ben. Logan wanted me to cheer for him near Ben. I figured he wouldn't be that hard to find, seeing as how he'd be in all black.

Problem was, the school had voted last year to change our colors. Instead of brown and yellow, our Owls were now black, gray, and white. Which meant there was a very monochromatic look to the crowd.

One of the cheerleaders did a backflip, and that's when I spotted Ben. I found him standing at the bottom of the stadium, talking to Danielle. Who was, of course, an Owlette. She couldn't have been a stock villain from a 1990s teen rom-com without being a cheerleader, too.

I stood about twenty yards away from Ben, leaning against the railing and looking out into the field, where the team was doing some drills before the game started. Logan spotted me and trotted over.

I will admit that my heart did a bit of a crazy drum solo/dance watching Logan run over. Like a soldier running off the battlefield just to say hello before he had to return to combat.

"You're here," he said after he took off his helmet.

"As commanded."

He ran his fingers through his damp hair, and it was like it was happening in slow motion. I wondered what his hair would feel like. I guessed probably silky smooth. The fingers of my left hand curled in, wanting to defy my command to stay put. I put both of my hands around my hot chocolate so that I could force them to behave.

Logan stood on his side of the rail, crossing his arms and leaning them against it. "Do you see them watching us? Don't look. They are."

"How am I supposed to know if they're watching us if you won't let me look?" I asked, taking a sip of my drink.

"I know they are. Because this is kind of a big deal. I'm singling you out at a game. I've never done that before."

I wanted to make a comment that somebody had a high opinion of himself, but he was right. I'd been at all these games, and he'd never talked to some girl in the stands before. Probably mostly because he wasn't allowed to.

Logan needed to be careful. There was a fine line to walk between getting Ben's attention and making my dad suspicious.

But he wasn't careful. He reached out and grabbed my hot chocolate, drinking down a big gulp before handing it back. "Thanks."

He gave me a quick smile and then headed back to the field.

I looked down at my cup and realized that if I drank from the same spot he had, it would almost be like our lips were touching via proxy. Like a thirdhand kiss.

Well, that was pathetic. The Dream had really done a number on me. I was starting to depress myself.

"Jess! Jess!"

Someone was calling my name from the stands. I shielded my eyes from the brightness of the stadium lights and saw Keilani standing up, waving both of her arms at me. I glanced over at Ben, who was still deep in conversation with Danielle. I was supposed to sit next to him, but I didn't want to disappoint my friend, who was patting the bench next to her. I climbed the stairs and went to join her.

"I saved you a seat!" she declared, moving over. I sat down and could feel the cold metal through my jeans. I wished I'd brought a blanket with me.

Keilani was practically bouncing up and down in her seat. She loved football games, too. "Are you so excited? I'm so excited. We're going to kill those Titans!"

When I'd first met her four years ago, she had been studying sports medicine and interning with the team's sports doctor at Amarillo. Then, when my dad was fired, Keilani followed him to EOL and became his academic adviser. She said that what she liked was helping the team and that she felt like she could do more for the guys by getting them to graduate than in any other way.

"I'm excited!" I told her, and she grinned happily at me. She had painted the team mascot on one cheek and the word *Owls* on the other. She was the embodiment of team spirit.

A movement down on the field caught my eye and I saw Danielle kiss Ben on the cheek. He climbed the stairs and sat about five rows down from me.

The teams left the field as the scoreboard was reset with the information for the game. Danielle and her minions rolled out a big poster that said "Go, Fight, Win, Owls!" They split into two rows, one on each side of the poster, forming a tunnel. Some part of me hoped that Danielle would stand in the wrong spot and that she might get run over by a very large linebacker.

The Titans cheerleaders had the same sort of setup on their side of the field.

"Please welcome tonight's guests, the Sequoia Tech Titans!"

There was applause from across the field and some scattered boos on our side as the Titans burst through their poster, cheering and waving as they ran. When they went to the visitor's sidelines, music with a thumping bassline began to play.

"And please welcome your national champions, the Edwin O'Leary Owls!"

People in the crowd screamed and cheered, but most of them hooted loudly to their team as they broke through Danielle's poster.

Without running her over, I might add.

The team stood on the home sidelines, pumping up the crowd by waving their arms. The crowd hooted louder.

Logan walked out onto the field to do the coin flip with the opposing team's captain, and I wondered why I'd never noticed how nice he looked in his uniform before. All broad shoulders and big biceps and those tight leggings showing off every little bit of . . .

"Jess?"

I realized that Keilani had been trying to get my attention. "Yes?"

"You seem . . . distracted tonight."

"It's just now that I'm friends with Logan and I know how hard he works, I'm jazzed to see him play. I really want to cheer him on. Support him, you know? As a friend."

"Uh-huh." She made the two syllables sound as if I'd just said, "Aliens are landing later on tonight and I'm jazzed they'll be abducting me. Because we're all good friends."

I probably should have told her why I would be cheering so loud for Logan. She already knew that Logan was helping me win over Ben. I just felt . . . embarrassed by it. I didn't want her to witness the crazy lengths I was willing to go to. Lengths that were starting to seem not worth it.

The coin was flipped and the Titans won the toss. They elected to receive. As Logan jogged back to the team, I stood up and called out, "Yay, Logan! Let's go Number Eight!" I shouted it at the top of my lungs but surprisingly felt no satisfaction at seeing Ben turn slightly toward me. His eyes lit up with recognition, and he waved to get my attention. I ignored him.

Tonight I would be cheering for Logan.

And it was easy enough. Logan commanded the field like he was a kid playing with toy soldiers. Everyone lined up in just the way he wanted, and he stayed in that pocket until he was ready to throw the ball. Other quarterbacks would dance and hurry before they got hit. But Logan knew his line would protect him, and he had confidence in his actions. He didn't send that football downfield until he had his receivers right where he wanted them.

He never got sacked, although he was tackled a few times right after the ball left his hands. I was torn between wanting to shove the defensive linemen who were hitting Logan and remembering what it was like to accidentally tackle Logan myself. All that masculine strength underneath me, the coiled power I could feel in his hard muscles beneath my body. It had been intoxicating.

And then he'd looked at me like he was going to kiss me, and in that moment, I would have let him. I'd forgotten about Ben, forgotten about the other people in the room, forgotten about my dad and his rules. I'd wanted Logan Hunt's hot, hungry mouth on mine and nothing else had mattered.

I suddenly felt a little warm and cooled my flushed face off by waving my hand.

While Logan dominated the field every time the EOL offense was up, Sequoia Tech was no slouch. They played just as hard and just as well, and every time we got a touchdown, they got one, too. I started to get nervous. We needed to win this game or our shot at the national title this year could be over.

Halftime came and went and the nail-biting game continued. I cheered so hard for Logan that somebody probably should have given me an Owlette costume and sent me down to the field to do it in a formal capacity.

Not that I would have. I'd never do anything that would force me into working with Danielle.

There were seconds to go and the score was tied. We wouldn't get the margin we were hoping for, but there was still a chance to win the game because Logan was on the field. My dad had just used up his last time-out. This was it.

The game could have gone into overtime, but better to win it now and not chance it.

The tension was crazy. I had half-moon shapes in my palm from digging in my fingernails so tightly as I prayed to whoever cared about football games. "Please let him score. Please let him score."

The Owls set up their line and the Titans responded. Logan called the play and the ball was snapped to him. What would he do?

I realized he was going to throw it. He should have let someone run the ball in. Had his guys open a hole and had someone carry the ball to the goal line. We couldn't risk an interception or an incomplete pass. This was not the time to make a big move, but Logan was going for it. My heart was in my throat as I watched him.

Then Logan did what he always did: he lazily waited for an open man and then threw a perfect spiral into his arms.

On the other side of the goal line.

The crowd went insane as the referees declared it a touchdown.

We'd done it! We'd won! We'd beat Sequoia Tech!

Keilani and I hugged as we screamed and jumped up and down. I wasn't going to be able to talk tomorrow, but it was totally worth it!

People rushed down onto the field to congratulate Logan and the team. I saw someone pour a bucket of Gatorade over my dad's head as he went over to shake hands with the opposing coach.

"I'm going down there!" Keilani told me just before she started running down the metal stairs.

Part of me wanted to join her, but the other part of me wanted to sit here and bask in the glory of the Owls beating their biggest rival.

I also wanted Logan to have his moment in the sun, to enjoy all the adulation and praise that he so deserved without having to worry about me and my problems.

Someone sat down next to me on my right and I was a little surprised to see Ben.

He spoke first, which was good, because I didn't know what I was supposed to say. "That was some game, huh?"

"Yeah, it was amazing." My voice already sounded scratchy. "Didn't Logan do such a good job? He's an incredible quarterback. This school is so lucky to have him."

Ben didn't say anything. Just sort of nodded.

His lack of reaction irritated me. What, was he the only one allowed to be good at something? He didn't mind being complimented and praised but didn't like to hear it for anyone else?

"Don't you think he did good?" I pressed.

He shrugged. "I don't really know much about football. I thought it would be nice to support Danielle."

Maybe it wasn't a lack of enthusiasm on his part or jealousy of Logan. I shouldn't interpret it as some kind of sign that he was selfish and unable to compliment others. Maybe he really didn't know anything about football and had come to support a friend.

The same friend who was currently draping herself all over Logan. No wonder Ben seemed gloomier and more depressed than normal.

"Yeah, she seems really happy that you're here supporting her." Since she was busy ignoring him and all, but I kept my snarkiness to myself.

Ben shrugged and asked, "So, what are you doing after the game? Got any plans?"

Did going home and watching TV count as a plan? "I'm not sure yet. Why?"

"The Zetas are hosting a party to celebrate the win. Maybe you could stop by."

He wanted me to go back to my old sorority house for a party? There was no way. Even if I would get to see him and spend time with him and manage to annoy Danielle in the process. I had no desire to go to that house ever again.

Was it my imagination or did Ben's hand move closer to mine on the bench? Because if that kiss before the game had been any indication, he was still doing whatever with Danielle.

Although Logan did tell me that she'd said they weren't exclusive. But I wouldn't want to date Ben unless Danielle was totally out of the picture.

Yep, his hand was definitely moving closer to mine. I should have wanted that to happen, but instead I sprang to my feet.

I didn't know what to do about the invitation. Logan and I hadn't discussed this possibility. "Let me talk to Logan. He and I didn't have any set plans, but I want to double-check with him."

That seemed like a safe way out of it—no confirmation that Logan and I were "dating" but enough of an implication that we might be. And if Logan was right, then it should have bothered Ben.

Ben stood up, too. "Oh. Yeah. Sure. Hopefully I'll see you there."

He was standing really close to me and it was making me feel weird. I turned to leave, maybe head out onto the field to ask Logan his opinion. My feet got caught up in Keilani's blanket and the straps of her tote bag. I fell forward and hit the cold metal flooring with my side.

Ow. I let out a little groan. That had really hurt.

"Wow. Are you okay?"

Ben leaned over to help me up, his hands on my arms, pulling me back to my feet.

"Yeah, I'm fine." And I was in the middle of a mini freak-out because Ben's touch was . . . nice. Vaguely pleasant. It was nothing like the raging infernos Logan had created. I should have been thrilled and giddy that Ben had his hands on me and instead it was . . . nothing. *Nothing like I imagined,* I corrected myself. I had just thought there would be . . . more.

More sparks, more chemistry, more fire.

Logan's touch isn't nothing, that little evil voice inside me said.

"Jess!" I turned to see Logan waving to me from the railing.

I smiled quickly at Ben. I'd figure out what had just happened later. For now I needed to get clear and do some thinking without him around. "Sorry, I have to go. I'll see you later!"

Logan's grin as I raced down the stairs toward him was so charming, so full of happiness, so inviting, that it took all of my willpower not to launch myself over the railing and hug him tightly.

"You were so great!" I told him. The black grease under his eyes had smudged; his hair was damp; his skin was glistening with beads of sweat.

How was that sexy? I was seriously depraved.

"Thanks!" His glance drifted up to where I'd left Ben. "What happened there?"

"Ben invited me to a party at the Zetas' house."

Both of his eyebrows shot up. "That's very interesting."

"Should we go?"

He leaned his head to one side, thinking. "No. Your dad always hosts a dinner after the game that he expects the team to show up for. We won't go to the party and then Ben will spend the night wondering what we're up to."

"Oh." Much as I hadn't wanted to go to the sorority house, I was strangely disappointed at not getting to spend more time with Logan. And I knew better than anyone that my dad presided over a get-together after every game. But it was like being around Logan's shiny handsomeness made me forget basic stuff. "Okay. Well, enjoy your dinner. I'm headed home. And great game!"

Logan opened his mouth as if he wanted to say something, but instead he just smiled at me and waved.

I had left my car in one of the faculty parking lots, wanting to avoid the lines to exit the stadium lot. It didn't take me long to get home, and, realizing that I'd have the place to myself for a few hours, I decided to make some popcorn and watch one of the Hallmark movies I'd saved on my DVR. To make the living room even cozier, I started a fire in the fireplace and grabbed a fleece blanket, and then settled in on the couch.

Suzette jumped up next to me, laying her head in my lap so that I could pet her while I watched my show. I'd just started the movie when the doorbell rang. Suzette jumped up, ran to the door, and started barking. At first I thought maybe my dad had forgotten his keys, but it was way too early for him to be home.

I went over to the door and looked through the peephole.

I rocked back on my heels when I saw Logan.

Standing on my porch.

What did he want? Why was he here?

A thousand other questions ran through my mind. Unfortunately, there was only one way to get some answers.

I opened the door to let him in.

CHAPTER TEN

LOGAN

"What are you doing here?" Jess hissed. Before I could respond she grabbed me by the front of my jacket and yanked me into the house, slamming the front door shut. Then she bolted it, locking us in.

A large white dog yapped loudly at me. "Suzette, hush! Sit!" The dog immediately quieted down and sat on her haunches. I held out my hand so she could sniff me. She did so a few times and then, deeming me not a threat, trotted off into another room.

Jess looked as appealing and inviting as ever in some fuzzy pajamas and with her hair up in a bun. She even had glasses on—I hadn't realized she usually wore contacts.

"Are you crazy?" she asked, interrupting my visual appreciation. "How many concussions have you had? My father is going to skin you alive if he finds you here."

"Whoa, hey." She was making this a little personal. "The dinner is still going on. I put in an appearance and snuck out. Your dad won't be home for a couple of hours. I was going to go back to my dorm but I'm too hyped up to sleep. I wanted to come see you."

I hadn't meant to say that last part, even if it was true. While walking back to my room I'd realized that I missed her and wanted to be with her. And Jess's downcast eyes and the tug of her teeth on her lower lip let me know that she wasn't sure how to react.

So I tried to cover it up. "You know, so we could talk more about our plan."

"Oh. Okay. Come on in."

I followed her into the living room, where it looked like I had interrupted some "me" time. Jess sat on the couch and, knowing it would be a bad idea to sit next to her, I headed toward the ugliest chair I'd ever seen.

"No! Don't sit there!" If she had been another girl, I might have thought it was a ploy to get me next to her. But she looked panicked. "That is my dad's favorite chair. He's had it since college. You know how football superstitions go—he thinks it brings him good luck. I feel like if you sat in it, he would somehow know."

I sat as far away from her as I could on the couch. "That chair is hideous. It looks like it's the result of hundreds of years of furniture incest."

That at least made her smile.

And there was something about her smile that made me forget myself. That made me want to reach over and tug her into my lap, hold her tight against me, and finally taste her. See how pink her cheeks would get when I kissed her.

"The plan?" she said, roughly bringing me back to reality.

"Right. I think it's going well. Ben invited you to that party. He seems interested. You're probably only a couple of events away from him asking you out." Why did that thought make my gut twist?

"Events?"

"Him seeing us together at events. Tonight could have worked, but I didn't want you to have to go to that sorority house."

Her eyes softened in a way that they never had before. She got up on her knees, facing me. "Really?" Her oversized shirt slipped slightly to one side, exposing the top of her shoulder.

I was tempted to sit on my hands so that I wouldn't reach out and touch her soft skin.

"Yeah." I had to clear my throat a couple of times so that I could talk. "I know how terrible it was for you there."

"That's just . . . really sweet."

I wasn't trying to be sweet. I was trying to behave. But after the game, it was like one of the restraints I'd had in place to keep myself in line had broken. And it was because of Jess cheering for me at the game. I'd heard her calling out my name, encouraging me. Everybody who had ever cheered for me before was a stranger or an acquaintance. Tonight was the first time somebody I cared about had rooted for me. And even though she was only doing it because I'd told her to, it had still felt amazing.

That glowing feeling that came from thinking she was on my side, cheering me on, hadn't diminished. If anything, it had doubled as soon as I saw her again.

If I was being honest with myself, it had started long before the game. Like when I ran into her at school and shamelessly flirted with her. I shouldn't have done it. I knew I shouldn't have been doing it while it was happening. But it was like I couldn't stop. I wanted to tease her. Wanted to see that light in her eyes, hear the sound of her laughter.

She coughed, and I realized that I'd been sitting there staring at her for a not-normal length of time.

Then she spoke, which was good, because I couldn't remember where we'd left off in our conversation. "Did you forget that we were talking about what's next with Ben?"

Yes, but there was no way I was going to admit to it. "I think you could probably date Ben now. As Danielle has repeatedly reminded me, they're not exclusive."

She shrugged, pushing the collar of her shirt further down her shoulder. "I guess it doesn't really matter what Danielle thinks in this situation.

Only what Ben thinks." She took her hair down out of the bun, letting it fall against her back. The scent of wildflowers floated over to me.

My Adam's apple bobbed as I gulped. Hard. I tried to focus on what she was saying and not how good she smelled. What did that clown think? Did he care that what he had with Danielle seemed superficial? Ben couldn't have expected to ever go out with a girl like Danielle, and so he was most likely willing to put up with a lot to hang on to her. Probably because he knew it would never happen again.

Although Jess wanted him too, and she was a thousand times better looking and a lot more fun to be with than Danielle. How could Ben not see that?

Which led me back to my original theory about Ben.

I Am Ben was stupid.

And he didn't deserve Jess.

"I just don't want to be responsible for anyone cheating. I hate cheating," she said.

"You're not making anyone cheat. There's no relationship." I hesitated for a beat. "And I feel like there's more to this story."

Jess grabbed the fleece blanket and threw it over her legs, bunching the top of it against her chest. "That night, when the offensive line at Amarillo drugged me and dragged me off to a bedroom? I was seriously dating the center. Or at least, I thought we were seriously dating. Turns out that while that was going on, he was hooking up with another girl in a different room."

"That's . . ." Another idiot dude who didn't deserve Jess. "Terrible. Now I'm the one who doesn't know what to say."

Suzette padded into the room and jumped onto the couch, placing herself between me and Jess. I felt very grateful to this dog because my instinct was to pull Jess into my arms and hold her. Like I could hug away her pain.

"He also knew what they were planning on doing. They'd planned it out beforehand because they thought it would be hilarious to take advantage of the coach's innocent little girl. And he didn't say a word to me. Of all the things that happened that night, his betrayal was one of the worst. He didn't stand up for me or try to stop them. It was a long time before I felt like I would be able to trust a man again."

I hated that I couldn't help her. And, as illogical as it seemed, that I hadn't been there to protect her.

She gave me a weak smile. "And I know what you're going to say." That would have been a neat trick considering I didn't. "That I shouldn't let one bad apple spoil the bunch, right?" She half laughed, half sobbed.

"What as—idiot said that to you? No, I don't think that. And it doesn't sound like you were dealing with just one bad apple. You had a whole orchard of them."

She nodded, her eyes glistening. I put my hand on her still-covered shoulder. That seemed like a safe-enough place. I squeezed her gently, letting her know I was there.

Then she rested her cheek against my hand, and it took every ounce of control that I had not to stroke her face and kiss her forehead.

"Ben." I said his name both as a realization and a talisman to get her to stop cuddling with my hand.

It worked.

"What about him?" she asked, sitting back up. I yanked my hand back so fast it caught the dog's attention.

"That's why you like him. He's nothing like those guys." Nothing like me. "Sensitive, unathletic, nonthreatening, into poems." I couldn't bring myself to call him poetic. Because he wasn't.

"That's possible. But he's the first guy that I've been attracted to in years."

It felt like someone spiked a stone in my stomach—it hit hard and then sank, filling me with a heaviness. Did that mean she wasn't attracted to me? Had I been totally misreading our chemistry? Was she not interested in me at all?

That would have been a good thing, right? I knew I had to stay away from her and from developing any romantic feelings. Maybe knowing that Ben was the one getting her back out there would be enough to keep me away. Knowing that she didn't see me as anything other than her friend.

Which was what I needed to be. Just her friend.

Like right now. "If you really like him . . ."

"Well . . . yeah." Her voice was a mixture of wistfulness and something else I couldn't identify. It almost sounded like regret, but that couldn't be right.

"All right, all right, keep it in your pants."

She laughed and her dog sat up, barking along with her laughter.

Then Suzette cocked her head to one side and ran over to the door. Both Jess and I heard the sound of keys in a lock at the same time.

"My dad!" she shriek-whispered. "Come with me!"

She grabbed my hand and led me up the stairs. "Why is he home so early?" I asked.

"I don't know!" She threw open a door. This must have been her bedroom. It was a lot pinker than I would have imagined.

And a lot messier. "You are like one stack of newspapers away from being a total hoarder," I said in disbelief. "If someone lit a match in here, this house would go up like kindling."

"Can we talk about fire safety later? More hiding, less talking!" She shoved me into her closet and closed the doors. There were slats that allowed me to see into her room, and she crawled into her unmade bed and picked up a book to read.

"Upside down!" I said as loud as I dared and had to tamp down a laugh as she hurriedly turned her book right side up.

"Jess?"

What had seemed humorous a second ago now seemed kind of terrifying as I heard Coach's voice outside her bedroom door. I took a step back and knocked something off her top shelf. I froze, worried that he might have heard me.

Jess glared at me in the closet and called out, "Come in!"

"Hey, sweetie. How was your night?" He walked over and kissed her on the top of her head.

"Um, quiet," Jess said.

"Really? I thought I heard voices when I first came in."

I held so still I could have won a best-statue-in-Jess's-room award. It felt like back when I was a little kid—if I just froze and didn't move, nothing bad could happen.

"Hearing voices is the first sign of madness," Jess said, calm and smooth. "You might want to get that checked out at your next yearly physical. And congratulations on the win! Your team did so fantastic. Speaking of, shouldn't you be with them right now?"

While I was admiring Jess's ability to change the subject so easily and quickly, I noticed that there was a weird look on Coach's face. And an even weirder tone to his voice. "I needed to pick something up and then I'll be headed back out again."

Relief bubbled up inside me. It was a good thing he was leaving. It would have been excruciating trying to sneak out of his house while he was sleeping.

I could see from Jess's expression that she was torn—part of her wanted to interrogate her father, but the other part wanted him to leave so that I wouldn't be stuck in her closet all night. Her more logical side won out. "Okay."

"You'll be all right here?"

"Dad!" I could hear the eye roll in her tone. "I am fine. You don't have to worry about me."

"Privileges of being a father. I get to always worry about you. See you tomorrow." Coach kissed her again and closed her door behind him. I didn't know how long he'd be home so I slunk down until I was sitting on the floor, making myself comfortable.

I was tempted to take my phone out and play a game but didn't want to risk it, worried about some accidental sound. That prompted me to turn off my phone's ringer. I was lucky nobody had tried to call while I was hiding out. Jess ignored me, pretending to read her book. We were going to keep up the pretense until her father left.

Since he wasn't in the room itself, I turned on my phone's flashlight to see what I had knocked on the floor. It was a book. With a very interesting title.

From the hallway Coach Oakley called out a goodbye, which Jess returned. I heard the front door slam shut and then Jess was up on her feet.

"Stay there until I know for sure he's gone."

She ran out of the room and down the stairs, and I guessed she was probably checking to make sure that the coach had actually left.

I heard her running back up the stairs and watched as she came over and threw the closet door open.

"His car is gone and I locked the front door. I think we're safe."

I held up the book I'd knocked down. "*The Greek Tycoon's Forbidden Wife?*"

She blushed adorably as she grabbed the book out of my hands. "That's nothing! It's so very nothing. Just, nothing."

"So, what you're saying is that I should immediately go back to my house and buy an online version of this book and read it right away?"

"You can be so aggravating sometimes," she muttered, walking back over to her bed and shoving the book under her pillow.

"Aw, Jess. You seem upset with me. Do you need a hug?"

"Go hug yourself," she retorted, which made me laugh.

I stood up and walked over to some shelves next to her closet that had tiny houses on them. They were miniature but perfectly detailed. "Can I touch these?"

"What?" She straightened up to see what I was talking about. "Oh, yeah. I'm sure you'll be extra careful and won't break them." Which sounded like a threat.

"No, I meant more like, I can see the state of the rest of your room and I don't want to catch cancer if they're coated in dust."

"So I'm a little domestically disabled. The houses are clean. Ish."
I picked up one with a purple roof. "What are these?"

"Fairy houses. My mom used to make them."

I'd never heard the coach mention his wife, or Jess talk about her
mom. "Where is she?"

Jess sat down on her bed, looking at her hands. "She died when I
was thirteen. She went out for a run and got hit by a car and died from
internal injuries. One of those things that happens every day to other
people. Only this time we were the other people."

Knowing how special that made these houses, I carefully set the
one I was holding back down and went to sit next to her on the bed. I
definitely sat closer to her than I should have.

"I'm sorry."

"Me too. She was pretty great. I miss her every day. I put those
houses in my room right after the funeral, I think because some part of
me had always believed they were magic. That fairies would come and
live in them and I could catch one and ask for a wish. I was way too
old to believe something like that, but I think I hoped for a long time."

I put my arm around her shoulder, semi-holding my breath so
that I wouldn't breathe in her scent. "I know what it's like to hope for
something that you know will never happen."

Jess turned her face toward mine, her lips so close that my brain
started to sputter. If I leaned in slightly, we'd be kissing.

My breathing quickened and turned shallow. I had never wanted
anything more in my life, ever, than I wanted Jess in that moment. It
was consuming, making it difficult to think. I tried talking my way out
of it. "I still think magic exists. You just have to know where to look
for it."

That did not help my raging hormones at all, given the way she was
currently looking at me. Like I was magic.

But I was all too human. As my pounding blood and thumping
heart could easily attest to.

Needing some space, I stood up. "Your plan tonight was severely flawed, just so you know."

It was like she had a hard time focusing on me. It took her a second. "What plan?"

"The one to hide me from your father."

She crossed her arms and glared at me, annoyed. I realized that I'd said her plan was flawed specifically to cause this reaction because this version of Jess was a lot easier to resist. "How so? We didn't get caught. My scheme worked perfectly."

"That was luck. You could have hidden me anywhere in the house, but you chose your closet? Did you think that if your dad did find me, the best place would be in your bedroom?"

"Oh." She uncrossed her arms, like she was letting her guard back down. Which was dangerous. "That would have been bad. And yes, he would have been slightly less angry if he'd discovered you someplace else, like the pantry. But the point is he didn't find you and so flawed or not, I win."

"You win," I agreed.

I needed to go. I should have said goodbye and taken off.

"It's no fun if you agree with me," she teased.

I could bench press hundreds of pounds and I felt like I was no match for this woman's flirting. She made me weak in ways I didn't know existed.

"It's late and I should . . ." I gestured with my thumb over my shoulder.

"Yeah, I think it's been long enough that you can safely take off without my dad catching you. Where do you think he was going?"

Jess was walking me out and I wanted to tell her that it was unnecessary. I could easily find my own way to the front door, but I wanted these moments with her to last.

I was deeply pathetic.

"Wherever he was going, he put on some cologne. Can't you smell it?" The odor of it lingered in the upstairs hallway. My guess was a woman and a date, but considering that Jess hadn't figured it out, I wasn't going to be the one to burst her bubble. She could come to that conclusion all on her own.

"I can smell it. I didn't notice it at first because I'm kind of used to it. Maybe we could add that to our list of things to do," she said. "Find out what my dad is up to. He's been acting a little weird lately."

We reached the front door and Jess unlocked the deadbolt. I wanted to agree to her offer. I wanted another reason to spend time with her.

Which meant I shouldn't. So of course I said, "Maybe."

She twisted her mouth, as if she'd tasted something gross. "Never mind. I don't think I want to know what midlife crisis he's currently going through."

"That's probably a good idea." Why did I keep moving closer to her? Like she was the sun and I was an asteroid stuck in her gravitational orbit. Not just because she was beautiful and bright, which she was, but because I was going to end up exploding into a fiery mass, everything in my life destroyed, if I got sucked in.

We both put our hands on the doorknob at the same time, and we both immediately jumped back as soon as we touched. Rather than acknowledge the weirdness, I said, "See you in math lab!" and let myself out, shutting the door behind me.

I hesitated until I heard her lock it and then headed for the car my teammate Roman had let me borrow on penalty of death if I dinged it up, which I had parked across the street. Some part of me must have worried about being busted by the coach, and I was glad that I hadn't parked in the driveway and ruined my entire life.

Just because I couldn't stay away from Jess.

As I started up the car I resolved that from this moment on, I was going to spend a lot less time with her.

All I needed was for my brain to convince the rest of me that it was a good idea.

CHAPTER ELEVEN

JESS

Anxiety twisted and turned inside my gut at the prospect of seeing Logan again. The last time we'd been together was that entire weird and inexplicable experience at my house after the game. It had been two days, and he hadn't texted or called or tried to see me at all.

Which I knew was best for both of us, but I missed him.

And I was nervous about our session at the math lab today.

I arrived early, setting up all of the materials we'd need, including his new math packet. Keilani told me that Logan had earned a B on his most recent test, which meant we were on the right path. I was determined to help him get an A in that class and hit that 4.0 GPA that he wanted.

Then I had that prickly feeling I always got whenever Ben arrived. That flutter in my heart, the featherlight feeling at the back of my neck.

But when I looked up, I saw Logan instead.

Oh, this was not good.

I plastered on a smile that I hoped he couldn't tell was fake. "Hey! Long time no see, cowboy."

"Yeah, sorry. I've been busy."

"We should get started. Have you had a chance to read over chapter seventeen yet?"

Logan looked embarrassed. "Not quite."

That frustrated me, and I held on to that feeling. I also tried to dismiss the memory of him in my room, on my bed. How I'd wanted to throw myself at him and beg him to kiss me. So very mortifying. Neglectful Student Logan was easier to deal with than Understanding and Sympathetic and Highly Kissable Logan.

Then he went and screwed everything up. All of my resolve went out the window the second his knee brushed up against mine. The electric spark that movement caused surprised me so much that I rammed my leg straight up and into the table, shaking everything on it.

I wanted to let out a moan of humiliation.

"Are you okay?" Logan asked.

"Yep. I'm fine. So fine. Anyway, so you didn't read the chapter but that's okay. I can show you some of the basics here with the first problem." I got out my pencil and my calculator, ready to explain some theorems to Logan. Anything to distract from my hurtling myself into inanimate objects just because he accidentally touched me. Only I realized he wasn't listening.

Instead, he was watching Danielle and Ben. I wondered how long they'd been there. My Early Ben Detection System must have been down. I didn't know when he'd arrived.

It wasn't down for Logan. You knew exactly when he showed up.

My internal voice needed a serious smackdown.

Ben and Danielle were doing more of that angry whispering that I typically enjoyed. No wonder Logan was watching. This was more entertaining than most reality television. And I loved reality television.

"What do you think they're fighting about?" I asked.

Logan shrugged. "I don't know. Maybe she's telling him she got sorted into Slytherin House? And with him being such a Hufflepuff, they'll never be together?"

I choked back a laugh. "Or maybe she's telling him about her plans for his soul once she finishes sucking it out."

He started ticking items off on his fingers. "She has so many options available to her. She can use it in a spell, she can release it into the wild during a harvest moon, put it in a mason jar on her shelf . . ."

This time I did laugh, along with Logan.

When we finally stopped, Logan offered, "Actually, I think they're calling things off."

It didn't thrill my heart the way I'd once thought it would. It was more mildly amusing. "You can't possibly know that."

"I can read lips."

Could he really? And why did that draw my attention to his very masculine and tempting lips? "You cannot."

"You're right. I can't. But I'm a predictor of human behavior, remember? Plus, it's weird that she's not touching him. Danielle's very handsy."

Why did that bother me? It wasn't like I didn't know it already. "And you, what, don't enjoy it?"

A shudder ran through him and he shook his head. "I find it . . . unappealing. I hope you appreciate what a sacrifice I've made for you."

That made my heart brighten and sparkle in a way it shouldn't have. Logan wasn't attracted to Danielle? At all? "Really?"

"Yes, really. Not to mention that I think she's in the same boat. That she's only flirting with me to bother you. Or Ben. Anyway, it's bound to happen eventually. Ben's going to have to make a decision between what is clearly right and what is clearly Danielle."

I didn't even have time to respond to his joke because I saw out of the corner of my eye that Danielle and Ben had finished whatever conversation they were having. They retreated to opposite ends of the room when normally they always sat together. Huh. Maybe Logan's theory had some validity.

"Should I go over and talk to him?" I asked. "Find out if something happened to EOL's most ill-suited wannabe couple?"

"Nope. We always want to make him come to you. And he always will, as long as I'm by your side."

"Have I ever mentioned that your humility is one of the things I like best about you?"

Logan leaned forward, his eyes full of adorable mischief. "What else do you like about me? I mean, I have a lot of amazing qualities, but as you pointed out, I'm far too humble to talk about them."

Okay, time to put some distance between us. "I'm going to refill my water bottle. I'll be right back."

"I'm not going to forget about this. I expect a long and complimentary list."

I grabbed my water bottle from the side of my backpack. "Just start reading chapter seventeen. We should get some work done today."

"Tyrant."

Trying not to smile, I headed toward the door. Ben stopped me just as I was about to open it and walk through.

"Hey, can I talk to you? It's kind of important."

Ben had never asked to speak to me before. Despite my crush on him, all of our interactions had been totally superficial. Why would he want to talk to me?

"Um, sure."

The door opened and one of the math lab volunteers came inside. Ben and I moved toward the back wall so as to not block the walkway.

Ben awkwardly cleared his throat. "This might be kind of sudden, but there's something I wanted to say to you."

Then he just stood there, making everything weirder. Now I was feeling uncomfortable.

"Yes?"

"Danielle and I aren't going to hang out any longer."

My first thought was, *Aha! Logan was right!*

"I'm . . ." I knew I should have said that I was sorry to hear it, only I kind of wasn't. Was this an it's-okay-to-lie type of situation? Like when your best friend asked if a pair of jeans made her look fat? Instead of lying, I settled on, "What happened? Do you want to talk about it?"

"I don't know. I went to that party after the game and I realized that I would have had a lot more fun if you'd been there. I like talking to you. I feel like you get me."

Only we'd never had a deep or meaningful conversation before. All of our interactions had consisted of basically saying hello or goodbye. Him asking me a math question he didn't know how to answer. There was our really brief talk at the Corner when I'd told him he was brilliant, but that was it.

Unlike you and Logan, who have shared some very real moments.

How could I like Ben when I didn't really know him? And how could he like me? Had I been more into the idea of him than the actual guy himself? Maybe I was being too hard on him and on myself. Maybe there was something deeper between us. Some potential that I was too quick to dismiss.

In that moment I felt like I was stepping into an episode of *The Twilight Zone.* Everything I had wanted to happen was suddenly happening, and all I could think was that there had to be some kind of catch. Had Danielle put him up to this? Was this all some kind of elaborate prank where they'd point and laugh at me for being stupid enough to believe that Ben would ever choose me?

"I . . . I don't understand what you're saying." Was Danielle watching us? Waiting for some signal? I turned slightly to see what she was doing. What she was doing was sitting so close to Logan that she was nearly in his lap.

Ben reached over and touched my hair. He let his hand linger, his palm brushing against my cheek. Again I felt that mildly pleasurable sensation. Still nothing compared to the Logan tsunami that would happen just from our legs accidentally touching.

He held up a piece of white fuzz. "Hope you don't mind. This was kind of distracting."

I brushed my hand over my hair. I didn't know if I did it to see if there was still something there or if it was some nervous tic.

Because I didn't think Ben was flirting and pulling things out of my hair and touching me for my sake. I didn't know why he was doing it, but it felt like he was playing some game and I was his pawn. I didn't like how that felt.

Was he pretending? I wanted things to be real.

Like my feelings for Ben.

Because those were real. And I did like him. Right?

Ben cleared his throat. "So, anyway, like I was saying, there's this Halloween party happening the day after tomorrow at the Gamma house."

The Gammas were the brother fraternity for the Zetas. Which confused me, since Ben didn't seem like the kind of guy to go to a Greek party. "You don't really seem the frat party type."

"That's not usually my scene. But one of my good friends is deejaying and I promised him I'd go." He paused, as if considering his next words. "You should come. You and Logan."

Wait, what? Here I'd thought he was asking me out, but instead he was inviting both me and Logan?

"I wouldn't want to step on anyone's toes," he continued. "Or get in the way of whatever you guys have. But I think it would be cool if we could hang out."

Date or not? Gah. Why were guys so vague? "I'll have to ask Logan. See what he thinks."

I didn't say anything that implied we were together. Only that I wanted to get Logan's opinion. It was neutral enough to be ambiguous, but still truthful. If Ben wanted to think I was dating Logan, that wasn't really my problem.

Besides, my situation with Logan kind of defied definition at this point. What had started out as a mutually beneficial arrangement had quickly morphed into a slightly attractive friendship and then into something more.

Something more that I couldn't examine because I knew nothing could ever happen with me and Logan. Even if we both wanted it to.

It was time to retreat and get Logan's input.

"So, I'm going to head back over and see if Logan wants to go and then I'll let you know, okay?" I said, starting to walk backward.

Ben reached out and gently grabbed my wrist. "I may not have the right to say this to you given your situation, but I want you to know that you were one of the reasons why I decided to stop seeing Danielle."

This totally flustered me, to the point that speaking was currently not an option. Wasn't this exactly what I'd hoped for? What Logan had promised would happen?

Why was I not more excited? I should have been thrilled.

"So, thank you for that, uh, information, but I'm going to get back to work." There was probably something perfect for me to say, but I didn't know what that was and I needed Logan's help.

I totally forgot about filling up my water bottle and made a beeline straight for Logan. Fortunately for me, Danielle had already gone back to her table, so I didn't have to worry about her. I could just see what Logan thought.

But after I sat down I realized that Ben had followed me, because Logan said, "Hey, Ben. How's it going?"

"Not too bad. So, I was just talking to Jess and let her know about this thing that's happening night after tomorrow at the Gamma house. I know Halloween's not for another week, but all the frats and sororities want to have their chance to host a costume party. You two should stop by. I can promise you the music will be off the hook! Just fantastic. Really fantastic."

The way Logan's lips quirked, I could tell he wanted to mock Ben, but thankfully he kept it to himself. "That sounds interesting. You plan on dressing up?"

"Definitely. Everybody will. I'm thinking maybe a cool superhero. Like Batman."

"The Dork Knight," Logan agreed, nodding.

"I think you mean the Dark Knight," Ben corrected him, as if eager to show off his superiority with movie titles and completely missing the fact that he'd just been mocked. I put my hand over my mouth so that I wouldn't laugh. Logan had used that name for Ben before, and it was probably killing him right now that he couldn't say more.

"What about you guys?" Ben asked. "Will you wear costumes?"

"Oh, I don't know," Logan drawled the words out before he turned to hit me full force with one of his smoldering gazes that made me lose all the feeling in my toes and fingers. "I know somebody who's a big fan of cowboys."

The flush started in my cheeks, and then it traveled to every part of my body. A rushing sound filled my ears, making it impossible to hear as Ben and Logan exchanged goodbyes. Ben waved at me and I tried to wave back.

I didn't currently have total control over my limbs, so it didn't work out so well.

Logan started speaking so fast I could barely keep up. "Do you think the music will be off the hook in the same way his poetry was off the hook? Because in that case, I vote pass. Or maybe we should go because it's going to be so Bentastic. Also, I know Batman. Batman's a friend of mine. And that guy is no Batman."

He let out a loud, deep sigh after all his words tumbled out, as if he'd been holding his breath for too long and could finally breathe again.

"You feel better?" I asked.

Logan nodded. "Ben seems attentive. Which makes sense. Because guys always want what they think they can't have."

I caught my breath, my heartbeat thundering inside me. Why did it feel like he was talking about me?

A hidden message?

Or, more likely, I had an overactive imagination.

While I was wondering what was wrong with me, Logan kept talking while drumming his fingers against the table. "You don't seem too excited about Ben finally asking you out."

"He asked both of us out," I reminded him. "He also said I was one of the reasons why he considers himself single."

"That's great! Isn't it just what you wanted?" Logan had a big smile on his face that didn't quite seem to reach his eyes.

The fact that I noticed something like that was why I wasn't as thrilled about the Ben stuff. Because the reality was that I was starting to have definite feelings for Logan. Feelings that were interfering with my liking Ben. Which was so pointless and stupid because Logan and I couldn't be together. He knew it and I knew it. Nothing could or would happen.

And I kept trying to put some distance between us so that we wouldn't make a mistake. Going out with Ben would definitely help with that problem.

Maybe my feelings would revert, go back to what they were, if I spent time alone with Ben. Logan was inadvertently interfering with my previous crush.

I couldn't tell Logan any of that, especially if I wanted us to stay friends and nothing more. "I thought it was what I wanted, but I don't know how I feel about . . ." I let my voice trail off. Maybe I wasn't being open minded enough, because I had started to want something different.

"What's our plan for the party?" I asked, wanting to stop my train of thought.

"Go, find Benman, and make a big move. Like at the end of the Sequoia Tech game. Don't play it safe. Do something outrageous. Go big or go home, and all that good stuff."

"Wait, you're not coming?"

Logan started flipping pages in his math textbook. "I wasn't planning on it. You and Ben need some alone time."

No, I wanted him there. Actually, I needed him there. "You have to come and tell me what to do. I trust your judgment. I used to make all these decisions on my own before I met you. Now it's like I have to have your input. Which is weird for me."

He'd gone strangely still, his hand in midair, holding a page of his book.

"What?" I asked.

"Nothing." He shook his head as if to clear it. "I would, but it's scheduled on the same day that I don't want to go."

"Oh, come on. It's not like you're going to be doing anything else."

"I could have plans." He sounded affronted.

"Like what?"

He sat for a while, thinking. "I can't even come up with a good lie. Your dad's taken everything fun out of my life. And speaking of your dad, I don't want to go and get in trouble for being there."

"You're not going to get in trouble. If you're really worried about it, go as a masked cowboy. Like the Lone Ranger. But when you get there, you'll see that most of your teammates will be there, breaking the rules. I think they figure the likelihood of getting caught is so low that they don't worry about it."

Logan seemed shocked by this news. What kind of bubble had he been living in? Why did he think Danielle kept hitting on him even though everybody on campus knew about my father's rules? It was because most of the team ignored them and did what they wanted.

"I follow the rules. And so does Bash."

"You two may be the only ones."

"Even if that's true, it doesn't really matter what anybody else on the team is doing. I won't get kicked off. If I go back to Texas, I'm going to end up back in construction. And I don't even know how I would go back given that I sold all my tools." Logan leaned back in his chair, looking defeated. I had to fight the urge to wrap my arms around him and tell him everything would be okay. "Don't get me wrong—it's a perfectly honorable profession. It's just what my stepfather did when he bothered to work and I—"

"You don't want any part of your life to be like his."

Logan seemed surprised by my answer. "Yeah."

I didn't know why he was surprised. Anytime we'd talked about his stepdad, Logan had indicated he wanted to be the opposite of the man who had raised him. "You don't have to worry about that. From what you've told me, you're nothing like him. You're a good man."

He had to swallow, like something was stuck in his throat. "Thanks."

"Come with me," I pleaded, starting to feel a little desperate. "We'll have fun. And I admit that I need your help. Come be my emotional-support milk."

At that I got a grin, one that did reach his eyes this time. "All right, all right. You talked me into it. I'll be your emotional-support milk."

"Yay!" Without thinking, I threw my arms around his neck, hugging him tight. I only had a second to smell that heavenly combination he wore that was part sandalwood, part laundry detergent, and part Logan, feeling his skin against mine, fighting the desire to bury my face in his neck.

I let go before he could return the hug. Because once he wrapped his strong arms around me I'd probably never let go, and it would most likely be difficult for Logan to play this week with me permanently attached to his front like a baby monkey.

Turning my head so that he couldn't see my flaming cheeks, I said, "You have a test this week, right?"

"Yeah. So we should probably get to work."

I had to stop dwelling on my attraction to Logan. I couldn't date him. Ever. And if Ben and I did officially get together? I would have to let Logan go and stop relying on him so much. Ben and I would be a couple and Logan would have paid me back for helping him with his grade. There wouldn't be any room for him in my new life.

At least I still had math. Cold, dispassionate, logical math to remind me that one plus one plus one would never equal two.

CHAPTER TWELVE

LOGAN

"You okay, Hunt?"

I was lying flat on my back, looking up at the gray sky. I wasn't supposed to get hit in practice, in case it did any serious damage. Ford was yelling at the overeager defensive lineman who'd broken past his man and hit me hard instead of just tagging me.

My center, Rodriguez, was bent over me. "How many fingers am I holding up?"

"None."

"You're fine."

Rodriguez offered me his hand, and I stood up slowly. He was right, I was fine. Nothing bruised, broken, or sprained. I'd just had the wind knocked out of me.

We waited while the coach chewed out the lineman.

"What are you up to this week?" Rodriguez asked.

"Homework. Studying. Practice. The usual."

"Yeah, that sounds about right." There was a dismissive tone in Rodriguez's voice that irritated me.

"What's that supposed to mean?"

He shrugged. "It means whatever, man."

I knew what it meant. It meant he thought I was pathetic. I thought about what Jess had told me—that all the other players broke Coach's rules constantly in the belief that they wouldn't get caught. It had bothered me when she said that, because the rules weren't just about not doing certain things but about acting honestly and doing what we said we would.

But if Bash and I were the only ones behaving, did all the guys on the team feel like Rodriguez? It would be hard for them to respect me as a captain or a quarterback if they all thought I was some rule-abiding pansy suck-up.

"I'm also going to a party this week," I said.

"Really?" That grabbed his interest. "Coach's Pet Hunt is going to a party? Which one?"

"The one at the Gamma house." That sealed it. I'd already told Jess I was going, but now I would definitely have to make an appearance so that the guys would see me there.

"Right on. I'm going to that one, too. You do know there's going to be women and booze there, right? No monks allowed."

"Shut up," I said, shoving his closest shoulder pad.

Bash was over in the defensive backfield, yelling. I didn't know if he was mad about my getting hit or something else. But he was doing his version of faux cussing.

"What the mother-father bullsugar is happening out here? Seriously, somebody tell me what kind of Monday-flipping sugar is going on? Freaking Mormon fiddlesticks!" Bash got really passionate about his game, and recently it had only gotten worse. Which was probably due to one of the defensive coaches telling him they already had interest from four different Division I schools who wanted him on their team. He just had to make it through the year with that 2.5 GPA and keep from spontaneously combusting on the field from all the non-swearing he was doing.

He knew how close he was to having his life back, and it made him crazy when everything didn't go exactly according to plan.

Something I completely understood.

"Will somebody please tell me what kind of Canadian bullsugar that was?" His loud voice boomed and carried across the field.

"Now *Canada* is a swear word?" Rodriguez asked.

"It's Bash," I said by way of explanation. "The only thing better than his level of intensity is his creativity."

"O-line on me!" a coach called out. I fist-bumped Rodriguez before he ran off. "See you tomorrow night!"

I then saw Ford jogging over to me. "Does your head hurt at all? Sensitivity to light? Feeling nauseated?"

"No. I'm fine."

"Yeah, that's what I used to tell people, too. And I kept getting concussions, and now I'm a coach instead of an NFL star. Don't lie about it if it's happening."

"I swear to you, I'm fine."

Ford looked at me like he didn't believe me. "Coach wants you to be checked out. Go warm a bench until Atkins can come and examine you."

Sighing, I went over to the sidelines. I sat down, took off my helmet, and set it on the ground. I spotted a bottle of water, picked it up, and sprayed it into my mouth.

"You all right, Hunt?" Coach Oakley yelled his question at me from across the field.

"I'm fine, Coach!" I yelled back. I understood the precautions they were taking, better safe than sorry, but I hated sitting by when a practice or a game was going on. If I had my way, the offense would just play the entire time and the other team could try to stop me from scoring.

It would be boring to everybody else, but I would be happy.

"Stay put and wait for Atkins!"

I raised one hand to let him know I'd heard him and that I was going to be good and listen. Like always. My encounter with Rodriguez had given me a bit of an itch. I kind of wanted to be bad. Break a rule.

And, of course, my mind went immediately to Jess.

To be honest, it was where my mind spent most of its time these days. When we were in the math lab, when she'd said that Ben had asked her out, some part of me had wished Jess would say it didn't matter because she didn't want Ben. She wanted me.

Which was stupid, because the whole reason we started all this was her huge crush on Ben. But realizing that she still liked him was a little like making a ninety-yard run down the field, crossing the goal line, and thinking your team had made a game-winning touchdown, only to find out that a foul had been committed at the beginning of the play and the touchdown was no good. All that running and screaming excitement from the crowd for a big fat nothing.

Which was okay, I told myself for the millionth time. It was how things should be. Jess was my friend, helping me with my math. My math professor had even stopped me to tell me how impressed she was with the work I was turning in. It made sense that I was improving. Not only because of Jess's help but because the only ways I had to get rid of this pent-up want for Jess were working hard on the field and doing my homework. Studying sometimes even helped me get my mind off her for whole minutes at a time. It made it so I could stop wondering where she was and what she was doing.

Maybe that was the real reason I didn't want to be on this bench—being out there on the field helped me turn my brain off and not think about things I could never have.

Like how my entire world had come to a screeching halt when Jess said she trusted me. The girl who didn't trust men trusted me. When she'd said that to me? It was like someone had rammed into my stomach, helmet first. It took my breath away, and I'd never known that just words could do that.

It had taken all of my strength not to grab her then and there and show her what her words meant to me.

I realized that wanting Jess had nothing to do with her being forbidden fruit. Or her being warm, beautiful, sexy, and inviting. It had to do with what she made me feel.

I wanted to protect her. Take care of her. Keep her safe. Track down those players from Amarillo and beat them until they could never hurt another woman again. Especially that ex-boyfriend of hers.

Because I cared about her. Not just as a friend. I wanted to date her. I wanted to spend all my free time with her. I thought about her constantly.

And I, without hesitation, desperately wanted to kiss her.

It kept me up at night.

Atkins finally arrived and examined me while asking me all the concussion questions. I answered them all truthfully. I was fine, and unless he had some kind of medicine that would make me stop wanting Jess, there was nothing he could do for me.

Movement across the field caught my eye. I saw an older woman in a bright-red silk shirt and black skirt making her way over to Coach. She looked to be about his age and had this cool salt-and-pepper thing happening in her hair. I wondered what her job was. Scout? Recruiter? Reporter? A school administrator?

She had to be somebody important because Coach was actually smiling at her, and he didn't smile very often.

They chatted for a little while, and I was about to start making dialogue up for them when she reached over and hugged the coach.

So she was none of the above. Someone like Coach didn't go around hugging random women. She meant something to him. Especially for him to do it in front of his entire team.

Or maybe I was the only one who'd noticed.

Either way, this was definitely interesting. The woman waved and walked away as Coach watched her go in that way that men watch women leave. Because they appreciate the view.

Something was definitely up. Should I tell Jess?

It might hurt her. She'd told me how much she missed her mom, but she hadn't said anything about whether or not she'd be okay with her dad dating again. She did seem grossed out by the possibility, but I figured that was probably a normal reaction.

Selfishly, I realized that if I told her what I'd seen, then we could team up to stalk her dad and find out what he was up to. Even if it wasn't a good idea and even if I should spend less time with Jess and not more, I was down for playing Scooby-Doo and solving the mystery.

"You check out okay," Atkins said. "Be sure to let someone know if anything changes. If you feel dizzy or nauseated, get a headache, or suddenly develop a sensitivity to light."

"I will." Concussions were a serious business and I did take them seriously, but I was fine. I wasn't made of glass and wouldn't break every time I got tackled. I knew how to take a hit.

I put my helmet back on and went onto the field. Atkins would tell Coach I was clear to play. Right now I wanted to throw the ball.

And not think about Jess.

~

It didn't work. I still thought about her for the rest of practice.

Stupid, inane things. Like, what kind of costume would she wear to the party? We had an away game this Saturday. Would Jess go? She said sometimes she went to help out her dad with the mathematical parts of the game. Would we hang out if she did?

Where was she right then? Was she in class? Did she like it? Like her teacher?

Even after practice ended and we hit the showers, I was still wondering things like, did she like living at home with her dad? How long had she had her dog? Why was she such a messy slob?

I wanted to know everything about her. I'd never felt that way about any woman before, and it was honestly starting to freak me out.

Especially because I knew it couldn't go anywhere.

After I'd showered and changed, I waited for Bash so that we could walk back to our dorm together. He took more time fixing his hair than most girls, so he always took a lot longer than everybody else. My phone rang and I went outside the locker room to answer it.

The display said "Restricted," and an uneasy feeling started to churn in my gut.

"Hello?"

A robotic voice answered. "You have a collect call from the North Texas Women's Correctional Facility from . . ." There was a pause and my stomach knotted up tighter when I heard my mama's voice say, "Louanne Hunt."

"Do you accept these charges?" the robotic voice asked.

I hesitated. I almost never hesitated. My answer was always the same.

Today wasn't going to be any different.

"No."

I hung up my phone.

Sometimes I thought I might say yes. Thought that maybe she deserved the chance to explain herself. Maybe she even wanted to apologize.

I'd never given her that chance.

While I was growing up, my stepdad didn't take me to visit my mom in prison. I hadn't seen her or talked to her in eleven years.

Which had been my fault since I turned sixteen. My stepfather got me a phone. Not because he cared but because some government agency had given him one for each of us, and he said he wanted to be able to get ahold of me if he needed me to pick something up. Like his beer.

He'd apparently given my number to my mom, and she'd been trying to get in touch with me ever since. About once every other month or so. I never knew when it was going to happen and it always surprised me when it did.

I often thought about changing my number. Bash's psychology professor would probably have had a field day with the fact that I hadn't changed it. It would be so easy to switch. My mom would never be able to find out the new one. I wasn't even in the same state anymore.

Deep down, though, no matter what else had happened or how angry I was at her or how much I blamed her for the stuff that had happened in my life, she was still my mother, and it was like I couldn't cut the one tie that still kept us attached. Like some digital umbilical cord.

I wondered what Jess would think about my problems with my mom. What she would tell me to do. And it suddenly seemed super important to find out everything she thought about my situation.

Bash came out of the locker room and almost ran into me. "You ready to go?" he asked.

"Yeah."

"Why are you staring at your phone?"

"What?" Was I staring at it? "No reason."

We started walking, and I realized that not even my mother was enough to make me stop thinking about Jess.

As soon as the phone call was over, my brain had gone right back to all Jess, all the time. Thinking of her reminded me of the party and that I needed a costume.

And that I'd need to convince Bash to come. If the guys were down on me about not participating in their illicit activities, chances were they felt the same way about him. Bonding was important when it came to football teams, and we did not want to be the odd men out. Our very futures could depend on it.

"How do you feel about going to a Halloween party tomorrow?" I asked him.

"Isn't that kind of masochistic?"

"Ooh, that's a big word coming from you."

He slammed me with his shoulder while I laughed at my own joke.

"Seriously, though, you want to go surround ourselves with stuff we can't have?"

Two girls walked past us and one of them waved suggestively at me. "We're surrounded every day by stuff we can't have. I have to go to help out a friend. And it turns out the team goes to this kind of thing all the time, and it would probably be a good thing for us to make an appearance."

"All right. It could be interesting. Count me in."

"Cool. We have to get over into the main part of town and pick up some costumes. Maybe Roman can drive us."

"Aw, man, it's a costume party?" he whined.

"It's not like I'm asking you to dress up as Romeo or Prince Charming or something lame like that. You can pick out an awesome costume. I was thinking about going as the Lone Ranger."

"What's a loan ranger? Is that a cowboy who works at a bank?"

I almost stopped walking. "Seriously? Tonto? Hi-yo, Silver? Did you not have a TV growing up?"

Or maybe his mistaken idea had merit. That could be funny. Only it would annoy me to spend the entire night explaining my costume.

"We owned a TV, but I went outside and had what people commonly call a life. What are the details?"

I told him when and where but I left out the why.

Which he noticed. "Is this to impress some girl?"

"Why would you say that?"

"My mom always says that when someone answers a question with a question it means the person is hiding something. Fess up. Who is she?"

I was tempted to lie to him, but Bash was my best friend.

After Jess.

I ignored my brain's attempt to manipulate me. "There is someone that I could be interested in, but she likes somebody else, so it doesn't matter."

"Who? We'll beat him up and then we'll see who she likes better."

Outside of the football field, Bash wouldn't hurt a fly. Even a caffeinated one intent on destroying his concentration. Which I knew, because I'd witnessed it. I laughed at his bluff. "That's not really the point."

"What is the point?"

That suddenly seemed like a very big question. "Do you date a girl when there's no future in it? When dating her means your entire life comes crashing down?"

"Because you're worried about getting kicked off the team."

"Yeah. Slightly. Coach seems serious about his rules."

Bash let out a sigh. "How do you give up your scholarship, your chance to play for a Division I team again, for a woman? Trust me, I know exactly how you feel."

"You do?" How had I not known this? Bash told me everything all the time, including information I did not want. Such as how often he pooped.

"I don't really want to talk about it, but yes. There's a girl I like, but nothing's going on because it can't."

It was so surprising that Bash had left out such an important thing in his life that I wanted to press him to tell me more.

But I didn't want to tell him about Jess. It felt too personal and I didn't want to share it. Share her.

So I'd respect his boundaries.

And I needed to start respecting my own. I had to draw some lines and not go past them. Not flirt with her, not accidentally touch her, not get sucked into her beautiful, dark eyes and want to spend my entire day just—

I shook my head. I was doing it again. It had to stop.

Putting my arm around Bash's shoulders, I said, "No worries. I'm here if you want to talk, and it's fine if you don't. If nothing else, at least we still have each other. We can be each other's dates for the Halloween party."

"Yeah."

We walked about ten more feet, my arm still around his shoulders. He finally pushed it off.

"Even if I am your date, just so you know, I'm not gonna kiss you, dude."

I laughed. "Bash, I absolutely wouldn't want you to."

There was only one person I wanted to kiss, and she was the one person that I never could.

CHAPTER THIRTEEN

JESS

My phone buzzed and I snuck a glance at it. Professor Woolsey hated class interruptions. The text was from Logan. Against my better judgment, I unlocked my phone to see what he had to say.

What are you doing?

I'm in class. Busy.

I got my costume last night.

I rolled my eyes. Did he not understand the definition of *busy*? I was about to turn my phone off but couldn't resist the lure of another incoming message notification.

> Do you have your costume?

> Yes.

> What is it?

> A surprise.

> Come on, don't I even get a hint?

I was about to ask him if, in addition to not understanding the word *busy*, did he also not get the word *surprise*?

But then I found myself not wanting to disappoint him, so I decided to throw him a bone.

> Black faux leather.

I'd decided to go as Catwoman. It wasn't really in my comfort zone, but if Ben was going as Batman, we'd be in a sort of couple costume (because Catwoman was Batman's true love and Vicki Vale could suck it) and I hoped that appearing as if we were together might be enough to convince me to make the right decision in this situation. Ben was available and seemed to like me; Logan wasn't and didn't.

I saw his three dots scrolling as he typed a response. When it came through, it was worth the wait.

> I'm sorry, Logan Hunt can't come to the phone right now as his head just exploded.

I laughed out loud at his response.

"Something funny about linear regression, Miss Oakley?" Professor Woolsey stared down his beaklike nose at me.

"No, I'm so sorry. Please forgive me."

> You just got me in trouble.

> I'm the one whose head exploded. How are you in trouble?

> You just made me laugh out loud in the middle of my Stats and Probability class and now my teacher is giving me the evil eye.

> Meh. Sounds like a personal problem to me.

I wanted to laugh again. The laughter welled up inside me and I tried breathing deeply to quell it. It was like when the urge struck you at someplace inappropriate, like a funeral, and you knew it was totally wrong to laugh, only that made you want to laugh more.

Stop it.

Ooh! I have the best idea.
Ask your professor what the
probability is that I'll make
you laugh out loud in class
again.

That was enough for me. I grabbed my backpack and headed for
the doors. Professor Woolsey was sure to ream me out in our next class,
but I had to get out before Logan made good on his word.

I'll have you know you just
forced me to leave class and
I have a test on Friday.

I'm sure you'll do fine.

He was right. The hour was nearly up, and I'd already studied the
material. But that wasn't the point. I was about to tell him as much
when he texted me again.

You want to meet up? Since
you're done with class and
all. Maybe I can figure out a
way to get you to tell me
more about this sexy
costume.

Yes, I did want to meet up. Desperately, in fact. Which was how I knew it was a bad idea.

> How about I'll just see you when I pick you up for the party tonight?

> Spoilsport.

I would spoil just about any sport to keep Logan in school. I couldn't be the reason he didn't graduate. There was nothing that would make me selfish enough to want to mess up his whole life.

If I'd only known how quickly that was about to change.

~

I dressed up like the 1990s Catwoman with the full-on mask, tight costume, high heels, and bright-red lips. The costume had been my mom's, and I hadn't worn it in a few years. I was feeling pretty pleased with myself as I looked in the mirror. It had been a long time since I'd dressed up in anything that made me feel sexy. I had forgotten how good it made me feel. To put on something that affected how I saw myself in a positive way.

Not to mention how much I loved that my mother and I were the same size. My heart squeezed tightly. If she had lived, we would have probably shopped together and shared clothes.

Or not. If she'd still been alive, I probably wouldn't have been living at home. I was here because I didn't want my dad to be alone.

Before I could get too depressed by my own train of thought, my phone buzzed. I expected it to be Logan, begging for more details about my costume.

It was him, only with not great news.

> Practice is running long. I'm going to be late. I'll catch a ride and I'll text you when I get to the party. Sorry. Tell ReBenge of the Nerds I say hello.

I texted him back saying that was fine, but I put down my cell phone with a sigh. Some part of me had been excited to see his reaction to what I was wearing. Even if I had chosen it specifically with Ben's costume in mind.

But all that was beside the point. Despite how confident I was feeling at the moment, I didn't want to go to this party by myself. I'd thought I'd have Logan by my side, and there was no way I could voluntarily go into a frat house without some support.

I called Keilani, who picked up on the first ring.

"Hi, this is Jess, in case you didn't already know. I have a huge, huge favor to ask of you," I said.

"What?" Her response was not what I expected. It was actually the opposite of how Keilani typically behaved. I'd expected a peppy "Sure!"

"Are you okay?"

"I'm fine. It's just stupid Ford came by my stupid office and was all . . ."

"Stupid?" I offered.

"Why is he such a jerk?" she demanded.

As I kept trying to tell her, he was only that way with her. The guys on the team loved him. Logan had nothing but good things to say about him as the QB coach. Keilani rubbed Ford the wrong way, and given my extensive knowledge of romance novels and rom-com movies, I'd tried repeatedly to explain it to her, but she never wanted to hear it.

Plus, I could tell she just wanted to rant and wasn't interested in having reality explained to her. So I said, "I need you to go to a party with me so that I'm not alone. A party at a frat house."

"Oh? Really? A party?"

My favor seemed to flip a switch in her. Admittedly, I was not-so-subtly using the Amarillo incident to my advantage in this situation, but I really didn't want to show up there alone. "It could be fun!"

"I'm too old for a frat party."

"Please. You're only two years older than me. Twenty-four is not too old."

She kept resisting. "I'm a school employee. They would fire me if I dated a student. What if I started chatting up some freshman? How would that look to my boss?"

Who was my dad. And I knew it wouldn't look good. "Ask to see their ID."

"Yes, because nothing says romance like 'I'll need two forms of identification, thanks.'"

"And they'd probably just have fake ones, anyways." I figured it was better to lean into her crazy so she could tire herself out.

"Right!" she proclaimed, as if she hadn't considered that possibility.

"Ben invited me to this thing. I'm going to see him. Logan thinks I should make some big move tonight. I need you there as my wing-woman since Logan's going to be late. You can take off once Logan gets there. Please?"

There was silence from her end of the call. "You're on Ben still?"

"What do you mean, 'on Ben still'? He just broke up with Danielle a couple of days ago. It's my big chance to see what's there between us."

"I don't know. I don't think he's the guy for you."

"Why would you say that?"

She spoke slowly, as if choosing her words carefully. "Ben is a very nice guy. But he's not the kind of person you need. You need a man who makes you laugh. Who doesn't date women just because they resemble Barbies. Who has some depth. Who you can confide in and trust. Someone who challenges you, who can look into the darkest parts of your life and not shrink from it. Someone who is strong enough to support you and wants you to get everything you want from life."

"Are you talking about Logan?" Because it sounded like she was describing Logan, and it was completely freaking me out.

"What? No! Why would I be talking about Logan? If you guys dated, not only would your dad kick him off the team, but I'm pretty sure he'd find a way to get the State of Washington to close down the borders and not let Logan in ever again." She paused. "Why would you think I was talking about Logan?"

"No reason. Do you want me to come by and pick you up?"

Keilani let out a long sigh that had overtones of martyrdom in it. "Fine. Come get me. But if something happens and I accidentally seduce an eighteen-year-old, I'm telling your father that it's your fault."

"Yay!" I was so relieved she was coming. "And thank you for letting me guilt you into this. I'll be over in a few minutes!"

I grabbed my purse and headed out to my car. I'd been a little worried about explaining to my dad where I was going and why I was dressed the way that I was. In his mind I was perpetually six years old.

But since he was at the same practice that was keeping Logan, I left the house without any Guantanamo-level interrogations.

About ten minutes later I knocked on the door at Keilani's apartment. She answered it without a costume on. And she didn't look like we were about to go out and party. She was wearing yoga pants and a T-shirt. "Did I mention that this was a costume party?"

"I figured. And I have one." She reached over and grabbed a white sheet off her couch. Then she put the sheet over her head. "I'm a ghost. And you owe me twenty bucks for a new top sheet."

That made me laugh, and I hugged her. "You're such a great friend. Let's go!"

Keilani lived close to campus, so it didn't take us long to get to the Gamma house. There were a bunch of people on the lawn and on the porch. I recognized a few of them, but nobody said anything to me. Because they didn't know who I was. I liked the anonymity of being dressed up with a mask on. It felt very freeing.

Keilani and I made our way through the crowd of zombies, sexy nuns, vampires, and sexy nurses until we found the main room. I spotted the DJ and figured Ben would probably be somewhere nearby.

A guy in an Iron Man costume pushed past us, carrying a red Solo cup.

"I hope that if there are any team members here, they behave." Keilani had to lean over and yell the words in my ear. "I wouldn't want to have to report anybody."

She'd most likely have to report everybody. I hoped any players who showed up would keep their vices under wraps or, barring that, were at least wearing masks so that she wouldn't know who was who.

I'd never really given my dad's rules too much thought. They hadn't applied to me—I wasn't one of his players. But I'd never brought them up with him, either, because he got fixated on things and didn't let them go. Like this time my uncle had given my dad an old beat-up car from the 1980s. The thing didn't run. But my dad was convinced that he would fix it up. We had dragged it along with us from Texas to Washington. He'd never worked on it. Never bought a part for it. It just sat in our garage, gathering rust and dirt.

But every time I suggested selling it or donating it or scrapping it, he got almost hysterical. He wouldn't answer my questions about it. Dug his heels in and refused to discuss it. He had the car, he was keeping the car, and there was nothing I could say to convince him otherwise.

The same was true with his rules for his team. I knew better than anyone that there wasn't anything anyone could say that would make him change his mind or ease up at all.

I reminded myself that I was at a party and wasn't here to question my father's life decisions. Something in the doorway caught my eye. "Look at that!" I pointed.

It was a severed foot with mistletoe attached to the actual big toe.

There were several more just like it, one in every doorway.

"Why would anybody hang up mistletoe in October?" I asked.

"To encourage people to make out and hook up. Haven't you been to a frat party before?" Too late she realized her mistake. "I didn't mean—"

"Don't worry about it." One, I wasn't offended, and two, the severed feet were giving me an idea.

A guy dressed as Master Chief from *Halo* bumped into us. "Cute costume!" he shouted to Keilani. His costume was impressive—the armor pieces looked real, and he even had a microphone in his helmet. I wondered if the black visor covering his face went up and down. "Not many girls go with the cover-yourself-from-head-to-foot look!"

Yep. Halloween was all about exposing as much flesh as was legally allowed. I mean, I had a slinky costume on, but my bits were covered up. I was impressed that he knew Keilani was female. Did his helmet have X-ray vision or something? It looked like it could.

"Thanks!" Keilani yelled back.

"Can I get you a drink?" he asked.

"Sure!" She turned to me. "Will you be okay by yourself for a couple of minutes?"

"Totally! Go on! And don't forget to check his spaceman identification!"

Even though I couldn't see her face, I could almost feel her withering glance. I could stand here by myself for a while. Scanning the room. And while I'd seen multiple superheroes, no Batman yet.

I checked my phone to see if Logan had texted me. Nothing. I wondered who on the team had screwed up badly enough that my dad would keep them this late.

The party swirled on all around me and I watched as people laughed and talked and drank. I kept an eye out for Ben. I let my mind drift and thought about how excited I would be if I were meeting Logan here for a date. If this night were full of possibilities and it didn't matter how things went because I'd be with him. The two of us, having an adventure together.

Did Logan think about me the way I thought about him? Had his feelings for me started to change? I thought I'd detected some interest, but that might have been because my dad had forced him into a year-round fast from women. And I happened to be one.

Then why doesn't he like Danielle? that perverse voice in my head asked.

There was no possibility of Logan. It was better for me to focus on Ben. Figure out if there was something more between us without my burgeoning feelings for Logan messing things up. And maybe I wasn't as attracted to Ben as I used to be, but I told myself that that was better. When I was younger, I'd dated many a guy that I'd been wildly attracted to, and without exception, they'd all ended badly. Maybe it was time to make a more mature decision. I didn't need fireworks. I needed . . . something else. The other stuff, the Logan stuff, was just hormonal and would pass. Feelings like that had done nothing but get me in trouble.

It was better for me to put logic and thinking first.

And I knew what was best for me, even if my heart and other non-neutral body parts wanted to argue.

A black cape fluttered in the corner of my eye, and that's when I saw Ben in his Batman costume. The only Batman I'd seen so far all evening. Heading out of the main room and into a hallway. Right under some severed-foot mistletoe.

This was it. Time to make my big move.

I went into the doorway and called out, "Hey, Batman!"

He turned and began walking back toward me. My plan here was to maneuver Ben under the gross mistletoe and then I'd have a perfectly legitimate reason to kiss him and an excellent excuse/rationalization for how I hadn't known it was actually him and . . . I didn't know what I'd say after that.

My knees had started to shake; the inside of my chest felt hollowed out. My heart slammed into my ribs over and over again, so hard that I thought I might pass out from it. I'd never been the aggressor when it came to guys, and now I was going to just up and kiss one.

It was okay. I could do this.

He came and stood next to me and I kissed him. Threw myself against him and pressed my lips to his.

Ben seemed shocked for a moment, not moving, not reacting. He put his hands on my shoulders as if he was going to push me away. I threw my arms around his neck, pushing him back against the doorjamb. If this was my one chance to kiss him, I was going to make it count.

I felt his arms slide around my waist, and then he was the one who deepened the kiss.

This was happening.

I was making out with Ben, and it was everything I'd ever hoped it would be.

Ben's touch had always created such a mild reaction in me before, but here was all the fire I could ever want.

Raging, consuming, devouring.

It was easily the hottest kiss of my entire life.

He drew me flush against him, his mouth moving over mine again and again. I might have been the one to initiate, but he quickly took control in a way that I never would have expected. There was so much sensation that I felt like I was going to burst out of my skin.

Now he pushed me against the opposite wall, pressing into me, holding me in place. His body was a hot, hard line against mine. He continued to ravage my mouth, almost bruising in intensity, and it was the most incredible thing I'd ever felt. The stubble from his five-o'clock shadow rubbed my skin almost raw, in the most delicious way possible.

I clung to him, unable to move, only able to feel and respond to what he was doing to me. I began to completely drown in intoxicating sensation, losing all sense of time and place. The entire party could have stopped and watched us, and I wouldn't have noticed or cared.

My pulse beat hard and thick, a light-headed exhilaration swamping my brain. I let out a small moan of appreciation for how good he was making me feel, and it was like that sound did something to him. Somehow his kisses turned deeper, wilder.

There was both strength and desperation in his kiss, as if he'd waited a lifetime to do just this, kiss a woman into total oblivion, and I was the girl lucky enough to be the center of his devotion.

His hands were everywhere, in places I hadn't felt other hands in a very long time. Kneading, grabbing, exciting me with each movement. It was so hard to catch my breath, as if every time I tried to get air he was there, and I wanted him more than I wanted to breathe. Shallow pants managed to escape my mouth, and I could feel him breathing in the same way. Hard. Out of control.

My heart turned into Mount Saint Jess, volcanic lava spreading through my veins until I fully expected to become one giant puddle of myself, inert on the floor and unable to ever move again.

And just as that languid sensation threatened to overwhelm me, he shifted and did something new with his touch and his kiss that made me feel like a string pulled too tightly. There was something I wanted, something I needed from him, and kissing wasn't enough.

It would never be enough.

His mouth pulled back from mine and I let out a cry of desperation, not wanting this to ever end.

"Jess." The word, spoken in longing and frustration, was rough against my skin, his voice thick and heavy, and as it cut through the fog in my brain I realized his voice was . . .

Not Ben's.

That was not Ben's voice.

Who had I been kissing?

I shoved against his shoulders with what little strength I had left. Leave it to me to do what Keilani was afraid she might do. I'd probably been making out with some random and inappropriate freshman in this hallway, and what was I going to do when everyone found out? Logan would never let me live this down and would mock me endlessly and why did I agree to come to a party especially a costume party because OMG this was turning out to be a truly epic disaster and . . .

Batman stepped back, as if he could finally move away from me.

I leaned hard against the wall, afraid that if I tried to stand, my liquefied bones would deposit me on the floor in a heap.

He reached up and took off his mask. I gasped, both of my hands going over my mouth.

Logan. I'd been kissing Logan.

CHAPTER FOURTEEN

JESS

This was not happening. Was. Not. Happening. A buzzing sensation started in my ears and then spread throughout my whole body. It brought the blood back to my limbs, making it so I could stand on my own.

I'd been making out with Logan Hunt.

Logan freaking Hunt.

And it had been the most fantastic thing I'd ever experienced.

I said the only thing I could think of. "Why are you Batman?"

His voice still had that sexy, gruff quality to it. "I thought it would be funny. Because I make such a better Batman."

True. He didn't need fake musclesssssss. I shook my head. So not the point.

"You were supposed to text me when you got here!" How had this happened? I'd been so careful and tried hard to prevent this very event from happening.

"I wanted to surprise you."

"Yeah, well, mission accomplished!" He'd surprised me, all right. By not wearing what he said he was going to wear. "And you were supposed to be a cowboy!"

"I never said I was going to dress up like a cowboy." He sounded defensive. Admittedly, I had been the one who had thrown myself at him and ruined everything.

Because I didn't know it was him!

Or had I?

My brain was too muddled and confused from his touch to figure anything out.

I became aware of the fact that my lips still burned, still wanted him back. It had been better before the kiss. At least back then I didn't know how it would be between us. I could imagine, pretend, but I didn't actually know.

Now I knew, and the knowledge of what it was like to kiss him was eating me up inside. How was I supposed to walk away from him now?

"Jess, we have to talk about what just happened."

No, we did not. I happened to be excellent at living in denial. "It was an accident. I thought you were Ben. I was trying to make a big move."

He let out a short bark of laughter. "That was definitely a big move. You won the game."

"Only I was playing the wrong team."

"You knew I wasn't Ben."

His claim shocked me so hard that I couldn't speak, couldn't breathe. Because I'd just been wondering the same thing.

Was he right? Had I known all along he wasn't actually Ben? Was that a lie I'd told myself because the second his lips touched mine I knew it was Logan, felt it in every fiber of my being? Even if I pretended like I didn't? Had I wanted this for so long now that I was willing to lie to get what my body ached for?

"That's . . . that's not true," I said weakly.

"I don't know if you're trying to lie to me or to yourself, but that was you, and that was me, and we both knew it."

My head was swimming with self-recriminations and his accusations.

"Jess, what just happened, I've never felt that way with anyone, and I think that it means—"

"It didn't mean anything," I told him, panic threatening to drown me. How had this happened?

He took a step toward me. I held up both my hands to ward him off. He came to an immediate stop.

"How can you say that?" he asked in a tone that nearly broke my heart.

Didn't he know that I was doing this for him? That I would have happily driven him back to my place and let him spend the rest of the night making me feel the way he'd made me feel in this hallway? But I couldn't, because his future was at stake.

And my dad, OMG my dad, he would draw and quarter Logan. Destroy his career, his education, and everything else Logan wanted. He was the king of ridiculously overprotective fathers.

How could Logan have forgotten?

One of us had to be strong. My anxiety turned to resolve.

"We need to talk about it. Work this out," he said.

"Not now." I gritted my teeth together so hard I was surprised I didn't break them. "I can't talk to you about it now. Later."

Definitely not now.

Because right now, there would be no talking. Now that I knew exactly what I'd been missing out on, now that I knew how his mouth felt crushed against mine, his strong body wrapped around me, the scorching intensity of his lips, the way I felt like I'd been made to fit against him, I wouldn't be able to say a single word to him.

There would only be more kissing. More extremely hot, passionate, crazy, desperate kissing. And I couldn't be that selfish. I wouldn't.

"Tomorrow. Promise me we'll talk about this tomorrow."

I nodded. It had taken all my strength to resist speaking to him about it right now. I had nothing left to resist or deny him what he wanted. "Tomorrow. I promise."

I'd deal with this later. For now I had to escape. Get away from this party, away from him. My willpower was not something I'd ever been known for.

The tears started to well up and I took one last look at him. He was so gorgeous. And although his lips were stained red from my kisses and I should have thought he looked ridiculous, he only looked . . . tempting.

I couldn't do tempting at the moment.

What I could do was leave. Leave and regroup.

Without another word, I turned on my heels and walked away. The tears started blinding me, getting caught up in my mask. So I peeled it off and brushed the tears away. Sad tears? Angry tears? Disappointed tears? In that moment I couldn't tell.

I got out onto the lawn, and a woman in a sexy French maid outfit approached me. "Are you all right? Do you need help?"

"No. I'm fine. Boy troubles." I must have looked terrible, all of my makeup smeared everywhere. "But thank you." I wished someone had been concerned about me in the same way when I was a freshman.

She handed me a card. "This is my number. A few of the girls are staying sober tonight, and we're here to help anyone who needs it. We've got some of our brothers ready to help out, too."

I thanked her and tucked the card into my purse. The tears started again at the thought that tonight another girl wouldn't have to go through what I did. I should have brought tissues with me. I cursed my lack of foresight.

How could you have known that you'd be making out with Logan freaking Hunt? My contrary voice was right. There was no way I could have known. Everything had gone so wrong tonight.

And speaking of things going wrong, I spotted Ben. Sitting on the lawn. With a girl straddling him, kissing him. The idiot who had invited me to this party was in the middle of making out with someone else. What was happening here? I'd come tonight thinking that maybe we'd get together. That maybe this was the start of our adult, mature relationship.

Instead, he was kissing a sexy Harley Quinn.

I was the world's biggest moron.

Before I could get away, Ben spotted me. He dumped the girl to one side and came running up to me. "Jess! You made it! You're not leaving, are you?"

"Yeah, I think I should probably just go home. Tonight wasn't what I'd hoped it would be." Understatement of the year.

"That's too bad. We didn't get to hang out."

Right. In large part because he'd apparently spent his evening with his tongue down another girl's throat. That tended to make hanging out just a wee bit hard.

So did you.

That was totally different. I was sure Ben hadn't mistaken that Harley Quinn for me.

It was then that I noticed his outfit. He was not Batman. "Who are you supposed to be?"

"Nightwing." The name jogged my memory. Some version of Robin. Batman's sidekick. "I thought it was more fitting for my personality. Don't you think?"

As someone who was so much less than Batman? Yes, his costume was definitely more fitting.

"I'm heading out. See you at school," I told him. I walked to my car, got in, leaned my forehead against the steering wheel, and cried. For a long time. Again, I didn't know what I was crying about. That Ben was a hormonal idiot who couldn't keep the inner parts of his mouth to himself? That I'd ruined the friendship between me and Logan?

Or was it the bittersweet knowledge of seeing how things would be with Logan, if we were allowed to date?

Once I'd sufficiently dehydrated myself, I sent a text to Keilani.

I need to go. Do you want to come with me or catch a ride?

It took her a couple of minutes to respond.

> Are you okay?

> I'm okay. I just want to go home. I can explain later.

> Let me tell Master Chief goodbye. Do you want me to meet you at the car?

> I'm already there.

Her goodbyes with her masked man must have taken a long time because it was a good fifteen minutes before she showed up at my car. "Hi, sorry, but you will not believe what just happened to me." She noticed my tearstained face and stopped. "Oh, honey, what's wrong?"

"It's a long story." Not really, but I didn't feel like getting into it just then. I had finally stopped crying.

"Okay, let's go to my house. Text your dad and let him know you're spending the night. We'll talk this out, whatever it is, until we find a solution. We will also eat our body weight in ice cream. Sound good?"

I nodded. This was why I loved her. I couldn't have asked for a better friend. I started up the car and pulled out onto the street.

"And while we're driving, I can tell you how terrible my night was."

"What do you mean?" I asked.

"So, I'm sitting with Master Chief and we're having one of those conversations where it's like it just flows perfectly and you're vibing off each other and finishing each other's sentences and realizing how much you have in common and that you're even close in age. I was a little worried that when he pulled off his mask he'd be a troll and I was going to have to be an adult and date him anyways because of how well we got along and that I'd have to learn to love him despite the fact that he looked like he could live under a bridge."

"And?"

"And then I got your text and said I had to go and we agreed to exchange numbers and he reached up to pull off his mask and he wasn't a troll."

I was confused. "That's a good thing."

"It would have been if the guy under the mask hadn't been freaking Ford!"

Her confession stunned me momentarily, and I couldn't help myself. I started to laugh. After a second or two she joined in and then spent the rest of the ride complaining about how the universe was conspiring against her and forcing her into spending time with the one guy who hated her. "Isn't it just my luck that I think I've finally met a guy I could date and really like and it turns out to be Ford, of all people?"

I was too emotionally exhausted to tell her why she should just date Ford. In large part because I thought it would make them both much happier.

When we got back to her apartment, Keilani led me inside and lent me some comfy clothes to change into. I scrubbed my face clean, avoiding staring at my reddened lips. I didn't need the reminder that Logan had done that to me.

When I pulled out my phone, there was some part of me that hoped Logan had texted.

He hadn't.

I sent my dad a short text, letting him know that I was going to stay over at Keilani's house. He quickly responded that that was fine and he'd see me tomorrow.

Tomorrow. Promise me. Logan's words echoed in my head.

How was I going to face him? What could we possibly say to fix our situation?

Maybe Keilani would know.

I found her in the kitchen, opening up some pints of ice cream. "I have a plethora of flavors—pick your poison."

After a quick glance at the labels, I decided on Chocolate Brownie Decadence.

"An excellent choice," she proclaimed, grabbing a chocolate–peanut butter cup pint. She grabbed spoons from a drawer and handed me one. "Let's go into the living room and talk this out."

I sat on her armchair while she curled up into a ball on the couch. She draped a blanket across her legs. "Okay, spill."

"I kissed Logan Hunt."

She'd been about to take a bite, but her spoon hovered in midair as she froze. "What?"

"I kissed Logan. A lot." And it had been incredible.

She put the spoon back into the ice cream and set it on the coffee table. "You kissed Logan 'Oh, We're Just Friends, Keilani, Stop Freaking Out' Hunt?"

"It was an accident. Ben was supposed to be dressed up as Batman, and I thought I'd be bold and make a move, so I kissed a Batman under the mistletoe—"

"Only it wasn't Ben. It was Logan."

I nodded, miserable. "Logan was supposed to dress up as something else."

"Do you think he did it deliberately? Like, was he trying to trick you?"

It wasn't something I'd considered before, but it seemed so unlike him. I had believed him when he said he thought it would be funny to dress up as Batman and show Ben up. That was the Logan I knew and lo—

I caught myself just in time. What was wrong with me? Where had that come from? I mentally corrected myself.

That was the Logan I knew.

"I don't think he was trying to trick me." Because—and I wasn't going to tell Keilani this—he'd had plenty of opportunities to kiss me before tonight. I'd put out all kinds of signals and had been more than willing to lock lips, but he'd never attempted it.

"Then I don't get what the big deal is. If it was an accident, no harm, no foul, right?"

I wished that were true.

And although I hadn't said anything, Keilani seemingly read my mind. "Oh. It's a problem because you have feelings for him."

"I didn't mean to." I rushed to explain myself. "We've been just friends to this point. There's always been chemistry there, but neither one of us acted on it."

"Until when? Do you have some secret romance with him?"

"No!" I protested. "All this time we've been hanging out—I've been helping him with this math class and he's been helping me to get with Ben. Does that sound like we have a hidden relationship?"

"It could all be part of some master plan." Keilani unwrapped her blanket and put it around her shoulders. "'Help' you land Ben while plotting to have you all for himself."

Why did the idea of that give me a little thrill? "That's not . . . that isn't what's going on. Tomorrow we're going to sit down and talk like adults and work this out. I won't be the reason he gets kicked out of school and isn't able to graduate."

"What do you mean? Even if your dad kicks him off the team, he can't stop Logan from getting an education."

"He's mentioned before that he doesn't qualify for financial aid. I'm not sure why." I should probably ask him.

She tapped one finger against the back of the couch, thinking. "Interesting. But what are you going to say to him? How do you go from kissing each other to not kissing anymore? Because it's obviously something you both wanted to do."

That was true. It would be hard. "I don't know what I'll say. I know the smart thing would be to stop seeing him altogether." That would definitely make sure nothing else happened.

"I could reassign him to another tutor."

My heart lurched at her offer and cried out, *No!* I didn't want that. Even if that would have been best for us. "He's my friend. I don't want to lose his friendship."

I couldn't bear to cut him out of my life completely. Which suddenly made me wish that I could date Ben. That I still had feelings for him. Then everybody would be in neat little boxes—Logan would be my friend and Ben would be my boyfriend, and since I didn't cheat, I wouldn't have to worry. That commitment to someone else would be enough to keep Logan where he belonged. Firmly in the friend zone.

Only I didn't feel that way about Ben anymore.

"Other than that, I've got nothing." Keilani picked up her now-mostly-melted ice cream and had a few bites. "You want him in your life, but you can't kiss him. You have to stay just friends. For both of your sakes."

She was right.

I picked up my ice cream and ate a big spoonful. "We'll work it out."

We had to.

~

I couldn't sleep. Keilani and I had stayed up for hours, but going over it with her was not helping me. I had to talk to Logan.

She'd made up her couch for me and I just lay there, eyes wide-open, watching the shadows move across the ceiling. While I tried to keep my thoughts focused on what I'd say to Logan, all I did was relive that kiss. Over and over, in 3-D and high definition. His lips against mine, his arms holding me close, the roughness of his jaw. How he'd made me drown and then come alive again, over and over.

It wasn't just that it had been physically fantastic, which it obviously had been. Although I hadn't acknowledged it at the time, there'd been something more. As if our souls had been merging and connecting. Like we'd been wandering the world lost, and in that moment we'd found our perfect mates. The ones we'd been waiting for.

He'd been my Stavros, rushing into the gazebo to claim me.

Would I ever forget that kiss?

The greatest kiss of your entire life? Not very likely.

At about six in the morning I couldn't stand it anymore. I had to have this conversation and fix things between us. I texted him.

> Are you awake?

His response was immediate.

> Unfortunately.

> Are you alone?

> Also unfortunately. ;)

I was asking about Bash, but leave it to Logan to turn this moment into something flirtatious. It would not be easy to be strong against his teasing.

Can I come over?

Yes.

After stripping the couch and leaving the sheets and blanket in the laundry room, I went into the bathroom to brush my teeth and my hair. Not because I anticipated a need for it, but because I didn't want to offend with my gross smells. I sent Keilani a text, thanking her for our chat and for letting me stay over.

It didn't take me long to reach his dorm. One of the players leaving for the morning grinned at me and let me into the lobby. Which gave me a few seconds more to prepare as I walked down the hallway to Logan's room.

Please don't let me screw this up, I prayed to whoever was listening.

I raised my hand to the door, hesitating for a second. Gathering up my courage, I knocked softly.

He answered quickly. It looked like he'd just gotten out of the shower, his hair still damp, his gray T-shirt clinging to his perfectly formed chest. "Hi. Come in."

I walked inside, rebuking myself for not even being able to see him for thirty seconds without objectifying his beauty while he let the door swing shut. His room was as clean and immaculate as ever. Both of the beds were even made. I sat on Bash's and he sat on his, across from me.

Logan spoke first. "We should probably just get to the point. That kiss last night—"

"Was a mistake," I finished firmly. "And it can't happen again." No matter how much we wanted it to.

"I know that." He nodded and swallowed hard. "I logically understand it. But it doesn't stop me from wanting to—"

"I know," I said. Echoing his words. I felt the same way, but I couldn't tell him that. To admit that I was just as attracted to him would make it impossible to follow my dad's rules. "We can't. Your future's on the line."

He looked down at his hands as he rubbed them together. "I wish there were another way."

I thought of Keilani's question last night about financial aid. He would definitely have to stop playing football, which meant that the NFL was out of the question. He didn't seem to believe that was a possibility anyway. But his degree? I knew how important that was to him. "What about student loans?"

It was so wrong of me to even ask the question. To ask him to go into debt just so that we could make out. I'd never felt more selfish.

"My stepfather ruined my credit years ago. There's no private or federal loan that I would qualify for. Trust me, I've considered all of my options."

Despite the way my heart was breaking, it beat low and hard at the idea that Logan had been trying to find a way for us to be together. A rush of feeling pulsed through me, something I'd never felt before and didn't want to identify. This was already hard enough.

"I won't be the reason you lose your scholarship." It was all he had.

"And what are we going to do to make sure that last night doesn't happen again? Because since you walked in my room, I've imagined a thousand different ways that I want to kiss and touch you."

My mouth went immediately dry and my lungs tightened, making it impossible to breathe. I knew exactly what he meant. Because while we were talking, I'd imagined walking across the room to his side. Sitting down next to him on his bed. The way that we would slowly lean into each other, when there's all that anticipation of knowing not only exactly what's about to happen but how good it will be when it finally does.

Then, when his mouth finally touched mine, his kisses would be slow, deliberate. Thorough. We didn't have to rush. We had all the time in the world to explore one another. I thought of how those kisses would build, like someone creating a campfire. There would be kindling in the beginning, little flames here and there that set the path for the next stage. Building to something bigger, better.

We'd pile up our kisses like small sticks, the fire intensifying with each one added on, until the logs were added, causing a blaze that could consume everything in its path.

I thought of how he would kiss my neck, my jaw, my cheeks, the way he would run his fingers through my hair, how he would feel pressed up against me. I thought of how we'd lean back slowly until I was flat on his bed, him hovering over me, his mouth still slowly exploring.

How I'd tug at the bottom of his shirt, getting him to pull it off, and I'd finally get to see and touch all those muscles I'd only been feeling through fabric and . . .

"Jess?"

"Huh? What? Yes?" I knew my cheeks were red. I hoped he didn't ask me why. Because I had no explanation for him that would make things better. I hadn't wanted to be with a guy physically in years. Ever since I was attacked, it had been like that part of me had gone dormant. And I'd thought Ben was the one who had turned it back on, the one who I was attracted to.

But it was Logan who made me remember, who made me want to feel that way again. He was the one I wanted to get closer to. I wanted to feel his warm skin on mine, our mouths pressed together.

We had to be friends and only friends. There was no other option.

"What do you think we should do here?" he asked.

Maybe I needed to give him up to make sure that his future was safe. It would hurt and it would be terrible, but I wanted to put his needs above my own. "Should we say this is it? Just walk away from each other?"

"Is that what you want?"

The words spilled out of me before I had time to consider them. "No, it's not what I want. I want you in my life. I don't want to lose your friendship."

"Good." He grinned. "I feel exactly the same way. You've become really important to me."

His smile lightened my heart, making me think that we could find a way to make this work. I was glad he hadn't agreed with my suggestion to end things entirely. Even if it was selfish of me.

"We can't kiss again. That's not a friendship," I told him.

"Well, it'd be a friendship with benefits," he said, his wry smile telling me he was teasing. "But I think we're strong enough to resist our chemistry. We can be just friends. Let's go play mini golf tomorrow after tutoring and practice."

"Excuse me?" What was he saying? "We decided to be just friends and you want to go on a date?"

"It's not a date. Let's prove to ourselves that we can do it. Hang out and have it not be romantic. We'll have fun. What do you say?"

"Yes." The word was out before I even had time to consider. Not that I would have turned him down; I had the worst time ever saying no to Logan.

"Great! I'll text you. We'll have a good time and we'll be just friends and nobody will kiss anybody else and everything will work out."

We said goodbye, and as I walked back to my car, I wondered what was wrong with me. The way to prove we could be just friends was not to go out on a date. Even if Logan denied that's what it was.

Why was I torturing myself this way? When had I become such a glutton for punishment?

At this point I deserved whatever bad things were going to happen next.

CHAPTER FIFTEEN
LOGAN

It was very hard not to be distracted by Jess. She'd had to explain this formula to me twice already, and she was heading into round three. But instead of concentrating, all I could think about was how I loved the way she smelled, how the overhead lights reflected off her skin, how she'd grab her lower lip with her teeth when she was deep in concentration.

And maybe I could have ignored all that if I hadn't kissed her.

That kiss.

It haunted my dreams. He—heck, it haunted all my waking hours, too. I only had to close my eyes, and I was back in that hallway at the Halloween party, her lips eager and inviting, her soft body quivering against mine, her breathy little sounds driving me absolutely insane—

"Logan?"

"Hm?"

"Should I explain it in a different way?"

It was a lost cause. "Maybe we should try the next problem."

"Or maybe you should pay attention. What's got you so distracted?"

She did not want to know. "It's all those bright, flashy colors Has Ben is wearing over there. How am I supposed to concentrate?"

Ben was dressed all in black, just like normal. Which meant I got a smile from her at my joke.

I'd hoped she'd given up on the reject from the Night's Watch. It was bad enough to want her, be close to her, and not be able to be with her. It would be miserable to watch her with him. Especially now that I knew what I was missing out on.

The thought of her kissing that reverse clown made me want to punch things.

Preferably him.

"If I was dating him, you wouldn't be able to make fun of him like that anymore."

That hit me like a punch to the throat. "Are you dating Ben?" I couldn't keep the surprise out of my voice.

"No. I'm not."

But did she want to date him still? No other woman I'd hung out with had ever made me doubt my own appeal. In fact, they spent most of our time together telling me how much they enjoyed it. But I never knew where I stood with Jess.

I'd let her know I was attracted to her, had thought about kissing her senseless again. But she'd never said the same back to me.

Although, if I'd had any question about whether or not she found me hot, the party kiss had settled the matter. She'd been into it. She'd been into me. She'd known exactly who I was, no matter what she'd claimed after the fact.

"I mean, I know that's the reason you and I started hanging out," she said, interrupting me before I could reminisce about that kiss again. "But I think maybe I should give up on the whole thing with Ben. I don't think it would work between us."

Was she serious? Hope fluttered inside me. But if we stopped trying to win Ben over, what would that do to our friendship? Like she'd said, that was the reason we had started spending time together. Even if I didn't like him, he did serve a purpose as a buffer to things becoming more serious between me and Jess. Much as I would have loved to remove him entirely from our lives, I decided that I'd have to take one for the team.

"Come on, quitting? When is quitting ever an option?"

"Opioid addiction? Cigarettes? New Year's resolutions?" She let out a sigh. "Not that it matters. I don't think he's that great of a guy."

"Why's that?" I started doodling in the margins of my scratch paper so that I wouldn't be tempted to gaze longingly into her eyes.

I was such a wuss.

"At that . . ." Her voice trailed off for a second, and then she cleared her throat. "At that Gamma party, I saw Ben making out with someone else."

"Who?"

"I don't know. Some random girl."

Really? My mouth hung open and I was temporarily unable to respond. How was that possible?

"What?" she asked.

"Nothing. I'm just dumbfounded by how much action this guy gets." It was one of life's greatest mysteries how any woman would want to be with that. "But it doesn't matter. You guys aren't dating. You're both free to kiss . . ."

Now it was my turn to let my voice trail off, as I realized too late what I'd been about to say. I tried to cover it up by more talking. "You're not together or exclusive."

But how could Ben want to kiss anyone besides Jess? Did he not realize what he was missing out on?

"That's true." Her phone rang, and she looked down at the screen. "It's my dad. Give me a minute."

She walked out of the math lab, ignoring both Danielle and Ben. I tried not to feel nauseous when I saw Danielle walking toward me. I wanted this game to be over. Jess seemed like she was over Ben, and I had never been interested in Danielle. I wanted them both to disappear.

I closed my eyes for a second, like I had when I was a kid: if I couldn't see the monster, then she couldn't see me.

She still saw me.

Danielle stared at me coldly, like a snake sizing up a mouse. She followed that with a chilly faux smile that showed all of her teeth.

Could she unhinge her jaw? I was suddenly a little afraid.

"Hey, handsome. Where have you been?"

"Around," I said. Her gaze flickered over to Ben, and I realized that she was now using me to make him jealous. Part of me wanted to tell her to stop, that the jig was up, but I figured that would probably make me a hypocrite, so I sat there and took my lumps.

"Like where?" she asked with a pout, running her fingers along the inside of my forearm. I tried not to grimace as she went on. "I feel like I haven't seen you in days."

"I, uh, I was at the Gamma party. Did you go?"

"I did. It was a lot of fun. I didn't realize you were there. You didn't see anyone dressed up as Batman, did you?"

I'd chosen that costume not only to slight Ben, petty as that was, but also to keep my face hidden. Was Danielle insinuating that Batman was me? Or did she really not know? The tone of her voice didn't reveal anything. Why would she care how I'd been dressed? Something told me to be cautious. "I didn't see anyone dressed as Batman at the party." Because I hadn't hung out in front of any mirrors. "Why do you ask?"

"Just something interesting I saw." She reached for her rose-gold iPhone and typed in her password. "Look at this."

All the oxygen left the room as I looked at a picture of me kissing Jess.

"I recognized the Catwoman costume. Jess wore it freshman year. She went on and on about how it had been her mother's. But I don't forget clothes. Or costumes. Anyway, that's a photo of her making out with some guy at the party."

The image had been taken when I'd pushed Jess up against the wall. You couldn't even really see her—I overshadowed her completely. You could see my back, my cape, and almost nothing else. Thankfully, it was a terrible photo.

I looked into Danielle's calculating, reptilian eyes to figure out what her game plan was. I almost let out a sigh of relief when I realized that she didn't know Batman was me. She was hoping I would either tell her the identity of the man or get upset that my "girlfriend" was cheating on me. She didn't know that Jess and I weren't actually together.

Danielle had nothing. I'd played poker with my stepdad's meth-dealer friends. I knew when people were bluffing.

"Can't help you, sorry."

"Worth a shot." She put her phone back down on the table. "It would be such a shame for her father to find out what his little girl is really like."

Anger, fast and fierce, burned inside me. Jess had done nothing wrong. And for Danielle to sit here and insinuate that she had?

"But I could be convinced to keep it to myself. Tell your little friend over there to leave Ben alone, and this stays safe on my phone."

What was wrong with this girl? I would not let her hurt Jess.

I couldn't even reply to what she'd said. Instead, I sat there quietly, taking in my deep, cleansing anger-management breaths the way I'd been taught as she left.

And I kept breathing hard until Jess returned to the table.

She took one look at me and asked, "What's wrong? Did something happen?"

"Danielle paid me a visit. Do you have any hand sanitizer?" I felt unclean after she'd touched me.

Jess picked up her purse and went through it, looking. "Maybe. I'm sorry you had to deal with her. I feel like I should make this better. Is there any way I can make it up to you?"

I couldn't resist as she handed me the sanitizer. "Yeah, but you won't do it."

She gave me a look of disgust, which made me laugh, helping to break up the rage I was currently trying to tamp down.

I considered not telling Jess about Danielle's veiled threat but decided it was probably best to be totally honest. And it shouldn't stress her out too much. Because what was Danielle going to do? Send the picture to Jess's dad with a note attached saying, "This is your daughter. I know you can't see her, but trust me"?

And Jess wasn't a football player. She was allowed to date and kiss guys. Even if the idea of it drove me insane. Problem was, even if she wasn't beholden to the rules, her dad was not going to be happy. I knew how protective he was.

Rules or not, Jess would still get upset. She might possibly go over and try to pull out some of Danielle's extensions. Much as I might have enjoyed the show, I didn't want to hurt Jess.

But she deserved to know the truth.

"Look, I don't know how else to say this other than to just say it. Danielle has a picture of us together. At the Gamma party."

She froze and blinked slowly. "What?"

"She showed it to me. She doesn't know I'm the guy in the picture. She recognized your costume at the party, but you can't see it in the photo. She says if you stay away from Ben, she'll keep it to herself. She's threatening to send it to your dad."

"I'm going to kill her." She half rose out of her chair.

I put my hand on Jess's arm, trying to calm her. Her skin was warm and soft. I ignored the burst of heat that exploded in my stomach. "Nothing's going to happen. She doesn't have anything on you other than suspicion. Please trust me. This will be fine."

She deflated back into her chair. "If you say so."

"I'm a big believer in karma." Not to mention that Danielle, for reasons unknown, obviously still wanted Ben, and not being with him was probably upsetting her. "But putting all that aside, are you looking forward to us hanging out tonight on our totally platonic and friendly not-a-date?"

"You did not just ask me that."

"What?"

"I think you need to forget that I'm a woman."

That was not possible. The swell of her curves under her clothes, the silky softness of her hair as it fell across my arm while we studied, the sway of her hips when she walked, the feminine slant to her lips, the taste of which I would never forget.

"Why do I need to forget you're a woman?" I asked, genuinely curious.

"Would you ask Bash if he were looking forward to hanging out with you tonight?"

"I don't know. It would probably depend on what he was wearing."

She tried to shove my shoulder while I laughed. I moved out of her way, which caused her to collapse on top of me, her face close to mine.

There was that overwhelming feeling again, that magnetic draw that wanted to pull me under.

Everything else stopped, and the only thing I could see was Jess.

Unfortunately, she came to her senses and sat up in her chair. "So, going forward, especially as we engage in not-dates, I think maybe we should set up some ground rules."

"I already have a lot of rules in my life," I reminded her with a groan.

"If we're going to stay friends and just friends so you don't break any of those other rules in your life, we need to have some boundaries."

"Like?"

"No flirting."

That might not be possible. "I make no promises, but I'll try."

"We can't be just friends if you're always flirting with me."

"It isn't always flirting. Sometimes I'm just friendly. Overly friendly. And I disagree with you. I think friends can flirt."

"Maybe some friends can." Her implication was that we couldn't. She was probably right. It was like I couldn't help some of the things that came out of my mouth when I was with her. I wanted to see how her eyes lit up in protest or delight, or if I could make her blush. It gave me the same kind of thrill as throwing a touchdown pass.

Jess wasn't done laying down the law yet. "And in addition to no flirting, we should probably avoid touching each other. No looking at me in that, you know, way that you sometimes do, and definitely, without question, no kissing."

"So what you're saying is that you have a really hard time resisting me and my charms." I was already breaking the no-flirting rule. I had to stop it. She was right. It would only lead to outlawed yet pleasurable things.

I tried not to smile when she rolled her eyes. "Is there anything you want to add?"

"No, I think you covered all the bases." I decided on my own to add a final rule—to never be alone with Jess again. If we could stick to public places, then I'd most likely be able to keep my hands and my lips to myself.

"Right. So things with us will be fine and you'll stay in school." She flicked her hair over her shoulder, exposing her neck. I tried hard not to stare in "that way" at her.

"And then maybe we'll figure out a way to get some Bengeance on Danielle. Or maybe finally end this Bendetta that you've had for years."

She just shook her head. "How long have you been sitting on those?"

"For a while now. Come on, that was funny."

"Let's just get you ready for your test next week, okay?"

"You're the boss."

As she tried for the third time to explain the same equation to me, I realized that maybe this was the solution. My academics. I needed to be reminded of why I was here and what I was doing. How I was securing my whole adult life in this one year. I wasn't going to stay at EOL forever. I would move on. Coach's entire program was designed for that purpose—to rehabilitate players and get them graduating or back playing at major universities. This wasn't going to be permanent.

Jess, no matter how much I liked hanging out with her, was going to be a story I told someone else someday.

~

"Why do you look so pretty tonight?" Bash lounged on his bed, watching me style my hair.

"Shut up," I told him, glaring at him in my mirror.

"Do you have a date? It better be with a dude, because Coach outlawed dating girls."

That made me pause and think for a second. That was true. Interesting. But now was not the time to think about loopholes and technicalities. I needed Bash to back off. "I don't have a date. I'm hanging out with a friend. Who happens to be female."

"You never get dressed up to hang out with me anymore," he said with a dramatic sigh, and I threw one of my pillows at him.

He caught it. "Yes! Interception!"

I grabbed my cologne and spritzed it on my shirt, hoping that maybe if I ignored him he'd lose interest.

It didn't work. "No way this isn't romantic. You don't put on cologne to go out with a buddy."

"Sure I do." Okay, maybe I didn't. And maybe I'd noticed Jess taking in a big whiff of me once or twice. She seemed to like the way that I smelled, and I wouldn't want to disappoint anyone.

"If it looks like a date and sounds like a date and quacks like a date, it's a date."

"I don't think that's how the saying goes."

There was the sound of a car door slamming shut, and I peeked through the blinds to see Jess getting out of her car. Usually I thought it was adorable that she came all the way to my door to pick me up, but today would have been a good day for honking. Because Bash was having way too much fun with this.

Then I felt him leaning over my shoulder. "Is that Jess Oakley?"

"Uh . . ." There was nothing to say. She'd be knocking on our door in a matter of seconds.

He gasped loudly. "Dude, you're going out with Jess? Do you have a death wish? Do you not remember the One Rule to Rule All Other Rules? No dating Jess! Coach has already proven he has zero problems taking out guys who mess with his daughter."

"If it were a date, which it is not, then I'd understand your concern. She's my math tutor. We're friends. We hang out. Tonight will not be romantic in any sense of the word."

"Is she a good kisser?"

His question caught me so off guard that I sputtered around for a response. "Wh-what? How would I . . . what would make you . . ."

"Oh, flipping Canada, I was kidding. You have kissed her. You are so going to die."

"It was one time and it was a mistake and it will never, ever happen again. Please, you can't tell anyone. I'm begging you."

Bash grinned at me, slapping me on the back. "I got you, bro. That just went into Bash's Vault of Secrets. I won't say a word. But I do have a very serious question for you."

"What?"

"Can I be a pallbearer at your funeral? You know, after Coach kills you."

There was a knock at the door, and I sent one final pleading look at Bash. The last thing I needed was for him to give her a hard time and make her think that this was an actual date. It was casual. We could do this. We could hang out and just be friends. I needed to prove it to her as much as I needed to prove it to myself.

When I opened the door, I wanted to let out a low whistle. I refrained, knowing it wouldn't exactly fit my whole "This isn't a date!" mantra. But she looked fantastic and again made it impossible to forget that she was a woman. I settled on "Hi. You ready to go?"

"Yeah. Hi, Bash!"

I blocked her view into the room, not wanting to give him a chance to say anything stupid.

"Bye, Bash!" she called out as I hustled her into the hallway and toward the exit.

My roommate foiled my plans when he leaned out the door and yelled at us in a cheery voice that made him sound like a TV housewife from the 1950s. "Have a good time, you two! Don't forget that it's a school night, so be home by curfew! And don't do anything that will get Logan kicked off the team!"

"What's going on with him?" Jess asked.

"Dropped on his head too many times as a baby? I don't know." I hurried her along before Bash's bellowing could draw our teammates out of their rooms. "Come on."

Thankfully, she responded to my prodding, and we were finally in her car and safely on our way. I let out a sigh of relief.

"Where are we going?"

"I'm not telling." I wanted it to be a fun and cheesy surprise.

"Um, I'm the one driving. You're going to have to give me directions."

"Already have them ready to go on my phone." A computerized female voice directed Jess to take a right onto the main road.

"The suspense will kill me, cowboy. You have to at least give me a hint."

"Nope." Was this date behavior or friend behavior? I decided not to think about it too hard and just enjoy myself.

"I could probably get it out of you if I wanted to." She meant it as a threat, but since I was starving for her affection, it sounded like an invitation.

"I'm sure you could." My voice sounded husky, even to my own ears.

Her cheeks turned pink in response. "How about some music?"

Music. Definitely. Friends listened to music, right? She turned on the local country station.

After about ten minutes, Jess said, "You're really not going to tell me where we're going?"

"I'm really not. Just follow the GPS. We'll be there soon enough."

I had directed her out of our small college town. I didn't want to run into anybody that we knew. Even though the two of us understood that it was an only-friends type of situation, that didn't mean other people wouldn't misinterpret what we were doing.

After we'd driven for about half an hour, the GPS told her we'd arrived at our destination.

"We're here!" I told her, unnecessarily, as I undid my seat belt.

She got out of the car and stared at the massive, blinking neon sign that promised a night of fun. "Where have you brought me?"

CHAPTER SIXTEEN

JESS

"Haven't you ever seen a mini golf course before?" he asked. "I told you what I wanted us to do."

"Yeah, but I thought you were kidding." Logan had told me to dress casual. I figured we'd see a movie or something. "Isn't this for little kids?"

"No way. Come on. It'll be a blast." He held his hand out to me and then immediately dropped it. "Whoops. Sorry. I forgot. Friend rules."

I curled up my fingers. I'd been totally ready and willing to accept his offer of holding hands. I fell into step beside him as we walked inside. He held open the door for me and let me go in first, which I thought was a sweet gesture. "This is the kind of stuff good buddies do?"

"Yep. And it's a school night, so we shouldn't be inundated by sugared-up tweens or exhausted toddlers."

We made our way over to the counter where they sold tickets and rented the golf clubs and balls. Logan took out his wallet. "Two, please."

"I can pay for mine!" I protested. Not only because of how datelike it felt, but because I knew how broke Logan was and I didn't want him spending what little money he had.

"Nope. I've got this, Jess. Next time we hang out as friends, you can pay. It'll all even out."

Here we were trying to make this not feel like a date, but he kept making it worse.

My impulses weren't helping the situation, either.

He'd been right about the course being clear. All of the kids who were here were inside at the arcade, winning tickets to buy junk. We headed out to the back outdoor area and the mini golf course.

The theme was "Wonders of America." The first hole was just a straight shot, and there was an outline of a mountain range surrounding the hole. The Rockies? The Appalachians? I wasn't sure.

"Okay, so this is a par three," Logan said, holding one of those tiny pencils and the scorecard the employee inside had given him.

"Are you really going to keep score?"

"Um, yeah. Supercompetitive athlete, remember?"

"Well, Mr. Supercompetitive Athlete, why don't you go first and show me how it's done?" I gestured toward the hole.

"I know I should say 'Ladies first,' but I'm going to own you and you might as well get used to it now."

That was a lot of smack talk from a guy who didn't know what he was up against. It took him the full three strokes—one to get the ball down the causeway, the next to get it closer to the hole, and the third to putt it in.

"Your turn!"

I lined up my ball, trying to get it perfectly parallel with the hole. "Did I ever mention that putting like this is basically all math? Figuring out the correct angles and reflections? That it's just geometry? Which I happen to be fantastic at?"

Then I hit my golf ball with what I hoped was the right amount of force, and it went sailing down toward the hole. It was about to go in when Logan blocked it with his club.

"Defense!" he called out.

"What? What do you think you're doing?"

"I don't understand games without an offense and defense," he said with an apologetic shrug.

"The course is the defense!"

"That doesn't really work for me."

"Because you know you're going to lose," I said, walking down to get my ball. I put it back in the spot where he'd blocked it. "This is the line of scrimmage. You can't go past it. I know you'll at least understand that."

He nodded, and I stood between him and the hole when I putted my ball in. He wasn't going to get another chance to stop me.

"Two strokes. That means so far I'm winning."

Logan sported a crafty smile. "We'll see about that."

"Yes, we will."

The next hole was the New York City skyline. The path angled and turned, and I quickly calculated how I would need to hit the ball to try to get a hole in one. As long as this overgrown cowboy didn't try to stop it.

Since it was his turn, I figured turnabout was fair play. I ran over to the hole and lay down in front of it. "See how you like it!"

He did some combination of laughing and muttering under his breath the entire time, but six strokes later he'd finally gotten the ball into the hole.

When it was my turn, I waited to see what he would do. He stood off to the side, his arms folded. My whole body tensed up in anticipation as I waited for him to make a move.

Finally I just hit the ball. It bounced off the wall at precisely the angle I'd hoped for and was about to get me a hole in one.

There was motion off to the side, and I turned to see Logan running after the ball and then throwing his entire body on top of it. He rolled over twice and then jumped up, holding my ball aloft. "To quote my roommate, interception!"

I couldn't help it. I started laughing harder than I could ever remember laughing in my entire life. "I can't believe you just tackled my ball!" I said in between my laughs.

At that point, all bets were off. At Mount Rushmore, he kicked my ball off the green while it was rolling. At the giant Las Vegas roulette wheel, I hit the wheel with my hip to make his ball fall off before it reached the right slot.

He wasn't able to get in the way of my ball at the Grand Canyon hole, and I finally got my hole in one. I celebrated, pumping both my arms in the air. "Yes! In your face!"

"You have an unfair math advantage."

"And you have an unfair athletic advantage, so I think that gives us a level playing field." I went over to retrieve my ball.

"I never understood that saying. Are there uneven playing fields? Are there football players who are getting career-ending injuries because they stepped in some hole? All those poor twisted ankles because somebody wasn't doing their job."

Everything he did and said tonight made me want to laugh. I loved the way his mind worked. The only way I could think to describe what it was like to spend time with Logan, laughing and joking with him, was that my body felt effervescent. Like somebody was filling me up with delight bubbles so that everything was fizzy and fun.

I was quite possibly drunk on Logan Hunt.

Which led to irresponsible behavior. At the California beach hole, as I squared up to putt, Logan grabbed me by the waist and spun me around until I was dizzy and breathless. When he finally put me down, I had to hold on to his shoulders to regain my balance. We were both laughing, both out of breath, staring into each other's eyes, and the urge to kiss him again was so overwhelming that it took everything I had inside me to step back.

"No touching," I reminded him in a breathy voice that made his Adam's apple bob in a really appealing way.

"Sorry. I just couldn't help myself."

Was it bad that I wanted him unable to help himself all the time? Yes, yes it was.

But did that stop me from doing what I did next to distract him? No, no it didn't.

We were at the entrance to what I could only surmise was the amber-waves-of-grain hole, long stalks of some yellow plant blocking us from view and making me feel like we were the only two people in the world. As he got ready to putt, I stood right next to him. When I saw his muscles tense, as if he were about to hit the ball, I leaned over and blew softly into his ear.

He must have jumped four feet straight up in the air.

"What," he said with a laugh, "was that? It was a total friends-only-rule violation."

I blinked at him innocently. "I didn't kiss you or touch you or look at you in that way, so . . ."

Logan stood so close to me that I could almost feel his heartbeat against mine. Racing. It was thrilling. "Is that how you want to play it?" he asked in a low voice.

Was that how I wanted to play it? Um, obviously. But somehow logic managed to return to my brain and remind me that friends didn't blow in each other's ears.

"So maybe that falls into the no-flirting category," I conceded. "But since you flirt with me all the time and basically ignore that rule, I'm not in violation."

Logan shook his head. "I understand that I'm partly to blame for you not being able to control your hormones. Not only am I devastatingly handsome and too sexy to handle, but I've brought you to one of the most romantic places in all of Washington."

"Mm-hmm," I agreed, not able to keep the saucy tone out of my voice. "This is super romantic, with the buzzing fluorescent lights, the algae-covered water in the beach area, and the menacing Statue of Liberty over there."

"She does look like she's going to kill us. Is that a torch or an axe in her hand?"

While I stared at the statue, trying to figure it out, Logan leaned over so that his words were hot against my ear. Icy shivers sprinted down my spine. He was giving me a taste of my own medicine. "And you probably shouldn't do something like that again unless you're prepared to deal with the consequences."

Problem was, I wanted the consequences.

Badly.

Even more when he looked at me that way. The way that set my toes on fire. There he went, ignoring another rule.

We continued through the course, still kicking and blocking each other's balls, doing our best to make the other one mess up and take more strokes. We talked about so many things, like our theories on why Ford was so mean to Keilani.

"Maybe she reminds him of his seventh-grade math teacher and he had a crush on her. But then his teacher ran off and married the assistant principal and Ford never got over it," I suggested.

"Or, she looks like the hit-and-run driver who smacked into his dog and caused the poor thing to lose his leg and now he hobbles around so Ford can never forget what happened."

"Does Ford even have a dog?" I asked.

"I don't think so."

I hit Logan's ball with my club, knocking it off the green. "Personally, I think he's in love with her and can't admit it."

"I think you're probably right. Maybe Ford thinks he doesn't stand a chance with someone like Keilani and he acts this way so he won't get hurt. Even though he really wants to be with her."

Then Logan again gave me the look he wasn't supposed to give me, and I nearly melted on the spot. Was he talking about me? About us?

I couldn't let myself read too much into it. I tried to ignore the heavy feeling that settled in my chest. Was this even more serious than I'd let myself believe?

Fortunately, he lightened the moment when we got to the Golden Gate Bridge. He started stomping around and roaring like he was Godzilla.

"It would be a lot more believable if you were dressed up in a green monster costume," I said.

"Yes, because authenticity is what the Godzilla movies were really going for. Come on. Hit that ball so I can make it into monster chow."

Despite Logan's best efforts, by the time we reached the White House hole, the final one, I was still winning.

As long as I got two strokes or under, I would win. A fact he was all too aware of. Before I could swing, he hit the ball from behind me, rolling it the opposite direction.

"What did I say about the line of scrimmage?" I asked, going to retrieve it.

"I'm playing defense."

"Well, cowboy, you should have stuck to your strengths." I kept my eyes on him, not breaking the contact so that he wouldn't notice my hitting the ball at the same time. Just as I'd figured, the ball bounced off two walls and then went straight into the hole.

"I win! I win!" I ran around, holding my club over my head. "I am the grand master champion of mini golf!"

Logan laughed, clapping for me as I did a victory lap around our nation's capital. "I think we both win."

That made me stop. "How so?"

"Well, I don't lose. Ever."

"Ha. I don't know what you want to call it, but you most definitely did not win. I did!"

He grabbed my ball from the hole and then came over to take my club. "What do you say to some ice cream?"

"I say yes. Always. I would never, ever say no to ice cream. And since I'm such a gracious winner, you poor loser you, I'll even pay for it. As friends so often do."

We returned our equipment and Logan said, "The place I have in mind isn't very far. Do you want to walk?"

It wasn't raining or drizzling, and the whole evening had been unseasonably warm. A walk sounded nice. A chance to chat. "Sure."

When we got out onto the sidewalk, I asked him, "How do you know where all this stuff is?"

"Some of my teammates and I have found it good to get away and explore."

"Away from my dad and his staff's prying eyes?"

"Something like that," he nodded. "Bash and I found this ice cream place by accident. We were walking along and it started raining really hard, so we ducked inside. The owner is from this small nation called Monterra, which is right next to Italy. And he makes the most amazing Italian gelato you'll ever eat."

"I've never had gelato before."

"You are in for such a treat."

Logan was right about the distance and we reached the shop quickly. He held the door open for me, letting me in first. It was tiny, almost unnoticeable from the outside, but the inside was warm and inviting and had been lovingly decorated. The counters that had the ice cream practically sparkled, everything was so clean.

"What can I get you?" the young man behind the counter asked.

"You should try the chocolate," Logan said.

"Okay. Two scoops of the chocolate, please."

"And I'll have the same."

Logan reached for his wallet, but I got to mine first and pulled out my card, handing it to the clerk. "Nope. I've got this. I hope."

"You hope?"

"I may love math, but I'm not always so great with my money. Sometimes using my debit card is like trying out a gift card you've already used once. I'm not sure how much is actually on it, but we'll give it the old college try."

He chuckled while we waited to see whether the card went through.

"Approved!" the clerk said, and Logan and I cheered. I put my card away while Logan gathered up the ice cream. We headed over to a small table for two, and we had the entire place to ourselves. Even the clerk disappeared into the back.

I realized that Logan was waiting and watching me. "What?"

"Take a bite."

"Okay." He was being kind of weird.

I got a spoonful and put it in my mouth, and then I immediately understood his knowing smirk.

"Oh . . . my . . ." It was velvety and smooth and creamy and chocolaty and quite possibly one of the best things I'd ever eaten in my entire life. It was like eating a chocolate cloud. "You have officially ruined me for all other ice creams. This is amazing."

"Told you." Then he wolfed down most of his in about three bites.

I wanted to take my time and enjoy each and every bite, but I found myself eating mine nearly as quickly as he'd had his. "My mom used to take me out for ice cream all the time." I didn't know why I'd said it, other than the fact that chocolate had always been her favorite and she would have loved this.

"I'm glad you have so many good memories of your mother," he said.

"Do you have any of yours?"

"The main thing I remember is that my mom used to not come home for days at a time."

Guilt for my own good fortune swirled around inside me. "That must have been rough."

"You get used to it. You can get used to anything if it happens often enough."

That struck me as unbearably sad. "Do you still talk to her?"

He finished the final bite of his gelato. "I haven't seen or spoken to her since I was eleven years old."

"Why not?"

"My stepfather didn't ever take me to visit her, and even when I got old enough to travel to the prison on my own, I didn't. I've been so angry with her for so long. She's the reason our lives were the way they were. Every chance she got, she chose drugs over me, and I've never forgiven her for that."

Even though we had the no-touching rule, I couldn't help myself. I put my hand on top of his. "I'm so sorry."

Logan stared at my hand. "Me too. She still calls me every so often. In fact, she called me a couple of days ago. I never take the call. Although sometimes I'm tempted to. I want to hear her voice again. See if she has an explanation for me. Or wants to say she's sorry. But I'm afraid I'll just be disappointed."

Even though I couldn't possibly have understood everything that he was feeling and everything he'd gone through, I did have to tell him, "She's still your mom. Maybe you should give her another chance."

"Maybe."

I was about to tell him that I'd give anything to be able to talk to my mom again, but I stopped myself. Our two situations were nothing alike, and I was in no position to tell him that he should let his mother back in his life after everything she'd done to him. I finally moved my hand away and felt the loss of his warmth immediately.

"I wish I'd had a mom like yours," he said.

"Me too. And I'm not trying to be trite here, but in life we get what we get, and somehow we have to figure out a way to move on."

"Speaking about moving on, I have an early class in the morning," Logan said as he gathered up his trash and stuck it inside his empty cup.

"Oh, right." I knew that at some point we'd have to call it a night. I was just having such a great time with him that I didn't want it to end.

We cleaned everything up, throwing it away in a trash can, and went back out onto the street, heading for my car.

Wanting a change of pace from the more serious stuff we'd been talking about, I asked him what he thought about the upcoming Seahawks-Jacks game. Neither one of us were Seattle natives, so we felt free to root for the Jacks and for Evan Dawson. All the way home Logan was animated, talking about how he thought this year's offenses and defenses would line up in the game.

I hated that anyone had ever hurt him. I wished I could take that pain away so that he could always be as light and carefree as he was in that moment.

When we got to his dorm, I thought it would be best for me to stay in my car.

"We did it," Logan said. "Friends only, rules mostly intact."

Ha. We'd broken every one of our friend rules that night, except for the no-kissing one. Which, to be fair, was probably the most important of the bunch.

So I just agreed with him. "Yep. Our not-a-date was a success."

In some ways it was. We hadn't kissed again, we'd had a really fun time, I'd gotten to eat some of the best ice cream known to all mankind, and now I knew how to play full-contact mini golf.

"We leave for Idaho the day after tomorrow," Logan said.

Right. The away game. I nodded.

"I'll text you when I get back. Maybe we can hang out. As friends."

"Sounds like a plan, buddy."

"Good. I'll see you around, chum." Logan got out of the car and waved to me briefly before jogging inside to his dorm.

Four days without Logan.

Why did that prospect seem so bleak?

CHAPTER SEVENTEEN

LOGAN

I was feeling pretty pleased with myself. I'd managed to (mostly) keep my hands off Jess on our friendly buddy hangout. And while traveling out to Idaho for our away game, I also stopped myself from texting her at all, let alone every five minutes like I wanted to.

Because I wanted to tell her about how Douglaston had managed to lock himself in the bathroom in the back of the bus and how three coaches had had to remove the door to get him out.

Or how I was pretty sure O'Malley had an illegal girlfriend, given how often he scrolled through the images on his phone, over and over again, sighing each time he started over.

Or that I had become convinced that Jackson was hungover, given how loudly he was snoring behind me.

But I didn't call or text. I thought it might be a good idea for us to take a little break from each other. To prove to myself that I could do it. I could go four days without talking to her. I hoped maybe it would give me a chance to toughen up. To not feel so weak every time I was around her.

Because that night we'd played mini golf . . . that had been some next-level entertainment. I'd had more fun with her at that cheesy course than I'd ever had hanging out with any other girl.

There'd been so much damage and so many problems in my life that Jess was like this big, bold, beautiful sun that chased away every cloud. She made me laugh in a way that I hadn't in a long time. She made me feel like a kid again, wanting to run around and play and just enjoy myself. She made me feel light. Happy.

It was a dangerous feeling because the more I had it, the more I craved it. I wanted to feel normal. To feel as if I could be with a woman like her and make it work. Maybe even someday we could settle down and have a family. That could be my reality.

I believed it when we were together. I wanted it when we were together. More. A future. A promise of things to come.

My thoughts were totally freaking me out. I'd never felt that way, had never considered that kind of possibility. A total commitment? I wasn't ready for something like that. I decided to ignore my brain and focus on the upcoming game.

The guys on the team also did their absolute best to distract me by discussing offensive strategies and playing pranks on anyone stupid enough to fall asleep on the bus, and there may have been one or two sing-alongs. For the most part, it worked. We had a more-than-twelve-hour bus ride each way, which was exhausting. Coach wanted us to arrive a day early to give us time to settle in and rest before the game. I figured it was probably an unnecessary precaution. The ICC Leopards were ranked almost last in the league. We could have probably literally done a one-hand-tied-behind-our-backs sort of thing and still won.

Which left me in a motel the night before the game with a bunch of bored football players who decided the best thing to do was to create as much mayhem as possible. They ran up and down the hallways like a bunch of inmates who'd just been loosed from the asylum. Nothing got destroyed (other than Franklin's practice jersey, which somehow accidentally caught on fire), but they spent the evening playing pranks on each other and smuggling beer into their rooms.

It made me wonder where the coaching staff was and what they were doing. Coach Oakley wanted us to be respectful, and at the moment, there wasn't a lot of respect happening. For the motel or the other people staying there.

I spent my time with Bash in our shared room, watching a rerun of a Raiders game. Something crashed hard against the wall behind the TV, making it wobble.

"If those idiots don't calm down, someone's going to get hurt, and then we really will have to play ICC with only one hand," I muttered.

Bash was chewing on a Snickers bar and grunted in response. He loved watching football almost as much as he loved playing it. He probably hadn't even heard what I'd said.

I picked up my phone when it beeped.

It was a text from Jess.

> How are things going? Have you recovered from your crushing mini golf defeat?

My thumbs hovered over my phone's keyboard, tempted to respond.

Nope. I didn't have to talk to her all the time. I could go a few days Jess-less.

"You talking to your girlfriend?" Bash asked, muting the TV since the game was on a commercial.

"I don't have a girlfriend," I reminded him for the millionth time. He thought it was a big joke, but one of these days he was going to slip up around somebody in charge and I'd be in trouble.

"You're wearing that big, goofy grin you get when you text with Jess."

"I don't—" I cut myself off, not knowing if what he was saying was true. Was I already that whipped?

"Do you have any requests for your funeral arrangements? The type of flowers you want? Any particular songs you have in mind? Who you want to deliver your eulogy? I think it should be me, by the way. I have this already prepared: 'Here lies old Logan Hunt, who never knew quite when to punt. Then he chased after Jess, made everything a mess, and Coach buried him with a grunt.'"

"You need a hobby," I told him. "Of the non-limerick variety."

"At the moment my hobbies consist of football and gossip. Speaking of, did you hear about Rodriguez?"

"What about him?"

Bash took another bite of his candy bar, chewing quickly and swallowing. "They're saying Coach booted him off the team."

I sat straight up in my bed. "What? Why?"

"Failed a drug test. Zero tolerance, remember?"

Why wouldn't Coach announce that to the players? It wasn't an especially effective scare tactic if kicking rule breakers off the team happened quietly and behind closed doors. "Did the coach say something about it?" Maybe I'd missed it somehow.

"As far as I can tell, his roommate came home and found Rodriguez packing up all his stuff. That's how everyone knows."

The news was bad, not only because I was sad to lose Rodriguez, but also because it let me know just how serious Coach was about his rules. I had thought that if I couldn't break his rules, maybe I could bend them a little.

I was realizing that there was no give whatsoever.

The commercials ended and Bash turned the sound back on.

"I'm going for a walk," I said, but Bash did that grunting thing that meant he wasn't really listening to me.

I grabbed my jacket and my room key and headed down the hallway, avoiding the obstacles, which consisted of empty pizza boxes, a couple of toilet plungers, and Colnetti passed out on the floor.

I'd almost reached the door when I heard someone calling my name. I turned to see Coach in his room. It surprised me; with how everyone was acting, I'd assumed that he was on a different floor. But he was seated at the desk, the door open. Even if he wasn't intervening, he had to know everything that was going on. I wondered how many more guys would be gone come Monday.

He gestured for me to come into his room. "Shut the door."

Some panicked part of me thought, *He knows. He knows how I feel about Jess, and Bash really is going to be my pallbearer.*

I closed the door behind me.

"Have a seat."

Since he was in the only chair, I was forced to sit on the foot of his bed, which felt awkward.

"How are things going with you, Logan?"

Did he know? Was this all some elaborate setup? Lull me into a false sense of security before springing his trap? "Well, I think. I almost have straight As, and I've been doing my best to follow your rules."

The coach took off his glasses and set them on his desk, rubbing his eyes wearily. "Did you hear about Rodriguez?"

"I did."

"It was a shame. I didn't want to do it, but I can't be any more plain than I have been. I can't tolerate anyone taking illegal drugs. How has the team been taking the news?"

"Uh, I don't know how many of them actually know about it. It's more of a rumor at this point."

He nodded. "I was waiting to announce it until after the game. I didn't want to bring the team down beforehand."

"Why would you worry about that, given who we're playing?"

"You have to treat every game like it's your last, because you never know when that will be true. When an injury might end your career. Or when a low-ranked team might rise up and surprise you and cause an upset. Always give it your best effort."

"I will. Thanks, Coach." While I appreciated his words of wisdom, Coach didn't seem to realize that if he was looking to gauge how the team was feeling, I was probably the last guy he should ask. He'd made me captain, but following his rules meant that I'd set myself apart. Going to the costume party hadn't done me much good given that I'd worn a mask, things with Jess had gone badly, and I'd left soon after arriving.

I wasn't anybody's confidant.

Except for Jess's.

Coach looked at me strangely then, and it felt like Jess's name had been branded into my forehead and was flashing neon, warning him that I was thinking about his daughter for the thousandth time that day.

But I knew he couldn't actually tell what I was thinking when he added, "I'm looking to you to lead this team. You've been a shining example so far. I hear things. I know things. And I know that you've been acting with honor and integrity, just like I asked you guys to."

Was that true? For most of his rules, yes. But when it came to women . . .

Nothing's happened with Jess.

I hadn't broken his rules. She and I were just friends, and we were both determined to keep things that way. "I appreciate that. I am trying really hard. It hasn't been easy."

He rested his elbows against his knees, leaning forward. "I know it hasn't been. I've asked a lot of you. But it's because I want what's best for you. I want you to have a bright and happy future. Do you think about what you'll do after you graduate?"

"Sometimes I feel like it's all I think about. The next steps."

"That's good. It's good to have a plan. But don't get so caught up in what you think has to happen that you miss out on what could happen. I wrecked my knee my senior year of college and ended my playing days. I'd planned on going on to the NFL. I'd been drafted. But it all ended just like that." He snapped his fingers. "And when everything was gone, I looked around me and made new plans. I married my college sweetheart and we had a baby, I got a coaching job, and it turned out to be the best thing that had ever happened to me."

"O-okay." I wasn't sure why he was telling me all this.

"I just want you to leave room in your life for all different kinds of eventualities." He sat back up, turning toward his desk. "Next week we'll be playing Western Washington Community College."

WWCC was ranked almost as high as we were. It was sure to be a difficult game.

Coach went on, "Given the level of talent that will be on the field for both sides, there are going to be a lot of recruiters and scouts in the crowd. Including Rick Hammerston, from the Portland Jacks."

My jaw might have dropped slightly. What?

He picked up the papers he had been working on and started writing on the top sheet. "Curfew's in an hour. Have a good night, Logan. Leave the door open on your way out."

Realizing that I'd been dismissed, I forgot about my walk and went back to my room. The news about Rodriguez paled in comparison to Coach's announcement.

But I couldn't figure out what the message was here. That I had a chance to play football professionally? Since the scout Evan Dawson had promised would come was going to show up?

Or was it the same thing I'd been telling myself from the beginning—that the NFL was a pipe dream and I should move on and forget about it?

Did Jess figure into this somehow? If Coach saw and heard things, did that include my hanging out with his daughter? Was that an issue? Was he telling me to give up on Jess and focus on my possible career?

I was tempted to turn back around and ask him what he meant. What was with all the crypticness? Why not just say exactly what he was thinking? Did he think he was being straightforward? Was this supposed to be some kind of life lesson where I had to figure things out?

Maybe he'd kept it vague because he wanted me to pass it along to the rest of the team without giving them false hope. No promises were being made, no offers. Just the chance to play well and possibly get noticed.

I thought of how Coach said he wanted me to lead the other guys. I was kind of feeling like it was all I could do to keep my own life on track at the moment. I didn't think I could serve as an inspiration for anyone else.

But the most important thing I could do was keep myself moving forward. Focus on graduating. Ignore the tiny chills happening along the base of my skull at the idea that Rick Hammerston from the Portland Jacks would see me play.

He'd see me win.

In just one week.

~

I told Bash what Coach had told me, and like the good little hobby gossiper that he was, he ran around telling the other guys. It immediately quieted everyone down and they turned in early. Maybe that had been Coach's intention: get us to behave by promising us our dreams.

Bash and I talked through how cool it would be to get offers, him from a Division I school and me from the NFL. Even if I needed to keep both feet on the ground, it was fun to spend one night dreaming about the possibilities.

Which, inevitably, led me to think about Jess. Dream about possibilities with her. And I didn't just mean the physical stuff. Don't get me wrong, I was thinking about that too, but it was more about what it would be like to be able to walk around campus with her, holding her hand. Letting people know that we were together. Watching Ben Is Stupid's face falling when he saw us as a real couple.

Being able to hang out with her without feeling any guilt or regret. She made it so easy to forget what I was supposed to be doing that I often did.

Bash passed out pretty quickly when we turned off the lights, but I stayed up and kept thinking about what it'd be like to have all my dreams come true. For both my career and my love life.

I heard the slam of two car doors. The clock on my nightstand said it was nearly two o'clock in the morning.

Out of curiosity, I got out of bed and crept over to the window. I didn't really have to worry about being quiet since Bash slept like the dead. I wondered who would be returning to the hotel this late.

Some part of me that sounded an awful lot like Jess whispered, *Maybe it's Ford and Keilani.*

Now I had to know, if only to tell her. She'd be thrilled.

I pulled the curtain back slightly, and out in the parking lot there was a couple talking in front of a black four-door car.

The man was Coach.

The woman was the same one I'd seen him with on the field not too long ago.

So no good Ford-Keilani gossip, but what was going on?

If it hadn't been Jess's dad, I would have gone back to bed. This was absolutely none of my business, and I was basically being a reverse peeping Tom, since I was inside, which was also unlike me.

But Jess had some kind of hold over me, and it was like I had to know what was going on so that I could tell her.

Nothing about their body language said they were on a date. They didn't touch at all, didn't kiss or hug. They just seemed to be making one another laugh.

I knew exactly how dangerous that could be.

But it was two in the morning. What else could I be witnessing except the end of a date?

And how was Jess going to take it?

CHAPTER EIGHTEEN

JESS

I was in my room, getting ready for a date with Ben.

The whole thing had happened so quickly that it felt like I hadn't had time to process it yet. Earlier that afternoon I'd gone by the math lab, just to see if they needed any extra tutors. I knew Logan wouldn't be there, because he was in the middle of returning home after their victory in Idaho. And I only knew that because my dad had texted me to say they were headed back to school.

No texts from Logan. Even though I had texted him once, asking how things were going and giving him a hard time about my mini golf win. Nothing.

Which I shouldn't have felt hurt over. Friends didn't have to respond to texts right away. He had probably been really busy.

Despite reassuring myself that I was fine, I still found myself headed to someplace that we'd spent time together. In a pathetic attempt to feel closer to him? Possibly. But I did it anyway.

I had run into Ben at the math lab, and after chatting for a couple of minutes he'd said, "Hey, there's a new movie being shown down at the student center. Do you want to go?"

There were no angel choruses swelling, no parting of the heavens, no ticker tape parades with a marching band carrying banners that spelled out "Ben and Jess." Those were the things I'd been expecting when Ben finally, officially, asked me out on a date.

And I had a pretty good idea who was to blame for my current lack of enthusiasm.

I'd hesitated before I said yes. I'd had to remind myself of all the reasons why it was a good idea. First, I'd had a crush on Ben for a long time and had always wanted to go out with him. Yay for wish fulfillment. Second, it was going to bother Danielle. Which was reason enough, in and of itself. I knew how immature and petty it would sound if I said that out loud, but it was true. Third, and probably most important, if it turned out that I'd been mistaken in my impressions of Ben and I could like him and date him, I wouldn't have to worry about being responsible for messing things up for Logan.

It seemed like a sensible choice to make. I wanted to give myself the chance to actually go out with him once and see whether or not I could still have feelings for him. Feelings I'd had up until a certain Texan cowboy rode into my life.

As I got dressed, put on some makeup, and fixed my hair, there was none of the anticipation I'd felt getting ready to hang out with Logan.

Of course, it didn't help that I'd had the Dream again last night, once more featuring Logan as Stavros. And while the grand kiss had always been amazing, now that I had actually kissed Logan? The gazebo kiss was beyond amazing. When I'd woken up, my lips had still been tingling.

But maybe that would change. Maybe I'd be so blown away by the kind of guy Ben was, when I got to really know him, that I would get excited to spend time with him. The Dream would once again feature Ben and not Logan.

Problem was, he'd have to be pretty special to outdo Logan.

Since Ben didn't have a car, I volunteered to pick him up. That was a little disappointing too—part of my initial fantasy involving Ben asking me out was for me to make a grand entrance. Like it was the prom or something. Yes, it was stupid, but most of those kinds of daydreams usually were.

When I got to his apartment and knocked on his door, no one answered. I knocked again after waiting about a minute, and finally there was some movement as the dead bolt was unlocked. Ben opened the door, his hair messy, one side of his face creased. He looked like he'd been sleeping.

All of my optimism started to flee.

"Hey. I'm here to pick you up?" *For our date, that you just asked me out on a few hours ago?*

"What?" He blinked a couple of times, as if trying to get his bearings. "Oh. Right. Come in. Let me get cleaned up."

I walked inside his apartment, and it had that boy smell. Like it wasn't quite clean and there were probably piles of dirty laundry somewhere.

"I'll be right back," he said.

Which left me free to look around. Problem was, I didn't really want to. I was irritated that Ben had been sleeping and had forgotten all about me.

So much for starting off on the right foot.

Not having anything else to do, I started checking my social media and email. On Instagram there was a picture of Logan on the bus, smiling with a bunch of his teammates. It made my heart twist a little uncomfortably. I missed him.

I had missed him a lot more than I'd thought I would.

While Logan had been in Idaho, I'd put up a picture of me and Suzette that said, "Missing the rest of our family." There was a notification that Logan had liked the photo.

Which made me feel a little manic-depressive as my mood shifted from sadness to almost elation. I told myself to calm down. Just because Logan liked my picture didn't mean that he liked me in that way.

But maybe it's a click in the right direction.

I immediately felt guilty that I was thinking about another guy when I was supposed to be going out with Ben. Who had been in his room for over fifteen minutes.

"Ben? Are we going to miss the movie?"

There was no response at first, and it was starting to feel like I'd wandered into a *Twilight Zone* episode. "Ben?"

He came back out wearing the exact same clothes he'd had on when I arrived. In fact, he looked the same. His hair was still messy, and I wondered if he'd even felt like I was worth bothering to brush his teeth for. "Let's go."

He opened his front door and walked out, leaving me to close it. I wondered if I should lock it, but Ben was already heading toward the parking lot. So I just pulled the door shut and decided to hope for the best.

I felt a little silly at the prospect of driving over to the student center since it was only about a three-minute walk from the apartment complex. "Do you want to walk over?"

"Why?"

"Because it's not too far?"

"No. Let's drive."

Okay. So we were driving. I'd thought walking might give us a chance to chat for a little while. Fortunately the parking lot wasn't as packed as I'd thought it would be, and it was easy to find a spot close to the theater.

We got out of the car and walked up to the student center. Ben got there first, opening the door and letting himself in. I'd grown so accustomed to Logan always opening doors for me that I almost walked face first into the heavy glass. Obviously I could open my own doors and I didn't need help, but my dad had always opened doors for my mom. I thought it was a sweet, romantic gesture.

One I was apparently not going to see tonight.

In the lobby there was a sign above the ticket office that announced the movie was *La vie non examinée.* I said the words aloud, figuring I was probably butchering them. "What does that mean?" I asked.

The pained look on Ben's face let me know that I had indeed done a poor pronunciation job. "It means 'the unexamined life' in French."

We got into line to buy our tickets. "The movie's in French?"

"Yes." He said it impatiently, like I was a little kid. Annoying. Especially since I wasn't really a subtitles kind of girl. But I should give it a shot. Maybe I'd really like it and it would broaden my horizons. Make me become more cultured. This could be a good thing.

We reached the front of the line and Ben told the guy in the booth, "One, please."

Oh. I guessed I was buying my own ticket.

Which was fine. To be fair, he was probably a broke college student like the rest of us. Theoretically, I was okay with paying for my half. Tonight it irked me. It was probably the effect of having been raised by an old-fashioned father, but I always thought the person who asked should pay. If Ben had told me we'd be paying our own way, I would have brought some cash with me.

And while I was in the middle of paying for my ticket, Ben went into the theater without me. I crossed my fingers that my debit card would work. It did, and I went inside to find my date. Even though it frustrated me that he hadn't mentioned the financial arrangement, I was a lot more bothered by the fact that he'd basically walked off without waiting for me.

Logan would never do that.

I can't date Logan, I tried telling that contrary voice of mine, but it didn't care.

Ben was standing in a middle row, looking around at the people who'd come to see the show.

"What are you doing?" I asked him.

"There's someone that I thought was coming tonight, but I don't see he—them."

Her? Was that what he'd almost said? And who was "her"? Danielle? This didn't seem like something she'd be into. Maybe I didn't know her evil ways as well as I thought I did.

Wait. Did this mean he'd brought me here just to make her jealous? That it wasn't about me or us? Which was the height of irony, considering how often Logan had used similar tactics to get Ben to show interest in me. I wanted to laugh at the farce I found myself in, but I refrained.

And maybe that was an unfair conclusion to jump to. Obviously I didn't have all the facts. I didn't even know if he'd really been about to say "her." I should stop rushing to the most negative conclusion and just try to enjoy myself. Ben sat down and I took the seat next to him. The house lights slowly turned off and the movie started.

It was in black and white. A man was riding a bike through Paris while chain-smoking. For, like, a long time. Just riding and smoking. I was so glad when he stopped at a café to drink coffee and smoke that I almost called out, "Finally!" Anything to get him off that stupid bike.

Only now, instead of pedaling around, he was drinking coffee, people watching, and still smoking.

I didn't get it. We were half an hour in and the man hadn't spoken to another person. Just said cryptic things that didn't make a lot of sense in English.

I tried really hard to like the movie. Or, if not like it, to at least tolerate it. This did not happen. My horizons were not being broadened. They were being shrunk. Like I had somehow been lessened as a person by being forced to watch this movie.

No wonder French people were depressed and had a lot of affairs and ate so much bread and cheese. If this was their life, I couldn't blame them.

There came a point where I was so completely bored that I considered just leaving. Ben could walk back to his apartment. I would tell him that I had to go to the bathroom and just never come back. The idea held a really high degree of appeal for me. But I thought about how it would make me feel if somebody did that to me, and I couldn't go through with it.

I also thought about texting Logan. I even pulled my phone out, but the ball was in his friendly court. I didn't want to seem desperate or pathetic.

"Put your phone away," Ben whispered.

I was simultaneously embarrassed that he'd had to correct me and irritated at the thought that he had the right to. I did put it away, but mostly so I didn't bother anybody who was actually enjoying this succubus disguised as a movie.

Not only was it sucking my soul; it was sucking my will to keep existing.

I'd never been so happy for a movie to end. I nearly applauded, but I didn't want anybody in the theater to get the wrong idea. The lights came back up and Ben asked, "Do you want to head over and grab a coffee?"

At this point I mostly wanted to watch a good movie in color, just to wash away the bad taste of this one from my brain. But I had been here to give Ben a chance. To see what might possibly exist between us. Even if every single one of his actions so far screamed that he was a selfish jerk, there could be reasons for his behavior. Explanations. The only way to find that out was to actually talk to the guy.

"I guess."

We headed over to the campus coffee shop, which was in the student center as well. It was busy, as always, but not overcrowded. Ben ordered his drink, a nonfat soy no-foam latte with extra caramel drizzled on it. He paid for his. And I paid for my hot chocolate, again relieved when my debit card worked successfully. I didn't know how he could order caffeine so late. I wanted to be able to fall asleep tonight and not lie awake in my bed reliving the nightmare that was the movie he'd taken me to.

We found a table and sat down.

"What did you think of the movie?"

The question I'd been dreading since it had ended. "It was very . . . French."

"Oh, I agree. Quintessentially French. That's what makes it so appealing, *oui*?" I probably should have found it sexy for him to say a word in French, but all I could think of was Miss Piggy.

Not wanting to keep following this particular conversation thread, I said, "So tell me about yourself, Ben. Where are you from? What's your story?"

It was a mistake I would soon come to regret.

"Well, I'm from the Seattle area. Born and raised. And I decided to attend EOL for financial reasons."

That was fine. Normal, even. But then things took a sharp turn for the weird.

Because he started telling me stories from his childhood, like from kindergarten on. Who his friends had been. His teachers' names. His hobbies and interests as a kid. Like some kind of chronological chart that he decided to share with me. And we went through year by year until I wanted to pull out all my hair and run around the room screaming.

He never stopped to catch his breath, never gave me the chance to end this hellish date and escape with what little of my sanity I had left.

Ben did not deserve a chance. I should have believed what he'd been telling me all along—with both his actions and his words. This was not a man I wanted to date. This was not a man I could fall in love with.

I never wanted to speak to him ever again.

We sat at that table until almost closing time as Ben guided me through his life story with all the boringness of, well, a subtitled French movie. He had no charm, no wit, just apparently a fervent belief that I would find him as fascinating as he found himself.

When he finally (FINALLY) paused to take a breath, I said, "Wow, would you look at the time? I need to get home."

I stood up and went over to throw my cup away. If he wasn't following me, then he could find his own way back to his apartment. I turned around to see Ben get up slowly, stretching as he did so. He headed toward a different trash can and I went over to the front door, waiting oh so impatiently.

The door swung open behind me and in walked my dad.

"Jess, what are you doing here?"

"I could ask you the same thing!" I said, hugging him to welcome him home.

"I decided to grab something to drink before going home," my dad explained, shifting his duffel bag strap higher on his shoulder. He could drink caffeine at all hours and didn't have any trouble sleeping. I wished I'd inherited that from him.

"I'm on a—that is, I'm here with a friend. Ben."

Ben came over, holding out his hand. "Nice to meet you, sir. I'm Ben Edwards." It was the most charm and personality that he'd exhibited the entire evening.

My father shook his hand, raising both eyebrows at me. "Nice to meet you, too. I don't think Jess has mentioned you before."

"Jess can be a private person."

He was telling my dad this. Like my own father didn't know me. But Ben just kept talking. Much as he had the entire evening.

"She's a tough nut. Sometimes it's hard to find out anything about her!" he said with a smile.

Maybe if you'd asked me about myself instead of running a night-long monologue, you'd know more.

"That's the point of dating, I suppose." My dad sounded . . . amused. Why was he amused? Why was he okay with someone like Ben but not someone like Logan?

"Speaking of dating, I know it's kind of last minute and you might already have other plans, but Jess, if you're free, I'd like to take you to the homecoming dance on Saturday."

What?

"I'm sure she'd love to go!" My dad was full of an enthusiasm I'd never seen from him before. "You're not already going with someone else, are you?"

Was there something in his voice suggesting that he knew more than he was letting on, or was that just the result of my guilty conscience?

"What do you say?" Ben looked so hopeful about it. "We even have your dad's seal of approval."

No thank you.

"Come on, sweetheart, I think you two will have a great time." My dad was basically my hero, and the fact that he was so gung ho about it made it hard to say no. I even found myself wanting to forgive some of Ben's earlier behaviors. Maybe he'd felt nervous and that's what had made him carry on a one-sided conversation the whole night. Maybe my feelings for Logan were so strong that comparing them side by side meant that Ben didn't stand a chance. Maybe I was looking for reasons not to like him instead of looking for ways to give him a break.

Regardless, I didn't want to go with him to homecoming. "Actually, I was hoping to go as your date, Dad." I slid my hand through the crook of my dad's arm. "Remember when you asked me to come along with you? To help fund-raise from the alumni?"

My father was not a stupid man and caught on quickly. "I do. Yes. Let's go together."

"In that case, I insist that you save me a dance," Ben said.

I hated that politeness/civility forced me to say, "Sure." Ha. At this point I would probably cut off my own feet before I danced with him.

"Great!" Ben exclaimed, patting me on the back like I was one of his guy buddies.

I kind of wanted this weird little trio to end, so I told my dad I'd see him at home. Ben and my father shook hands again, and we finally headed out to my car. Where Ben was again the only person talking as he laid out his plans for Saturday. His DJ friend was doing the homecoming event, too, which was why Ben wanted to go. He was going to help him set up.

We pulled up to his apartment complex and I parked the car, killing the ignition.

Ben smiled at me. "Thanks for the great time. I really enjoyed myself tonight."

Yes, I was sure he had. He loved to perform for other people, and I'd basically sat through several hours of *The Ben Show.*

But instead of getting out of my car, he looked at me with an "I'm going to kiss you" look, and I wasn't sure what to do.

It wasn't much of an internal struggle as I quickly decided to kiss him. I needed to see if something more was there. If I had mistaken an outfit of black clothes and his tendency to spout off bad poetry as indicative of a deeply interesting, artistic, and sensitive personality that probably didn't exist. Maybe I had just wanted him to be that way and had decided that's who he was without really even knowing him.

It wasn't like how it was with Logan, where I lived in anticipation of kissing him every moment we were together, even though I knew it couldn't happen. I still desperately wanted his kiss and spent every second hoping.

But being with Ben? This felt more . . . scientific. Like an experiment. This was necessary, I decided. I had to know.

Then he kissed me, and it was . . . fine. I wasn't grossed out by him, which I always figured was a good thing. And it was technically okay.

There was no nose or teeth bumping. He didn't lick my face like my high school boyfriend Tom had the first time we kissed. No overabundance of saliva. No chapped lips.

But there were also no boiling seas, no whirling tempests, no melting bones of any kind.

It was sweet and fine and utterly forgettable.

Ben pulled back from me, his face still close. "Hey, do you want to come upstairs?"

Nothing he had just done would even make me start to consider such a thing. "Nope. I mean, no thanks. I should get home. With my dad just getting back and all."

"Oh, sure. Well, have a good night. I hope I'll see you again soon."

As soon as he shut the passenger-side door, I started my car up and headed back to the main road. I probably should have been thinking about that kiss, wanting to relive it and gush about it to Keilani tomorrow.

But that very un-Stavros-like kiss would have to wait. Because there was something I hadn't allowed myself to consider until after I'd dropped Ben off.

If my father was back, that meant Logan was, too.

I could hardly wait to see him again.

CHAPTER NINETEEN

JESS

When my dad told he'd be at the school late watching game film, despite the fact that it was Halloween (which he said was a little-kid holiday and that since neither one of us was a little kid, it wasn't really something for us to celebrate), I decided it was time for my Logan drought to come to an end.

I texted him.

> What are you doing tonight?

No more subtlety for me. I'd just be direct.

His response was immediate, making me giddy with relief and excitement that he wasn't ghosting me.

> Let me check my calendar.

The three dots scrolled as he wrote, and I could hardly wait to see what he said next.

> I have dinner with the Queen of England, and then I'm off to a peace summit in Hawaii where I plan to spend my time relaxing on the beach. You?

> Same.

He sent back a laughing emoji as his response.

> But if your plans fall through, you could come over here and we could hang out.

Then I added on another message, to put his mind at ease.

> My dad won't be here. I thought we could pass out Halloween candy together.

An innocent, wholesome activity. I held my breath, waiting to see his response.

> Sounds fun. Count me in.

Yes! I threw both of my arms up in the air and might have danced around my room for a minute or two.

Okay, it was for ten minutes. I was so happy.

I kept an eye out for him on campus that day, but I didn't see him. And not wanting to seem too stalkery, I decided to not go looking for him (though I could have weaseled his schedule out of Keilani) and settled on seeing him later that evening.

And it wasn't a date. It was us just hanging out. I had just gone on a date with Ben; I was hanging out with Logan. World of difference.

Especially when I compared the two, as I'd been doing since last night. Which wasn't fair because only one of them could result in an actual relationship, but I still did it. My time with Logan had been fun, lighthearted, and enjoyable. Ben was just . . . the opposite. He'd been boring and self-centered, and I was done with him. It was like after you'd had authentic Italian gelato and then had to go back to the cheap store-brand ice cream. They just didn't compare.

If Keilani had come to me with this problem, the answer would have been obvious. Date the hot guy you love being with.

Or I would have told her that, except for my dad's superpesky rule.

I knew that it was a little dangerous inviting Logan over, just the two of us. We would be alone in my house. And the last time we'd been alone here, we'd almost kissed a couple of times, even with my dad nearly scaring us to death.

Was that why I'd done it? I secretly wanted the chance to be alone with him again? And if it led to another kiss . . . oh well?

I tried to rationalize my invitation by reminding myself that there would be dozens of trick-or-treaters interrupting us every couple of minutes. Even if a kiss accidentally occurred, it wouldn't be able to last for very long or lead to something more serious. I'd created a built-in safety net. So we would be okay.

But my net turned out to be unnecessary because Logan had thought ahead.

When my doorbell rang, I wasn't sure if it was Logan or the kids. The neighborhood didn't officially start trick-or-treating until five thirty, but sometimes the kids got started earlier than that.

I stood at my front door, not knowing who was on the other side, hoping it was him. I had so much nervous anticipation about seeing him again that I was actually shaking. Like an inbred Chihuahua with anxiety issues. Trying to push all that aside, I opened the door.

It was Logan.

My nervousness quickly turned to giddiness. My heart leapt and did a happy dance of joy at seeing him again. Handsome as ever, with that twinkle in his eye that let me know he was happy to see me, too. I wanted to throw my arms around his neck and hug him tight, but I refrained.

And I was glad I did when I saw who was standing behind him. Bash.

Logan had brought a chaperone.

I tried to hide my surprise. "Hey, you guys."

They both smiled and said hello and came inside the house. I offered to take their jackets and I hung them up on our coatrack.

It was then that I noticed that Logan was wearing a Jacks jersey.

"Is that your costume?" I asked.

"Yep. I'm going as Evan Dawson this year." Ha. Evan Dawson had nothing on Logan. "What about you? Where's your costume?"

"Oh." I looked down at my clothes. "I'm going as a college student, I guess."

"So original," he teased.

I'd briefly considered donning my Catwoman costume again. But then I'd thought about all the implications of wearing it, what it would remind both of us of, and decided that putting it on would be a very, very, very bad idea.

Or a very, very, very good one. It depended on whether you were asking my head or my heart.

Bash interrupted to ask, "You have ISEN, right? Logan said you had ISEN."

"Bash was in the middle of watching a Patriots game. I told him he could watch the rest of it here."

"Yeah, sure. Follow me."

I led him into the family room, turned on the TV, and found ISEN. Bash settled onto the couch, his eyes glued to the screen. "Thanks," he murmured in a way that let me know he'd already forgotten about me. I considered explaining how the various remotes worked but figured he'd yell for me if he needed something.

"I ordered a pizza from Gino's. I didn't know if you guys had already had dinner." I hadn't even known that Bash was coming—I hoped one large pizza would be enough for the three of us, because I had seen those boys eat, and it was a little like when killer whales came up on shore to eat seals. "I'll bring you a couple of slices, Bash." I figured he wouldn't want to move.

Logan followed me into the kitchen, but I busied myself with getting out three plates and putting them on the table. I wasn't sure what to say to him now that we had a guest. It changed the whole dynamic of what I'd thought might happen tonight.

Which was, again, both a good thing and a bad thing.

I took three slices out to Bash, who absentmindedly thanked me, and returned to the kitchen. Logan had sat down at the table. "Hope you don't mind. I helped myself."

Grabbing two slices, I sat down next to him. "Of course not." Deciding to just take the bull by the horns, I added, "I was surprised when you texted me earlier today. Because it meant your phone is still working. Hint, you didn't text me the whole time you were gone."

I hoped I sounded breezy and not hurt. I was shooting for playful. I might have missed.

"I'm sorry I didn't text you back. It was just because of some excuse I'm trying to make up right now."

What else could I do but laugh at his joke? "Let me help. Did the bus break down? Or did Bash's appendix blow up?"

"My appendix is fine," Bash called from the other room, making me think it had to be a commercial. "And this pizza is really good. Thanks!"

"None of that happened," Logan said. "I did try stopping by the excuse store before we came over, but they were all out."

"So what was the real reason?"

He must have heard the seriousness in my voice. "I figured friends could probably go four days without talking. And I was right. We survived."

Huh. Looked like I wasn't the only one conducting some romantic experiments.

"Although you should remember that we did have a game to play, where we destroyed the other team, thank you very much. And somebody had to babysit Bash. He requires constant supervision."

"I'm incorrigible!" Bash added. The commercials must have ended, because I could hear the announcer from the game again.

Which meant he was no longer listening in on my and Logan's conversation.

"So, what did you do for fun while I was gone?" Logan asked.

"Actually, you being gone was kind of fun." That was such a lie.

Which he totally saw through. "You didn't miss me? Even a little?" He had that charming glint in his eye that made my knees feel hollow.

"Maybe a little," I conceded.

His hand lay next to mine on the table, and if I just moved my littlest finger over slightly, we'd be touching. We were dangerously close to slipping off track, even with Bash in the next room. I decided to tell Logan about Ben. "I did go out on a date with Ben last night."

"What? Really?" I could tell that Logan was trying to act excited for me, but there was a note of pain in his voice that just crushed my spirit. "How did that happen?"

I told him how I'd run into Ben at the math lab, leaving out the reason I'd gone there in the first place because I knew how pathetic it would sound. "Then he just sort of asked me, and we went to see a French—well, I hesitate to call it a movie since it bore no resemblance to anything that I would call a movie. And then out for coffee. Where he told me his life story. His literal, entire life story."

"Did you have fun?"

"It wasn't . . ." I'd been about to say it wasn't fun, that I hadn't enjoyed myself. But I figured it was probably better if Logan didn't know the full extent of the crappiness I'd endured. "It was fine."

"There's a ringing endorsement. 'It was fine.' Come on, it couldn't have been that bad."

If he thought that, I wasn't telling it right. "My dad seemed really excited about him." I told Logan how my father had shown up at the coffee shop at the end of the date.

An expression I couldn't identify crossed Logan's face. "Then maybe your dad and Ben should be the ones dating."

"I don't know what they'd talk about. Ben's not into football." Not just football. As he'd told me last night, at age fourteen he'd decided he had moral and ethical issues with all organized sports.

My guess was that his issues were that nobody would let him participate in them.

"Not into . . ." Logan's voice trailed off and he sounded aghast. As if I'd just announced that Mickey Mouse wasn't actually a mouse. "How can you date him? Doesn't that go against your genetic programming? Your family's religious beliefs?"

I let out a little laugh. "It's not that bad. And since you brought up me going out with him again, he asked me to go to homecoming this week. I said no thanks, but I promised to save him a dance."

His face was shuttered, like he was trying to keep his reaction from me. "He asked you out again? Haven't you already Ben there, done that?"

"You're hilarious," I told him sarcastically.

"Yep. I was thinking of making up some T-shirts." He shifted his gaze, not looking at me. "And at the end of the night?"

My heart beat fast and hard in my chest, and a metallic taste filled my mouth. I put my pizza down. I knew what he was asking. I also knew I wasn't going to lie to him about this. "I kissed him."

"You kissed him," Logan repeated.

"Sort of." The last thing I wanted to do was hurt Logan, but it had happened and I felt this compulsion to tell him about it. It wasn't any of his business, but it was like the words had just spilled out of my mouth.

I tried to pretend that I didn't see the disappointment in his eyes.

"Maybe we should be planning our next hangout," he announced, surprising me. It was totally off topic and out of the blue. Why had he said it? To compete with Ben? He didn't have to. Logan would always win. I just couldn't tell him that. To be sure that he would graduate.

I noted that he hadn't called it a non-date or rushed to emphasize that we were only friends. No qualifiers like he usually included so that I wouldn't get my hopes up.

"Yes. Let's do that."

"When? Where? Let's go someplace nice."

Someplace nice? My heart started to beat quicker. Was this approaching date territory? "We could go tomorrow night. The only nice place nearby is Madison and Main." I shifted in my seat, wondering what he would think about my next statement. "Which is the restaurant Ben works at. But he shouldn't be there. He typically works on Thursdays and Fridays starting at five o'clock."

It wasn't until Logan asked, "How do you know that?" that I realized how bad it sounded.

"I just happen to know things. Random things. I used to be very observant of him. It's not because I memorized his schedule. I'm not a stalker. Shut up."

"I didn't say anything," he protested.

"You did with your eyes."

He laughed. "I'll try to keep my eyes in check from now on. So tomorrow night? Dinner?"

"It's a plan." I deliberately didn't say it was a date because I didn't know what his reaction would be, and I should probably have been trying harder to behave.

I wiped my mouth with a paper towel and threw it on top of my plate. I started to stand, intending to put our dirty dishes in the sink. When I reached for Logan's, he gently grabbed my wrist.

"Now what are my eyes saying?" His light-brown eyes stared into mine and said things I wanted desperately to hear.

I want you, Jess. I need you.

I love you.

That last thought made me nearly jerk free from his grasp. I wanted him to love me?

Did that mean I loved him? My heart hammered furiously in my chest, making it difficult to breathe.

The doorbell rang and I cleared my throat. "I think your eyes are saying I should go answer the door."

Forgetting about the plates, I grabbed the big bowl of Halloween candy from the counter. I didn't buy any of those cheap suckers or crappy mixed candy, which so many of our neighbors seemed to pass out. It was as if they'd forgotten what it was like to be a kid, when getting a chocolate bar was like the ultimate Halloween prize.

We were a fun-size-chocolate family.

Logan trailed behind me as I tried to focus on the holiday and making children happy and not on the fact that I'd seen things in his eyes I wasn't supposed to see.

Or things that hadn't actually been there. Because there was also a high possibility that I'd imagined it, given that I wanted him to feel that way about me. To know that it was killing him to stay away from me. That instead of opening the door for trick-or-treaters, he wanted to push me up against it and lower his mouth to mine and then . . .

Logan opened the front door.

The kids of our neighborhood had descended on our lawn like some kind of biblical plague.

"Trick or treat!" they chorused, and Logan and I hurried to put some candy in each kid's bag.

We got a ton of thank-yous and some excited exclamations when they saw what they had gotten from us. My dad was right—this was a little-kid holiday, but that was what made it so much fun.

When we finally finished with the horde, I went to sit on the stairs with the bowl. Logan sat next to me, and because the stairs weren't that wide, his side was pressed fully against mine, sharing his intoxicating warmth and making my belly flutter.

"Just FYI—you probably don't want to leave that bowl in the same room with Bash." He pointed at the candy.

"Good point."

The doorbell rang again and Logan took the bowl from me. "I'll get this one."

Just as I'd predicted, the built-in interruption system would keep us honest and keep things from getting too serious. It wasn't like Bash was any help in that regard as he seemed to be totally ignoring us.

I noticed the muscles in Logan's back tightening as he moved to each bag to drop in a piece of candy, and let out a sigh at how pretty and well formed he was. It was a little like going to a museum and see-ing a piece of art you absolutely loved but knew that you would never be able to touch. To own.

Absolutely out of reach.

That made part of me want to just say "Forget it!" and stop hang-ing around Logan altogether. But that made my stomach turn over and then squeeze painfully. I couldn't give him up. I just had to find some way to be around him.

Maybe it was like going to the gym and working out. It was painful and difficult at first, but the more you worked at it, the stronger you got. If I kept resisting him and kept myself in check, at some point it would become easy and second nature to be around him, right?

Logan closed the door and sat next to me on the stairs. "You know, I used to make myself sick every Halloween. I would eat candy the whole time I was trick-or-treating and then I'd come home and finish off the bag."

"Gross, even the Smarties and the Whoppers?"

"What are you talking about? I love Smarties and Whoppers."

"Weirdo." I nudged his shoulder with mine. I was enjoying teasing him until I remembered why he must have done it. He'd been hungry.

I again had to resist the urge to hug him and comfort him. A regular friend probably could have. But no matter what we said, we weren't just run-of-the-mill friends. Even if we pretended really hard.

There was something so much more here.

Someone knocked gently on the door. It was my turn. I stood up and went over to his jacket first. I slid a handful of the chocolate bars into his pocket. "For later," I told him with a wink.

We took turns answering the door for a while, but I had so much fun watching Logan interacting with the kids that I started letting him answer the door every time.

A group of color-coordinated ninjas came to the door.

"What's the password?" Logan asked before they could speak.

The kids lowered their arms slowly, their bags now brushing against the ground. Password? Their eyes all looked so confused.

"Uh, trick or treat?" one of the boys tried.

"Correct!" Logan said, giving them their candy.

Then there was a mixture of robots, soldiers, witches, and fairies. "Trick or treat!" one of the littlest girls said.

"I choose trick. What do you guys got?"

I stepped in and got them their candy, asking them to please not play any tricks on this house. Because I'd be the one responsible for cleaning it up.

A four-year-old princess came to the door with her parents.

"Princess? Is that you? I've been searching for you everywhere! I'm Prince Charming."

Well, he wasn't wrong. And apparently I wasn't the only one who thought so, because the little girl took the candy while looking up at him through her lashes and smiling playfully. Her dad had to pull her off the porch while she blew kisses to Logan.

I totally got where she was coming from.

A pirate came to the door with his obligatory "Trick or treat." He sounded bored.

Logan fixed that quickly. He folded his arms. "Sorry. That's not how a pirate asks for candy."

The boy smiled up at him and said, "Give me yer booty, or else I'll make ye walk the plank!"

Logan saluted him. "Aye-aye, Captain!" And he passed over the mini candy bar.

He really was going to be a good teacher. The kids would love him. He'd make learning fun.

Watching him, I realized that I'd spent the last few years with tiny fissures covering the entire surface of my heart. From losing my mother to the attack and its aftermath, I hadn't ever quite felt whole since. But here was Logan with his superglue, filling in each and every crack with his laughter and kindness and healing my heart.

When I hadn't even realized that it had been broken.

I'd balked earlier when I'd realized that I wanted him to say that he loved me, because the implication that I might love him terrified me. I'd already lost one of the people I'd loved most in the world, and I never wanted to go through that pain ever again.

But for him? I would take that risk.

Because I did love him.

Thanks to the rules, I just couldn't ever tell him.

It took a couple of hours, but eventually the stream of trick-or-treaters turned into a trickle. I kept having a great time, talking to Logan in between runs to the door until we were out of candy. I turned off the porch light to let the children know we were out and brought the empty bowl back to the kitchen.

Where it looked like a tornado had hit. Bash had apparently helped himself to the leftovers in the fridge, which was fine, but he'd left a pile of dishes on the counter that even my dad was sure to notice. I set the bowl down on the counter and started rinsing dishes to stick in the dishwasher.

"See?" Logan said, coming up behind me. "I told you. He needs constant supervision."

"Your best friend ate enough to feed an entire platoon of soldiers," I said.

"He would have cleaned up. Eventually. After the game was over. I'll go grab him."

"Don't worry about it," I said. "Let him finish watching the game. I can get it this time."

Logan stepped up next to me to help out, which made it go twice as fast. We rinsed and scraped in a companionable silence until he said, "I wanted to mention earlier, I noticed that the house is clean. Didn't you say something about how I should be worried about how angry you are if things are cleaned up?"

"Usually, yes, but I did this for you. I know you like things clean."

He went still. "For me? You did this for me?"

"Oh, don't get a big head. It wasn't that hard to make the effort. And if it makes you feel any better, my bedroom still looks like I'm on day seven of fighting off a band of poltergeists." I splashed some of the faucet water on his face when he laughed.

He grabbed the bottom of his T-shirt to dry off the droplets I'd flicked him with, which exposed his very fantastic abs for my eyes to feast upon.

And feast they did.

"Hey," he protested. "You can't look at me that way, either."

Gulping, I nodded and turned back to face the sink. This would all be so much easier if he were a lot less gorgeous.

Or if I were less easily swayed by muscular muscles.

We finished loading the dishwasher and I started it up. Logan went and sat at the kitchen table while I grabbed the pizza box and threw it into the trash can. Without the kids interrupting us every minute or so, I was suddenly feeling that nervous anxiety from earlier and wanted to be doing something with my hands.

Logan reached out as if he were going to grab me by my wrist again, but he let his arms fall back into his lap. "Hey, sit down for a second. There's something I wanted to ask you."

Why did that ratchet up my anxiety level to, like, an eleven? "What?" I had the feeling that if it was a yes-or-no question, my answer would be an immediate yes. Would I be his forever? Yes. Would I like to know how much he loved me? Yes. Would I like to sneak upstairs with him? Also yes.

"How would you feel if your dad started dating again?"

Oh. Of the many fun questions I'd run through my mind, that one certainly hadn't made the cut. "Um, in theory I think I'd be okay with it. I'm going off to graduate school next year, and I don't want him to be alone. I mean, I like the idea of him falling in love and finding someone; it just sort of grosses me out."

"Okay. Because I think he's dating someone."

"What? No way. I would know."

"How?"

"He would have told me." Wouldn't he? I had to concede that he might not have. My dad was super protective of me. Maybe he would be afraid that I'd be upset because of my mom. But she'd been gone a long time. It would be good for my dad to move on. My mom would want him to be happy. I wanted him to be happy.

"The thing is, I've seen him with the same woman twice now. Once she came by practice and they hugged. I got a vibe that they were something more, but I didn't have anything concrete to go on, so I didn't really think it was report worthy. Then the night before the game in Idaho, I saw them in the parking lot together at two in the morning. Again, nothing was technically going on, but what else could they have been doing at two a.m.?"

He had me there. A million questions swirled in my head. Who was this woman? What was she like? Why hadn't my dad told me? Was it serious? Were they even actually dating? How long had it been going on? "I can't believe this. I know where he is. He tells me what he's going to do."

"Okay. So where is he tonight?"

"He's staying late to watch game film. Sometimes he doesn't even come home because of how late it gets. He just sleeps at the office."

Logan gave me an incredulous look. "Have you been to his office?"

"No. It's in the back of the locker room."

"There is nowhere for him to sleep in that office, unless he likes sleeping on the floor. There're no couches in any of the offices. They're not big enough." Logan said this like I should have already known this.

"Oh. Ew. Ew, ew, ew."

Logan laughed as I tried not to gag. I couldn't even accuse my dad of lying to me, because knowing him, he technically hadn't. He was watching game film tonight and would stay up late to do it. And then he'd go out with his . . . friend. He'd just left that last part out.

Probably to spare my feelings or something.

Bash wandered into the kitchen. "Hey, guys, sorry, I was going to clean that up."

"No worries. We got it."

Logan stood up. "Now that the game's over, we should probably head back."

"Do you want me to drive you?" I offered.

"It's okay. We borrowed Roman's car."

I walked them out to the front door, waving goodbye to Bash as he went down the sidewalk. "Thanks for all the food!" he called out.

"Thanks for all the mess!"

Logan stopped on the porch. "So, I'll see you tomorrow night? Maybe six or so?"

"I'll come pick you up."

"How about this time I pick you up? I texted Roman while we were talking and he said I could borrow his car again as long as I filled up the tank."

"Oh. Yes. That sounds great." Only now I'd have to figure out a way to either get my dad out of the house or prevent him from answering the door.

"Good night. Happy Halloween."

"Happy Halloween!" I called back, watching as they got into the car and drove off.

I closed the door and locked it. Much as I was excited about my kind-of-a-date tomorrow with Logan, I was more focused on the fact that my father might actually be dating someone whom I knew nothing about.

Someone he might be falling for.

But maybe if he was falling in love, he wouldn't freak out so much when I told him that I was doing the same with one of his players.

CHAPTER TWENTY

LOGAN

I got to Jess's house to pick her up for our dinner at the restaurant when I suddenly realized the potential danger I was placing myself in. What if, when I went to the door, her dad answered? How would I explain myself? I sent her a text.

I'm here. Is your dad home?

No. He said he had plans. I didn't ask what they were, and he didn't tell. I think we're both happier that way. I'm here all by myself.

That was a relief. I got out of Roman's car and ran up to the front door. I had just barely rung the bell when Jess threw open the door.

She looked . . . phenomenal. My mouth went dry at the sight of her, my heart beating an unusually hard rhythm. She wore a long, silky dark-blue dress that looked totally impractical for October in Washington State, but I was glad she'd picked it out. I'd never seen her in a dress before, and I loved how soft and feminine she looked in it. It woke up some caveman part of me that wanted to throw her over my shoulder and carry her off to my lair.

Her hair was down and hung in long waves. She'd even put on makeup. And I only noticed it because her lips looked slightly pinker than I knew them to be.

It was kind of embarrassing that I knew the exact shade of her lips. It meant I'd spent way too much time studying them.

Much as I was doing at this very moment.

"Is this a dress-up place?" I asked. I was wearing a button-down shirt and jeans. It was my attempt to be a little more formal while still being casual. "Should I go home and change?"

The question seemed to startle her. "What? No. You look . . . perfect."

I should have said it to her first, but I'd been so stunned by her beauty that I'd stood on the porch with my mouth hanging open, like some kind of pathetic moron. "So do you" was my inadequate description of what I thought of her.

Because she looked better than perfect. She looked like every wish I'd ever made.

"The restaurant's not that fancy," she said, looking sheepish. I didn't understand why. "I just wanted to dress up."

Was there a "for you" missing on the end of that? Or was I imagining it?

"Shall we?" I asked.

"Let me just grab my coat."

Jess headed over to the front closet and took a long coat out. I couldn't have explained what possessed me to step inside and take the coat from her and say, "Here. Let me."

Wanting an excuse to touch her? To be close to her?

She turned her back to me and threaded her arm into one sleeve, and then the other. I pulled the coat up so that it fit snugly and left my hands on her shoulders. Allowing myself to smell her hair, to feel that magnetic warmth that always called to me. She tugged her hair out of the coat and it cascaded over my hands, all smooth and sleek, and I wanted to run my fingers through it.

Jess pivoted around, my hands still on her shoulders. I could hear that her breathing was fast and shallow, and suddenly my legs didn't feel so steady. I swallowed down the lump in my throat, ignored the desire that was swirling in my gut and threatened to take over. Her big, dark eyes looked up into mine, and something clenched inside me, freezing me in place. She trusted me. Even now, when all I could think about was that we were alone together and we could go up these stairs, head into her room, and . . .

I let go and took a step back. I was twisted, torturing myself with something I couldn't have.

"We should go." And whether that was just a reminder to her or a warning to myself, I wasn't sure.

"Right." She nodded and we walked outside. Jess used her keys to lock the front door, and I noticed the way her hands were trembling. If I'd bothered to look, I probably would have seen the same thing in my own hands. She drove me crazy.

What was it about her that made me feel like I was fourteen years old and going on my first date, about to have my first kiss?

We walked over to the car and I rushed over to open her door. I'd already put the GPS coordinates in my phone, and while I was aware of the fact that we were making small talk as I drove, all I could think about was how much I wanted her.

How much I loved her.

I accidentally jerked the wheel when I realized this. I was in love with Jess, and probably had been for a long time. She was the best thing that had ever happened to me. She was my sunshine, the one who soothed my soul and healed my hurts. She made me want to be better, stronger, faster. To succeed and show her that I was worthy of her.

It was also why I didn't want to keep my hands off her, even though I knew I had to. I loved her and I wanted so much to show her just how I felt. As if words couldn't be enough.

"Logan, what is it?" Jess asked, her hand on her heart. I'd probably really scared her when I moved the car the way that I had.

"Jess, I lo—" It was like now that I had officially recognized my feelings for her, they were dying to spill out of me. But I couldn't say them. It wouldn't be fair to either one of us. "I mean, I looked and I thought I saw a cat. But it must have just been a shadow."

"I'm glad you swerved. Squishing someone's pet would have really put a damper on our evening."

That made me laugh, and it was like it relieved the tension I'd been feeling. It allowed me to feel like myself again as we found Ben's restaurant. There was no parking out front, but the restaurant offered a free valet service. I felt a little uneasy turning over a car that wasn't mine but figured it would be fine.

When we walked in I saw that Jess was right—there were people here dressed up, but there were also plenty of people in jeans and leggings. It was a nice place, but not formal or too upscale.

The hostess walked over. "Two?"

"Yes, please," Jess said with a nod.

I caught a brief glimpse of Ben as he headed into the kitchen. Despite Jess's "observation" that he wouldn't be here. His schedule must have changed. Just a short time ago I would have made tonight about letting him be the jealous one for once, rubbing his nose in the fact that I was here with Jess and he wasn't. But something had changed. Ben didn't matter.

Even if it felt unfair that he'd been allowed to date her, with her father's blessing. He could have been affectionate with her. Which I couldn't do. I couldn't hold her hand right now the way that I wanted to. Put my hand on the small of her back as we followed the hostess. Lean over and tell her how beautiful she was and how I couldn't wait until we were alone together later.

We were seated in a small booth in the corner of the restaurant. The lights were low, making everything seem nicer and more romantic than it probably actually was. Jess slid in first, and I scooted over so that we were close together.

The hostess handed us our menus. "Your server's name is Claudia, and she'll be by to take your order soon."

My eyes went wide at the prices on the menu. Everything looked delicious, but it was definitely more than I'd budgeted to spend. "Wow. This is a lot."

"Don't worry about it," Jess said. "I'm treating you tonight. And I checked my account balance beforehand, so we won't be stuck washing dishes or anything."

"No, I can . . ." Well, I couldn't pay for both of us. "I can help out. I donated plasma this week."

"You are not spending money that you earned by donating vital bodily fluids. Keep that kind of money as a nest egg for when you graduate. You're going to need it while you're earning your teaching certificate." She sounded exasperated. "Stop insulting my generosity and let me just do this, okay?"

"Okay." I hated charity, but it somehow felt different when it was the person you loved doing it. Then it just felt like you were being cared for, in the same way that you cared for them.

"Huh. I really expected you to put up more of a fight."

"I don't look a gift horse in the mouth."

"Listen up, Seabiscuit—" Jess had been about to go off on me for my joke when our waitress came to the table. She put down some napkins.

"Hi, I'm Claudia. What can I get you to drink tonight? Would you like to see our wine list?"

I'd just figured out that I was in love with Jess. The absolute last thing I needed was alcohol to loosen my tongue. It already wanted to tell her.

Plus, the rules. And I was driving. "I'll have milk, please."

Jess gave me a funny look. "I'll just have water."

Claudia asked if we wanted an appetizer, and Jess ordered some spring rolls for us to share. "I'll get that put in for you and then I'll be right back to take the rest of your order."

"Why did you order milk?" she asked. "It's not like anybody we know will be here. This isn't exactly a college hangout."

Obviously, since no one we knew could afford to eat here. "Because you never know where this night might take us. It might be necessary."

She rolled her eyes at me. "So other than stupid things like milk, what else are you going to have?"

I knew what I wanted to have, but she wasn't on the menu. "I'm always a sucker for a good steak."

"Me too. Let's get that."

Why did I always feel like I was so in sync with this girl?

Our server came back with our drinks, and we told her which entrées we wanted. The New York strip sirloin for me, the filet mignon for Jess. We handed her back our menus, and as she moved away to put in our orders, I got a really good look at him.

Or at least some version of him. "Is that Ben?"

I'd never seen him in anything other than his crow outfits. And now I knew why he stuck to wearing all black. There was absolutely nothing distinctive about him. In khakis and a polo shirt, he was the blandest bland that had ever blanded. Like, he should be making plans to become a spy, because no one would ever notice him or be able to pick him out of a lineup.

"Look at him," I said in awe. "It's bad enough that he's boring and doesn't realize how boring he is. Like a textbook that made a wish to become a real boy. But he's just so . . . average. When they made him, they kept the mold."

Jess was laughing next to me, and I expected her to rush to his defense.

She did not.

Which I thought was interesting.

"He's noticed us," she said while she carefully rearranged her flatware.

"When?"

"Just now. He gave me a weird look."

"How could you tell? Everything this guy does is weird."

That set her to giggling and she picked up her linen napkin, hiding her face behind it.

Claudia brought back our appetizer and we both dug in. Pretty much as soon as we'd finished our spring rolls, she was back with our steaks. The service here was amazing.

It made me wonder how Ben had gotten the job.

I made a concerted effort not to look at him. I didn't want him to know that I was aware of him, that I knew he was watching us.

When she'd told me that she'd gone out with this fool and that he'd asked her out again . . . I'd really, really wanted to hit something. Hard. But instead I'd smiled and played along like it didn't bother me.

Then, when I'd found out she'd kissed him? I didn't know if I was more angry or hurt. Jess had a right to kiss whoever she wanted. We weren't together. It still drove me absolutely insane. I didn't want her to kiss Ben I Am. I didn't want her to kiss anybody else.

Only me.

Why did she like this tool? And why had she kissed him? I knew that her liking him had been the whole reason we'd started hanging out, but things had changed for me. And since she'd said no to another date, I couldn't help but wonder if things had changed for her as well.

While I was ignoring Ben, the conversation between Jess and me flowed effortlessly, as it always did. It was one of the things I liked best about her—we could talk about anything and everything, and I was always engaged. Even when we didn't agree, we found some common ground that allowed us to keep the conversation moving. She respected my viewpoints and I respected hers.

An unexpected crack of lightning lit up the window behind us, making Jess jump. I could see her rapid pulse pounding beneath the delicate skin of her throat, and I resisted the urge to press my lips against it. Instead, I said something inane like, "Boy, it's really coming down out there, isn't it?"

Rain had accompanied the lightning and thunder, a hard, driving rain that beat loudly against the windows. It wasn't uncommon for this area, but it was still a little surprising in its intensity.

Claudia came back to check on us. "Did you save any room for dessert tonight?"

"I'm good," Jess said. "Logan?"

"None for me." I was stuffed.

"And can you bring us a box?" Jess asked.

There wasn't much left on the table besides some broccoli and a few fries. I felt Jess's gesture in my chest. Like I'd been sacked and the wind had been knocked out of me hard. Here was a woman who didn't judge me. Who understood my weird quirks and relationship with food, which other girls had made fun of or ignored. She just accepted me for the man that I was, without question.

Man, I loved her.

"Sure thing! I'll grab you a box and I'll just leave the check with you. I can take care of it whenever you're ready."

While Jess took out a card from her wallet, I reached for some of the cash I had in mine.

"Nope," she said firmly when I put it on the table. She pushed it back toward me. "I'm not taking your money, and neither is Claudia. Put it away."

I was tempted to argue with her but figured it wouldn't do me any good. I sheepishly put my cash back, keeping out a couple of bucks to tip the valet with.

Our server brought us the box and took the little leather folder that had our check and Jess's card and promised to be right back.

While Jess started packing up the leftovers, I noticed a middle-aged couple enter the restaurant. Something felt familiar about the woman. A second later I realized why when I saw Coach Oakley's face as he put his arm around her waist.

The coach was here. On a date.

I was so dead.

"Jess, your dad is here. With that woman I was telling you about."

"Where?" she demanded, whirling around to search for her father. She peeked over our booth and spotted them. "That's her? She doesn't seem like she'd be his type."

Now was not the time to be discussing the type of women Coach was interested in! "What are we going to do?" I asked, feeling completely panicked. I slid down in the booth so that the coach wouldn't see me.

"I'm not sure how I feel about this now that I know it's true. He should have told me."

I tugged on her dress so that she'd stop staring at them. "He's allowed to have a life outside of you."

"Why? When I've basically constructed my whole life around him?"

"You're entitled to your own life, too," I told her. "You don't have to build your life around him. That whole parenting thing is supposed to be about raising independent adults. Or so I've heard."

"What are they doing now?"

I leaned up slightly to see them again. "Ugh. They're sucking face. Nobody wants to see old people making out. Talk about Fifty Shades of *Gray*."

She kicked me under the table, right on my shin. "My dad is not old."

"I know. I was trying to ease the tension. Obviously it didn't work. And ow."

"We should probably wait until they're seated and then sneak out. Hopefully they'll be far away from the door."

It wasn't much of a plan, but it was the only one we had.

"They're being seated now." And not in Ben's section, which was my other concern, which I'd been afraid to say out loud. Ben and Coach had met briefly—what if they started a conversation and Ben happened to mention that Jess was here on a date with me? While we were still in the restaurant?

I put on my coat and she did the same. Coach and his date were looking at menus. Time for us to make our escape. "Okay, let's go." We slid carefully out of the booth. I tucked her into my side, the one farthest from her dad, and put my arm up, like I was scratching the back of my head. Which blocked my whole face. I was also counting on the fact that Coach would be into his date and choosing his food and not paying attention to some random couple leaving.

"We made it!" I said when we had stepped foot outside. Now we just had to get Roman's car and we'd be home free.

Unfortunately, the weather had caused a huge pileup of people waiting for their vehicles, and the valets were soaking wet as they ran around trying to help everyone. The restaurant had no canopy or covering out front, and everybody was getting drenched. Including us.

"We have to get out of here," Jess said in a worried voice.

"We will. We just have to wait for our turn."

"Don't you watch movies? We think we're safe and we've gotten away with it, and that'll be the very moment my dad remembers that he forgot his wallet or his cell phone in his car and he'll come out here and catch us."

I risked a glance over my shoulder and saw Coach still seated in his booth. "Doesn't that seem a little paranoid to you?"

"We've come this far. We can't let him catch you now. Come on. There's a park across the street. We can hide there until this line dies down."

"Let's say you're right—"

"Yes, let's, because I am."

I shook my head. "Okay, fine. It wouldn't be worth the 'I told you sos' if he did." I grabbed her hand and we darted through the parking lot, then across the empty street. The park had plenty of big trees that could have offered us shelter, but all it would have taken was one good strike of lightning and that would have been the end of both of us.

Looking around, I spotted a building at the center of the park. "Let's go wait in there. Come on!"

"Is that a . . . gazebo?" Jess asked, and I didn't understand the tone in her voice.

"What does it matter what it is? It's shelter."

We raced over, and it looked like an octagonal gazebo that was walled in with panes of glass. I tried the door, worried it would be locked, but at some point someone had jimmied it open and now the lock was busted. I ushered Jess inside before joining her.

She started laughing as water dripped off us and onto the concrete floor.

I took off my jacket and tried to wring it out. "Is this funny to you?" I asked.

"I thought I made that clear with the whole laughing thing."

That made me start laughing, too, as all the anxiety rushed out of me, filling me back up with relief. No way would Coach know we were here. We were safe. For now. "I could have been kicked off the team!"

"But you weren't. We're fine."

We were not fine. She peeled off her coat and hung it on a piece of protruding metal to dry, and all I could do was look at the way her dress clung to her body, showing off all the gorgeous curves she possessed.

She was beautiful in a way that I didn't know women could be beautiful. She was so strong. A survivor. I wanted to protect her even though she didn't need my protection.

Maybe it was the adrenaline from nearly being caught, but it was like every molecule in my body had been switched on and was programmed to be totally aware of this woman. Just Jess, and no one else.

She was shivering from the cold.

Without my permission, my feet walked over to her, and my hands reached out of their own volition and began to rub her arms, trying to give her back some warmth. Then, without warning, I pulled her toward me, hugging her tightly. I rationalized that body heat was the best way to help her.

Not to mention what it was doing for me.

The rain had brought out the scent of her shampoo. It was like a field of wildflowers had suddenly bloomed all around me. "You smell"—like how I imagined heaven—"really good."

"Thank you?" She said it like a question, probably wondering where I was going with this.

So was I.

But something about this moment—the rain, being alone in this glass-paneled building, the way I couldn't keep my eyes off her—it was like something was knocking down every wall I'd built up in defense. Every promise I'd made myself, every threat that hung over my head, every rule I refused to break came tumbling down. I loved this woman with everything in me, and I wasn't going to be apart from her any longer.

Maybe common sense would return after. Maybe then I'd remember what I had to do, as opposed to what I desperately wanted to do. But I wouldn't regret a thing. Not ever, where Jess was concerned.

I decided on some honesty and to leave the rest of it to be sorted out later. "It's hard to be close to you and not touch you. Like, chemically hard. At a level I can only barely resist. I'm obviously not resisting well right now."

Her words were muffled against my shoulder. "Sometimes I think my hormones are staging a revolution against my brain and I'm losing the battle."

I reached over and caressed the side of her face, forcing her gaze up to me. "You know this is so much more than the physical for me, don't you?"

That trusting, serious look was back in her eyes. "I know."

Which sucked, because I was about to knock down every boundary we'd set up for ourselves. I couldn't stay away any longer. I needed her. Needed her to feel how in love with her I was.

"Do you think about our kiss?"

"Do I think about it?" Her breathy voice made parts of me tingle that should not have been tingling. "Do you?"

"Constantly." Without thinking, I bent forward to kiss the tip of her cold nose. "Every time I close my eyes and try to sleep. Every time I throw a football. Every time I sit in class and try to pay attention. That's what I'm thinking about. And the whole time I'm with you, all I can think about is how much I want to do it again. And again. And again."

"Oh."

I tightened my grip on her, pulling her closer. I wanted to melt into her so that I couldn't tell where I began and she ended. "It's necessary for me to kiss you now."

"Yes. Absolutely. Completely necessary."

That was all I needed to hear. Screw Coach, screw his rules, screw keeping away from this woman for a moment longer.

CHAPTER TWENTY-ONE

LOGAN

My instinct was to re-create that kiss from the costume party. Hard, driving, filled with a passion I could barely contain.

My Jess deserved more. She deserved to be adored and worshipped, which was what I was planning on doing now.

I'd kept myself in check this long. Surely I could keep a handle on my hormones for a few minutes longer.

Her gaze lingered on my mouth and I knew what she wanted. What we both wanted. I leaned forward and brushed my lips softly against her warm, soft, inviting cheek. I pressed butterfly kisses there, leading down to the curve of her jaw. I explored the feel and taste of the skin there before making my way down her throat. Her head lolled back like a rag doll's, and I used one of my hands to support her.

I found that throbbing pulse point from earlier, the one that had been beating erratically at the restaurant, and let myself kiss it gently, rubbing my lips against it, feeling her racing heartbeat against my mouth.

"Oh . . . Stavros."

I paused and pulled back slightly. "Did you just call me Stavros?"

Her gaze was hazy, unfocused. I felt it like a punch to my stomach. "What? No. And don't stop what you were doing."

"Yes, ma'am," I murmured against her skin.

She let out a breathy sigh as I continued loving her neck, her collarbone, the skin behind her ear. It was a sound that felt real and ethereal. Like she was giving up some part of herself to me just with that sound.

Not to mention that it was completely sexy and drove me crazy.

Her skin felt hot and feverish under my touch; her cheeks flushed a bright pink. "I'm glad you're enjoying yourself." My voice felt thick in my own throat.

"Just this once, could you possibly shut up and kiss me?" she demanded weakly, and I couldn't stop an amused chuckle.

I looked at her mouth, the perfect shade of pink. This was a mistake I shouldn't make. My body wasn't interested in a discussion about the best course of action, but my brain knew this was a mistake. I would never regret it, but all it took was this kiss to blow up my entire life. I should stop.

But it felt beyond possible to walk away now. I had wanted her every minute of every day for so long that I didn't know if I could hold back and make the responsible choice.

"We should stop," I told her. Nothing substantial had happened yet. We could still walk away from this. Still be friends.

"Probably," she agreed. Then she reached up and undid my top button, pressing her lips against the base of my throat, and my knees nearly buckled. "I really enjoyed what you were just doing to me. Do you think you'd enjoy it?"

My breath caught in exquisite agony at what she was doing. She charted the same trail I had on her in reverse, her soft, perfect lips pressing against my skin over and over until I thought I'd die from it.

She ended up on my left cheek. I only had to turn my head and I'd be able to capture her mouth so easily. With such little effort.

"Jess," I tried again, but I was losing this battle. And the war.

She ignored me.

Finally I said what I feared most. "I don't want to lose control."

At that, she pulled back, looking deep into my eyes, her arms wrapped around my neck. "I do."

Before she could finish the last syllable I did what we both wanted and pressed my lips against hers in a long, slow, intoxicating kiss. I was going to take my time. This might be the last chance I ever had to kiss her, and I was going to enjoy every second of it. I wouldn't rush to something more or create a fire that would burn itself out too quickly.

And if this was the only time it would happen, I was going to make sure she remembered it. With each kiss, each stroke of my mouth against hers, I wanted to leave an invisible imprint so that if she tried to be with any other man, she wouldn't be able to. Because she wouldn't forget me. Forget this.

Another sigh of pleasure from Jess that was nearly my undoing. I cupped her face in my hands, trying to bring her closer. I wanted to fuse us together. To turn us into one person so that we'd never be apart again.

Then it wasn't enough to kiss her. I needed to feel her, to touch her. My hands roamed, feeling the velvet softness of her arms, the silky wetness of her hair, the heat from her back. I'd never played an instrument before, but Jess responded to my touch like I was a master musician. Her body went fluid and pliant against mine, rising and falling in response to my fingers. I had to keep her upright.

Then, despite all my attempts to stay in control, the sensations began to overwhelm me. I'd always prided myself on my strength, but she had turned me weak and defenseless. Like there was nothing I could do to stop how much I loved her. What her touch did to me.

"Logan." She sighed. And I knew in that moment she felt the same way about me.

There was an intense burning in my chest that slowly snaked its way through the rest of my body. It was Jess's sunshine. She found every dark, secret, hidden place inside me and lit it on fire. She scorched me with her light.

And I wanted to burn.

My heart pounded so hard and so erratically that I worried briefly that I might have a heart attack. Jess continued unbuttoning my shirt, which set off a savage longing in my gut and made my blood explode into flame.

A shudder went through me and I wasn't sure my legs would keep supporting me. I walked us backward until my knees hit the bench, never breaking off our kiss. I sat down and Jess climbed into my lap, pressing herself against me. Her curves against my edges, feeling like they fit perfectly together.

She continued in her quest to get rid of my shirt, which was hindered by the fact that I couldn't stop kissing her long enough for her to see what she was doing. I deepened the kiss without meaning to, but I couldn't help myself. My stomach dropped down into my lap, taking my heart with it.

The passion I'd only ever felt with Jess reared its head, whipping through me like electricity. Electricity that had caught on fire. Desire for her beat through my blood in time with my thundering heartbeat.

No more slow and easy. Now it was deep and hard and bruising and intense in a way that I'd never experienced before. I started to shrug off my shirt, and her fingers left trails of sparks that made me growl in the back of my throat.

I became aware of a ringing sound that I thought I was imagining. There was a buzzing sensation against my leg. It was my phone.

"Let it go to voice mail," Jess said, pressing a kiss to my chest.

Who was I to disobey?

But it rang again, and I groaned in frustration as I reached for it. I answered it without even looking. "Hello?"

Jess nibbled on my earlobe, and my eyes rolled back in my head.

"You have a collect call from the North Texas Women's Correctional Facility from . . ." Of course. My mom had the absolute best timing. "Dr. Alan Friedberg. Do you accept these charges?"

Alarm slammed into me as my lungs tightened, making it hard to breathe. A doctor? From the prison?

"Yes, yes I accept." I tried to get my ragged breathing under control. What was going on?

Jess pulled back from me, her face marked by confusion.

"Hello? Is this Logan Hunt?"

"This is he," I confirmed. "Who is this?"

"My name is Dr. Friedberg. I've been treating your mother. She is very sick." Jess slid off my lap while the doctor continued talking. He used a bunch of big medical terms and jargon I didn't understand. It didn't help that my brain still felt muddled from making out with Jess. "To bottom-line this, your mother is fading fast. She doesn't have much time left. If I were you, I'd be on the next plane out here so that you can say goodbye. Let me hand you over to my nurse. She can give you the details."

I didn't speak. Couldn't. I just sat there and listened. The nurse told me the address of the prison and what I'd need to do in order to visit my mom.

"Can you, uh, can you text all that to me?"

She said that she would later that evening, that cell phones didn't work within the prison walls.

I thanked her and hung up my phone.

"Logan? What is it?"

"My mom." The words felt wrong in my mouth. This all felt wrong. "She's dying. I have to go to Texas. Right now."

I stood up, buttoning up my shirt and then reaching for my jacket. Jess ran over to grab her own coat. Thankfully, the rain had stopped and there wasn't a line for the valet. I walked quickly, with Jess hurrying to keep up.

"What did the doctor say?"

"A lot of stuff I didn't understand. He just told me I had to come right away." We crossed the street and the parking lot, and I gave the first valet I saw my ticket.

"I'll go with you," Jess said.

They pulled the car up and I ran around to the driver's side. I felt this real sense of urgency. Like if I didn't go as fast as I possibly could, my mother would die before I could say goodbye. But I couldn't let myself feel anything beyond that. No worry, no fear, no concern. I needed to go into game mode and just focus on the next play, and then the one after that.

"You're not coming with me," I told Jess as I drove onto the main road. "I'm going to take you home, go back to the dorm and grab some things, and then go to the bus station."

I hoped I'd be able to get there in time.

"Why don't you want me to go?" Her voice was small, and I felt like the world's biggest jerk.

"This is something I have to do alone." I wanted her to come, but she couldn't. I had to go face my past and my demons without leaning on Jess. It scared me how much I wanted to accept her offer. How much easier it would make everything. She would hold my hand on the bus, sit with me in my mom's hospital room. I could imagine her at every step of the way, and that's what worried me.

She'd already lost her own mother. I wouldn't selfishly make her sit with me while I lost mine.

I got on my phone and called Coach. We all had his cell phone number; he'd said to only use it in case of an emergency. I guessed this qualified.

He picked up on the third ring. "Hello?"

"Coach? This is Logan." I filled him in on the details I had, including my plans to go see my mother as soon as possible. "I'm sorry, but this means I'll miss the WWCC game."

"Some things are more important. Check in with me when you get there and when you get back to school."

I told him I would. It was a good thing I hadn't put too much stock in the maybe-I-could-play-for-the-NFL dream. Because that was officially dead. I wouldn't be playing in the WWCC game, and who knew if I would ever play again? If we won, there were only a few more games to go, and then my football career would be over. There wouldn't be another chance for me to perform for this many scouts and recruiters.

Jess got on her phone and started making calls while I got in touch with Bash. I told him briefly what was going on and then asked him if he would drive me to the bus station and then return Roman's car for me.

"Of course. Definitely. Whatever you need, man." It was the most serious I'd ever heard him.

I also called Ford to tell him. He said he was sorry and that he'd let the rest of the coaching staff know. I told him I'd already called Oakley.

I pulled up in front of Jess's house and didn't even turn the car off. I needed to go.

"Check your email," she said.

"My email? Why?"

"Keilani got you a plane ticket. So you can get to Texas faster."

My first reaction was to tell her no thanks, but if the athletic department wanted to help me out in this situation I'd take it—time was not on my side and I needed all the help I could get. I opened up my email app and found the one forwarded from Keilani.

"Got it."

Jess put her hand on the door. "I really wish you'd let me come with you. But I understand if you need to do this on your own. Be safe. Call me anytime."

She leaned over to kiss me on my cheek, and I let my eyes slowly close at her touch. I didn't want her caught up in this. That phone call had been a reminder of my past and how, even when I'd fooled myself into thinking that I could move beyond it, somehow it kept catching up with me. I tried fighting the tide, but no matter how much I struggled, I just couldn't escape. I wasn't about to suck Jess into that same whirlpool. I couldn't protect myself from it; how could I possibly expect to protect her? The only thing to do was to keep her far away from it.

We needed some space between us, especially after that kiss. I didn't want to be the one who dragged her down. "I need to go."

She sat in silence for a few more moments and then let herself out of the car. Part of me wanted to call her back, but I wouldn't make her a part of this.

The next couple of hours passed in a blur. I went home and packed a bag. Bash dropped me off at the airport, I got my ticket and went through security, and then I was sitting in a middle seat on a crowded flight.

It felt like I was in shock. I couldn't believe this was happening. How much my life had changed in the space of a few hours.

When I landed in Texas, I rented a car. The prison was about forty-five minutes away, and as I ate up the miles, I kept thinking, *What do I say to her?*

She was my mother, she was dying, and I didn't know what to say to her.

At the prison, after I went through security, they got me checked in and handed me a badge. The nurse I'd spoken to, Tracy, waited for me on the other side of a locked door. A buzz sounded, a light went on, and the door opened.

"Logan, I'm so sorry about your mama. If you'll follow me, I'll take you right to her."

While we walked down a stark white hallway, Tracy tried to warn me. "Your mama is hooked up to a lot of machines. The doctor predicts that her organs will begin shutting down soon. We're doing our best to make her comfortable. She hasn't been lucid for the last few days, so don't expect very much from her."

Tracy opened a door into a room with multiple beds. A few of them were occupied farther down, but Mom was in the one closest to the door. It was just as Tracy had described. She was hooked up to a lot of machines, and even though she had only just turned thirty-eight, she looked about twenty years older. She was so thin. She'd always been on the thinner side, but now she looked emaciated.

"Are you Logan?" A balding middle-aged man in a white lab coat came over to shake my hand. "I'm Dr. Friedberg. We spoke on the phone."

"Yes. How is she?"

"Not well. While there are some treatment options for someone with her cancer, she came to us too late. She was already stage four. We've just tried to keep her comfortable. Maybe if she'd come to us when she'd first started having symptoms . . ."

My guilt was swift and overwhelming. Maybe if I'd picked up the phone those times she'd called me, I could have talked her into seeking medical treatment. The eleven-year-old kid inside me told me it was my fault.

As if he sensed my internal struggle, the doctor said, "Even if we had started early, this is an aggressive cancer and most patients don't survive. There's really nothing any of us could have done."

He probably saw a lot of patients' family members who blamed themselves.

"Please let me know if I can answer any questions," Dr. Friedberg said.

"How long does she have?"

"I'm not sure. It's not an exact science. I'd say one day, maybe more. If you'll excuse me." He walked away to check on his other patients.

It seemed wrong that this was where my mom was dying. "She should be in a hospital," I muttered. Or a hospice.

Tracy gave me a sad little smile. "Compassionate release is rarely approved, and even after you submit the application it usually takes six months or longer to work its way through the system." She walked over to my mom's side. "Hey, Louanne. Your boy is here. Logan's come to see you."

My mother's eyelids fluttered and she turned her head toward me. She reached out her hand and I took it, trying to avoid wires and tubes.

"Logan," she whispered in a scratchy voice.

"I'm here," I told her.

And then she fell back asleep.

It was the last thing she ever said to me.

I stayed by her side. The warden granted me special permission to be with her until the end. I didn't sleep or eat. I just . . . waited. And held her hand.

I expected to feel more as I sat with her. She was my mom. But it was like I was sitting with a stranger. And I'd played a part in that—refusing to take her calls for all those years. Not coming to visit her once I got my license. I'd felt the justification only a teenager can feel. Now, as an adult, I wished I'd made different choices. She'd been a teen mother and an addict. Her life couldn't have been easy, either.

I told her all that. Apologized for not trying harder. Saying that I forgave her. But she couldn't hear me.

About a day and a half after I arrived, my mom's breathing began to sound weird. Like a rattling noise. I pushed the nurse's button, and I was relieved to see that Tracy was again on duty. "There's something wrong with her breathing."

"Oh, honey, she's at the end."

Tracy held my mom's other hand, and we sat there quietly as the pauses between breaths became longer and longer until she stopped breathing altogether. Tracy got up quietly and turned off the machines. "I'll give you a minute to say your goodbye."

"I don't know what to say," I confessed. This was all so final, and even though I'd expected it, I felt only a numb shock that this was the actual end. "I didn't get to talk to her."

"Sometimes we don't get to have the conversations we want to have. Life isn't always wrapped up in a neat little bow at the end. We just gotta keep moving forward, even if we don't get the answers we wanted." She squeezed my shoulder and walked out of the room.

I wanted my mom's apology. I wanted her explanations. Her excuses. Something. Anything.

But all I got was silence.

Someone came in to ask me about the arrangements for her funeral. Even if I'd emptied out my bank account, I wouldn't have had the money to pay for a burial. I told the coordinator that, and she said my mom could be buried in the prison graveyard at the state's expense.

Which was how on early Saturday morning, just before what should have been the most important game of my life, I watched as they lowered my mother into the cold ground. Her grave was marked with a cross that only had an identification number on it. Not her name.

I stood there, the only mourner at her burial. The woman who had given me life was now dead. The finality of it, the dismay at what I was witnessing, made me feel like I was waking up from a deep sleep. Like someone had flipped a switch, and I went from numb to feeling so many things at once that I couldn't sort them out. Regret. Guilt. Anger. Shame. Despair. There was this sense of loss, an overwhelming sadness for what could never be. My mom and I would never work things out, and that realization hit me like a defensive lineman spear tackling me in my gut. Any hopes I'd had were gone—I could never make things better for us. There would never be a happy ending.

We'd both spent our lives doing whatever we had to do just to survive. No one had ever expected more from me. Not until Coach Oakley. He was the first person who cared how I behaved. The first to tell me he expected more. And to really escape the past, to escape being buried alone in a prison graveyard, I knew I needed to be that kind of man. If I wanted a better life, I was the only one who could make it happen.

Life was so ridiculously short. No one knew when things would just be over. If I'd ever get that bright future I dreamed about. Did I really want to live half a life? Pretending that I wasn't in love with Jess? Maybe she did deserve better. When I'd gotten the doctor's phone call, some part of me had wanted to push Jess away. I'd told myself that it had been to keep her safe. But it was to keep myself safe. To avoid making some hard choices. It wasn't right. I shouldn't have been shutting her out. I should have been letting her in. I wanted her to be my partner. I wanted to support her when she needed it and let her do the same for me.

I'd been lying to myself and to Jess, downplaying my feelings. That was wrong. From here on out, there was no room in my life for anything but the total truth. And if that meant getting kicked off the team? Then that's what would happen. Jess and I would find a way to make it work.

I wanted to tell Jess what was in my heart. I needed to say everything I was feeling. I could never let it be too late again.

No more pretense, no more half-truths. No more hiding in the shadows, hoping not to get caught.

Not just with Jess, but with her father, too.

It was time for me to be the man he wanted me to be.

CHAPTER TWENTY-TWO

JESS

Everything about the homecoming dance seemed garish and overblown. Yes, it was oh so thrilling that we'd beaten WWCC and the players had a whole new stack of official offers, but what did any of this matter in the grand scheme of things?

How could I be sitting at this dumb dance when somewhere out there Logan's heart was breaking? It was killing me not to be with him, helping him through this.

I had lost my mother. Who knew better than me what that felt like? Who else could support him through this the way that I could?

Not to mention that I loved him and wanted to be by his side, supporting him. He would need it. I'd had my dad. Logan had no one.

No one but me.

I noticed Ben out on the dance floor, grooving by himself to his friend's club mix. Even the music irritated me. He boogied on over to where I sat and said, "Hey, you ready for our dance yet?"

He scanned the room as he talked to me. Looking for someone else. His next date? Or Danielle?

At least I had really liked him in the beginning. But at some point Ben had just become the excuse. It was about hanging out with Logan and spending as much time with him as I could. He was the one I wanted to talk to at the end of the day. He was the one I wanted to have dinner with. The one I wanted to see movies, even boring French ones, with.

The one I wanted to be at this homecoming dance with.

What had made me attracted to Ben initially? Was it really just that he was nonthreatening and semicute? Had that been the entire extent of it?

Even if my feelings had changed, Ben's were nonexistent. Had he even cared about me at all? Or was I always just the means to an end for him?

I wanted to know. "Hey, why don't you sit down for a second?"

Ben took a chair across from me, not the one next to me, as Logan would have. Fortunately, we were far enough away from the loudspeakers that we could carry on a conversation.

"Do you know anything about me?" I asked.

"What?" Ben said with a laugh, as if I'd said something funny.

"What do you know about me?" Every conversation we'd had was about him. His hobbies. His likes and dislikes. His art. I'd tried to excuse his behavior the other night as him being nervous or anxious, but tonight I'd realized that theory was wrong.

"Um, you're a math major."

Bzz. I sounded off a negative game show buzzer in my head. Too easy. "What else?"

"Your dad's the football coach."

Bzz. "And?"

"You don't like Danielle." Ben looked very self-satisfied. As if he'd cracked the code of my personality. He knew nothing about me.

"Do you know why my dad and I moved to EOL?"

"No. Why?"

That shocked me. Danielle hadn't told him? I found that hard to believe.

I'd been saying all along I wanted a guy who didn't know about the attack. And here was one. One I'd even found attractive at some point. That should have made me happy.

It didn't.

Instead, I thought of the man who did know, who had tried to be understanding about it and supportive. Who'd always been there for me. Who'd helped me win this guy sitting in front of me even though he didn't think Ben and I were a good match.

Turned out Logan was right.

"Is Danielle here tonight?"

Ben looked utterly confused. "I don't—what does she have to do with any of this?"

"I think she has everything to do with it. You don't want to be with me. I don't think we're a good fit, and I think what you really want is to date Danielle. So you should go do that. I hope you're both really happy." I wasn't even being sarcastic. I genuinely hoped they'd work it out.

Huh. Falling in love had made me magnanimous.

With that, I stood up, not giving him a chance to respond because, honestly, I didn't care what he had to say. All these stupid games seemed so petty and inconsequential. There were important things happening in this world, and none of this Ben stuff mattered even a little.

I went to grab my coat and then headed outside. Where I found Danielle sitting on a planter, looking miserable. She brightened a bit when she saw me.

"Hello, Jessica. I just wanted to let you know that I got that mentorship with Professor Gardiner. He wrote me personally to tell me."

That was probably something I should have cared about. Had once cared a great deal about, in fact. But in this moment, I didn't. There were other professors and other mentorships and other graduate programs.

"Did you hear me?" she demanded. She swayed slightly. I wondered if she was drunk.

"I heard you. Congratulations."

She seemed stunned by my response. I'd had so much anger toward her, and now it just seemed . . . pointless. Like a waste of energy. Why should I keep being mad at her? Yes, she'd done something terrible to me. And I could either dwell on that and keep letting her hurt me, or I could forget about it and move on.

"That's it?" she asked. "That's all you have to say? Are you going to run in and tell your new boyfriend Ben about how I beat you again?"

"Ben is not my boyfriend, and I am not going out with him again. To be honest, I think he only went out with me to make you jealous."

To my surprise, her eyes welled up with tears. She unsteadily got up and walked over. The smell of alcohol slammed into me. Yep. Definitely drunk. "I dated him just to bug you. I knew you liked him. But then I started having real feelings for him. I think I might be in love with him."

I probably understood that better than anyone else. I'd hung out with Logan to get Ben's attention, and now . . .

I didn't get why she wanted to date Ben. Maybe he was different with her than he was with me. Just because I didn't want a relationship with a guy like him didn't mean that he wasn't right for somebody else. He and Danielle might be soul mates for all I knew.

"Then you should tell him."

"Ben's the only one who understands me. Some of us don't get rescued like you. When I told him about what happened to me freshman year at that Gamma party, he was the one who got me to see the counselor and helped me consider reporting . . ." Her voice trailed off in horror as she realized what she'd just said.

And it made everything click. Why Danielle had been so mean to me. Someone had hurt her, and it sounded like they'd gotten away with it. Nobody had saved her, and she'd lived with it. Unlike me. I totally understood for the first time why she had treated me the way she had.

I didn't know what to do. Pretend like I hadn't understood her? That didn't seem right. So I said what some of my friends had said to me. "I'm so sorry that happened to you. I believe you, and if you need someone besides Ben to talk to about it, I'm here."

She looked at me incredulously. But I truly meant every word. And I felt bad for every mean thing I'd ever said about her.

"Oh, because that's so what I needed. Your validation. I'm going inside." Danielle stomped away, not looking back at me.

She'd been overly truthful because of whatever alcohol she'd been drinking, and I'd been truthful because I didn't have any more time for, as Bash would say, bullsugar in my life. I hoped Ben and Danielle would reconnect and be stronger than ever.

It was so freeing to let them both go. Like a huge weight had been lifted from me.

Danielle's confession made me think about Logan. Not that I needed the excuse for my brain to go there, but what she'd said about Ben reminded me of Logan. One of the things I loved best about Logan was that he'd never tried to fix me. My dad had tried to in the beginning, not really seeing that what I needed was not to hang out with my friends or go to parties or pretend to be normal. I couldn't blame him for not understanding my needs. Not only because I didn't tell him, but because that's what he did as a job. He fixed teams and players, and he won. Logan just accepted me for who I was, and what had happened to me was just that—a thing that had happened to me but didn't define me.

I'd never really discussed serious things with my father. Ever. Maybe that's why I hadn't approached him about Logan. And why he didn't tell me about the new woman in his life. Even though we loved each other, we just didn't have that kind of relationship.

I pulled my phone out of my purse and checked it. Something I did multiple times a day to see if Logan had called. I didn't know what was happening with him, and I didn't want to intrude. He'd wanted to visit his mother alone, and I felt like it would be selfish to demand that he pay attention to me.

I'd be here when he got back, and we'd figure things out from there.

My phone buzzed as I was putting it away. I drew in a shaky breath when I saw that it was a text from him.

> You look beautiful. Red is definitely your color.

He could see me. Where was he? I spun around and then spotted him at the edge of the parking lot, walking toward me. I ran in my heels, my dress dragging along the concrete sidewalk, but I didn't care. I had to get to him.

As soon as he was within reach, I launched myself at him and threw my arms around his neck. His went around my waist, holding me tight against him. "You're here! How are you? Are you okay? What happened?"

"Do you want to go inside? It's a little cold out here."

I slid down him until my feet landed on the ground. "Yeah. Let's go." I took him by the hand. I probably hadn't needed to, but I wanted to. I wanted to touch him and reassure myself that he was real and that he was here.

As we walked into the student center, I found a study area that was empty, given that it was Saturday night. I got my first good look at him. There were deep bags under his eyes. I wondered when he'd slept last.

We sat down, and I tried to figure out what to say. But Logan spoke first. "My mom died. Which you probably already guessed. They buried her in the prison cemetery."

"I'm so, so sorry." I squeezed his hand and kissed the back of it. "What can I do for you? How can I help?"

"I don't know if anyone can help me. I've been feeling so guilty because I haven't cried. I feel like I should cry. That I should be devastated. But I realized that the feelings I had for her died a long time ago. She was never really a mom to me. It's like she died years ago. I'm sad that she died, but I feel like I already mourned her. So I'm not destroyed, and it makes me feel like I'm a terrible person."

"You're not a terrible person," I told him. He was one of the best men I'd ever met. Especially with everything he'd had to overcome. "Are you glad you went?"

"Yes. It was a good thing that I went and saw her. That I got to say goodbye. She woke up long enough to say my name, and I'm glad that she knew I was there. I hope that it brought her some peace."

"Did it bring you any peace?"

"It did. There's more a sense of closure than anything else."

"Are you going to take some time off?" I asked.

He shook his head. "I don't need any time off. I realized that life is too short. I think I've witnessed one of the worst things that can happen to a person. Dying in a prison hospital, being buried in a grave that doesn't even have your name on it. It made me realize that it's time to move forward with my life. Which is why I'm going to tell your father about us."

Panic shot through me. "Why would you do that?"

He looked deep into my eyes and raised my hand to his lips. "Jess, don't you know? I am in love with you. I want to be with you. No more hiding or waiting. I love you."

So many conflicting feelings hit me at the same time. Sympathy for what he'd gone through, guilty excitement that Logan had just said he LOVED ME, and then sheer terror at the idea of him saying as much to my dad.

All we'd done was kiss a couple of times, but it was more than that. My dad probably could have forgiven the kisses. But the no-girls rule wasn't only about the physical. He didn't want his players distracted by relationship drama. For Logan to have fallen in love with me . . . it was so far beyond what was allowed. My father would never forgive him. He would dig in his heels and wouldn't even speak about it. Just like how he was about that car in our garage. Logan would ruin everything if he went to my dad. "You can't tell my father."

He took both of my hands in his. "I can. And I will."

"I won't be the reason you destroy your life. I won't. You can't ask me to be."

"I'm not asking that of you. Loving you is not going to ruin me. I have too much ambition and self-respect for that. I'll find a way to make things happen for me. For us. Because it won't mean much of anything if you're not there to share it with me. I love you, Jess. I want to have a life with you."

Frantic, I tried to find a way out of this. There had to be an alternative. "We could date on the down low. Keep it a secret. My dad doesn't suspect anything. And it would only be for a few more months. We could do that."

"I can't. I can't live a lie anymore. Neither one of us should want that. We shouldn't start a relationship based on deceit."

"But you're on the one-yard line. Everything you want is right there. Just past that line. You only have to wait and make the right play. Don't rush it."

"That's not true," he said. "Everything I want is right here. We'll work the rest of it out."

"We can't. You don't understand my dad. He's like a brick wall. He'll never understand. He will kick you off the team." Logan didn't get it. He only knew Coach Oakley. But I knew the other side of Dad. I knew how formidable he could be when someone crossed him. I'd spent my entire life trying to please the man. Especially after my mother's death. I had always tried to be the perfect daughter, never causing him any trouble or upsetting him in any way. Following all his rules. This wasn't a boat we could rock and hope to remain unscathed.

Logan would not give up everything for me. Even if he quit football, there was no future where we could just be together. My father would never get over the betrayal from either one of us. And he was the only family I had left. I couldn't lose him.

It was becoming agonizingly clear that there was only one way to stop Logan. To make sure both the men in my life would be happy. Better for Logan to play and graduate and have a chance at his dreams than for him to wreck everything. I took my hands away from his, ignoring his questioning look. "No, we won't work things out. You shouldn't tell my dad anything because we're just friends. Only friends." That was our arrangement. We needed to stick to it. For his sake.

"That's not true. We're so much more than that."

He wasn't going to give up. I could see it in his eyes. "We're not." I almost choked on the lie I'd just told him. I tried to remain calm. I couldn't cry. Couldn't react emotionally in any way or else he'd know the truth.

"I don't believe you."

How could I sell this when I didn't believe it either? "I'm not denying that there's a physical connection between us, and we are friends. But there's nothing beyond that."

I don't care that you're kind and smart and funny or that you make me feel like I'm the most important thing in your whole world.

He didn't say anything. He just sat there and stared at me. Daring me to go on. I couldn't admit that I loved him, too. If I did . . . there'd be no going back. He wouldn't graduate, and I couldn't let him make that kind of sacrifice for me.

"Much as I wish I could say the same, I just don't have the same kind of feelings for you." They were the only kind of feelings I had for him, but somebody had to put Logan first, and I had no problem doing just that.

No matter what it cost me.

"I don't know what you want me to say to that."

I wanted him to say that he'd walk away and that this was over, and I'd take my broken heart and go cry a lot and he'd keep playing football and win the national championship and graduate with a degree. That's what I wanted.

But that wasn't what he said. "Even if you don't feel the same way, it doesn't matter. I broke the rules. I fell in love with you. I didn't mean for it to happen, and I don't regret that it did. I never will. And I'm still telling him."

He stood up and started walking away. Wait. He hadn't agreed to stay just friends. He was going to talk to my dad and ruin everything. Panic gripped my heart hard and my stomach turned over. He would ruin everything.

"Don't do this! You said no girl was worth giving up your future for!"

That made him stop, and I hoped that it had been enough to make him reconsider. That he'd turn around and tell me that everything would be fine and we just wouldn't see each other anymore. Instead, he kept walking until he went out the double doors.

I took out my phone and frantically texted Bash.

> Your boy's going to tell my
> dad that he's in love with me.
> You've got to stop him.

Maybe that would be enough. He would go home, come to his senses. Bash would talk him out of making this life-altering mistake. Logan would do the rational and logical thing.

He had to.

Even if it destroyed me.

Then I made a phone call to Keilani. "Can you meet me at my house? I really need you. Something terrible has happened."

She promised to be right there, and I picked myself up and went out to the parking lot to my car. I drove home, the mascara blinding me. I pulled over more than once to wipe away tears and snot and makeup. I was glad my dad was busy with some of the biggest alumni donors for the school tonight, schmoozing them into giving him more money for the team. I could not have dealt with him right now.

Keilani had a key and let herself in. She found me on my bedroom floor, still in my homecoming dress, curled up in a ball.

"Oh, sweetie," she said, coming over to crouch down next to me. "What's wrong? Why have you gone full fetal?"

"I told Logan we were just friends. He said he was going to tell my dad that he loved me and I tried to stop him by telling him that I didn't have any feelings for him at all."

I heard her mumble something about "martyr complex" before she sat all the way down. "Did he believe you?"

"I don't know. Thus the fetal position and the floor." I let out a shuddery breath that had the edge of a sob on it. "I hurt him so much. If you could have seen his face . . ."

"My mom always says, 'Could be worse.'"

"I don't think so. If this isn't rock bottom, it's close enough that I can smell the biotite."

"Tell you what. You shower, change into something that lets you breathe, and I will go find a snack for us. Do you have any ice cream?"

"No!" The word was more of a wail than I'd intended. How could I not have ice cream in the house?

I'd never done drugs, but I imagined the high would be a little like when I suddenly remembered that we had chocolate chip cookie dough in the fridge. The promise of white sugar made me feel slightly better. I told Keilani about it. She said she'd go downstairs and get it all ready for me. She helped me get to my feet, unzipped my dress, and pointed me in the direction of my shower. I didn't linger there. I needed carbs and I needed them now. If I stayed in the shower for much longer, I would just stand there and cry.

I towel dried my hair and went into my room to put on some comfy clothes. Clothes that I could be sad and eat a lot of food in.

Keilani was in the kitchen. She'd washed a load of dishes and set them out to dry, and she was in the middle of sweeping the floor.

"You don't have to do that," I told her.

"I don't mind. Now about that cookie dough." She turned to the fridge and found it on the back of the second shelf. Being out of sight was what had made me temporarily forget that it was there. I handed her a knife from the butcher's block, and she sliced the packaging off. She handed me half of the dough and kept the other half for herself. I knew I should probably get a plate or something, but instead I took a big bite from my half of the log. So good.

She picked up the plastic wrapping. "Hey, have you seen this before? It says right here on the package 'Never consume raw cookie dough.' Ha. The cookie dough patriarchy is not going to win today!"

I wasn't too worried. Even if I got salmonella, it couldn't possibly be as bad as how I was already feeling.

Keilani did get a plate and picked off small chunks to eat while I treated my half like a giant, thick ice cream cone and took bites off the top.

"Tell me what else is going on. What happened with his mom?"

I filled her in on the details between bites until the cookie dough that I shouldn't have been eating raw was gone and I was sad again. But between the sugar rush and being able to share the burden of my story with someone else, I was feeling a tad bit better. Keilani was so sweet; she just sat and listened. No "I told you so" or reminder that she'd warned me to steer clear.

Her expression was thoughtful, and I could hear how guarded her tone was. "Do you think maybe you didn't have the right to make that decision for him?"

"What?"

She shrugged, not quite making eye contact with me. "Maybe instead of lying about your feelings you should have been honest. Maybe you wanted to push him away first. Before he pushed you away."

I blinked at her in surprise. That was so untrue. I was being noble and sacrificing my own happiness for his. I did a *good* thing, and she was making it sound like I'd screwed up. "It was the only way to make him stop."

"You can't control other people and their choices. I understand your fears and concerns. I know you don't want to lose anybody else the way you lost your mom. But the solution isn't to preemptively kick them out of your life."

My mouth hung open and I couldn't respond. Because she was so, so wrong.

But what if she wasn't? What if everything she was saying was a hundred percent right? That I'd made a unilateral decision to protect my own heart? I hadn't been noble. I'd been selfish.

But I was in no emotional state to examine my feelings any further. "Okay," I said. "I don't want to talk about him anymore. I'm all tapped out."

Thankfully, she nodded. She understood and didn't press the issue. She was a good friend. Keilani still had most of her raw cookie dough left, and she cut it in half and handed one piece to me. Correction, she was a *great* friend.

"We're bad females," she said. "We should talk about something besides boys."

"Like what?" I asked with a sigh as I threw another chocolate chunk in my mouth.

"I don't know. Quantum physics?"

"What about it?"

"Um, it's the physics that is the most quantum-y?"

I shook my head, a small smile threatening to break out on my lips. "I did find out more fun news tonight. Danielle got the mentorship with Professor Gardiner."

"That's okay. Maybe you weren't meant to go to UW. There are lots and lots of schools with excellent math graduate programs."

"I know. That was kind of my feeling about it, too. But I wanted this one so that I could stay close to my dad."

"You shouldn't be basing your future on what your dad might or might not do. You need to make your own decisions on what's best for you and your life."

It sounded so much like the advice Logan had given me at our dinner at Madison and Main that I almost doubled over in pain. "I did get early admission to the University of Oregon and the University of Portland. That wouldn't be too far. But it isn't what I wanted."

"Well, we don't always get what we want."

Something I knew all too well.

CHAPTER TWENTY-THREE

LOGAN

Bash finally admitted that Jess had texted him in an attempt to enlist him on her side. He tried to talk me out of going to Coach, too, saying it was pointless since Jess had friend-zoned me.

"What do you have to gain?" he asked.

"My self-respect," I told him. That finally got him to stop. I'd grown up with people who would lie at the drop of a hat to get what they wanted. I'd always thought I was so much better than my mom and stepdad. But when push came to shove, I'd made the same kind of decision. When I realized that, I knew I had to be better. In order to look at myself in the mirror every morning, I had to do the right thing.

I decided to tell Coach at practice on Monday. That gave me the entire weekend to think about my last conversation with Jess. How she'd said she didn't love me. Some part of me, some neglected, abused little kid part of me, wanted to believe her. To believe that I wasn't worthy of love. Not good enough for her. But I also realized that she wouldn't be going to this effort to stop me if she truly didn't care about me at all.

She's never said "I love you."

No, she hadn't. But I still felt it. In her kiss. In her smile. In the way she looked at me like I was her favorite hero.

Once the damage was done and I was kicked off the team and out of school, I'd figure out a way to work things out with Jess. She'd probably be mad at me for a while, but once she saw how I had my life fixed, she'd get past it and we would be together.

Oh, I also had to fix my life. I wasn't sure what that would look like yet. I would probably need to get a job. With a sinking feeling in my gut, I got on Bash's laptop and started looking for local construction crews that were hiring. I could probably go to a thrift store and pick up some decent tools and earn first and last month's rent.

I didn't go to my Monday classes, figuring there was no point. Instead, I looked online for a cheap car. I'd need it to get to job sites. I narrowed it down to three, and Roman promised to drive me around later that evening to choose one.

I put my jacket on to walk over to practice. I stuck my hand in the pocket and felt something there. I realized it was the mini candy bars that Jess had placed there on Halloween. I'd worn this jacket to Texas. It was like a piece of her had gone with me. A sharp pang pierced my heart.

When I got to the locker room, I didn't bother getting changed. I touched the outside of my locker for what I figured was the last time. Bash was across the room, putting on his shoulder pads. He glared at me before yanking them down, hard. He was still mad. He didn't want me to go.

Coach came into the locker room and used his hands as a megaphone. "If I could have everyone's attention, please!"

The guys quieted down and looked at him expectantly.

"The rankings have just been posted. EOL is ranked number one, which means we are going to the national championship game!"

Loud cheers broke out, and some part of me wanted to join in as the guys slapped each other on the back and threw up high fives.

Just put this off. Play in the national game. Then tell him the truth.

I'd made a commitment to follow all of Coach's rules, and I was going to see that through to the end, no matter the cost. I would be better than my past and the people who'd raised me. I had to tell him now.

I pushed through my teammates, trying to get close to him. "Coach!" I called out several times until I got his attention. "I need to talk to you!"

"Suit up and come talk to me on the field."

"No, it needs to be private. Like in your office."

But he wasn't really hearing me. "Talk to me on the field, son. Let's go."

Then he left the locker room, with me still calling after him. Sighing with frustration and left with no other option, I went to my locker and changed into my practice gear. I left my shoulder pads off and hurried to get my cleats on. I carried my pads and helmet out on the field with me, just in case Coach insisted I put them on before he'd speak with me.

I stopped when I saw Jess on the sidelines. Was this her plan? To just shadow me and do what she could to stop me from talking to him? It wasn't going to work.

She tried to approach me, but I shook my head at her. This was happening.

Keilani was there, putting her arms around Jess. I was glad she had someone to support her since she wouldn't let it be me.

I stalked over to Coach Oakley, more determined than ever. "Coach, I really have to talk to you right now. It's important."

He took off his sunglasses. "I know you've been through something terrible and I hate to say this, but if you're going to ask me for some time off, I can't. It has to be all hands on deck for this game, and we need every minute of practice we can get. Southeast Missouri Junior College is too good. They're number two, right behind us. I'm going to need a hundred percent from you for this game so that we win. And the entire country can watch you lead us to that victory."

This was going to be harder than I thought. My pulse ricocheted around inside my body. I didn't want to do this, but I had to. "This isn't about the game. Well, in a way it's going to be about the game. Look, Coach, there's something I have to tell you. I'm in love with your daughter. I'm in love with Jess."

It was like every coach and player on the entire field went completely silent.

"What did you say?" he asked. I heard the shock and anger dripping from his words.

Some part of me yelled, *Abort! Abort! Abandon ship! Tell him you were kidding!*

But now was the time to be a man.

"It wasn't intentional. We were friends. Good friends. And we did our best to stay away from each other so it wouldn't turn into something more. And I could have lied to you. I could have lied to myself. But I promised when I first came here to follow your rules. All of your rules. I understood that was the price I was going to pay to be on your team and accept your scholarship. Because you said you wanted a team full of men with honor and integrity."

Coach had turned into a stone version of himself, and I briefly wondered if he'd take a swing at me. If he did, I probably deserved it.

"When I was in Texas, I realized that I'd never been that man. I'd lied, stolen, cheated, did what I'd had to do to survive. But being here on your team, I wanted more. I looked at where I'd come from and where I wanted to go. And I knew that I wanted to live a life with honor and integrity because I never had. I wanted to be the kind of man who would be good enough to date your daughter."

Still he said nothing, his mouth compressed into a tight line.

"I take full responsibility for my actions," I said. "I know what this means. It means I'm done on this team and that I'm done at this school. I accept that. And Jess has told me she doesn't love me, and I accept that, too. This wasn't about trying to win your approval or get you on my side.

It was about doing what was right. And I have you to thank for teaching me what that is. So thank you for that, thank you for letting me be a part of your team, and thank you for all the opportunities you've given me."

"Opportunities that you're now wasting." He spat the words out.

"That's out of my control. I wouldn't if it was my choice, but I respect your rules and I respect you. I'm sorry that I didn't hold up my end of the bargain, and I'm sorry if I let you down, but I'm not going to apologize for loving Jess. She's the best thing that's ever happened to me." I glanced over at her on the sidelines. "So I'm going to go get changed and withdraw from my classes. I should be moved out of my dorm tonight. Thanks again, Coach."

I walked past Ford, who stood there with his mouth hanging open. I patted him on the shoulder. "Thank you for all that you've done to train me. I really appreciate it."

He nodded.

Jess was my last stop. She had tears in her eyes, and I wanted nothing more than to soothe them away. "I know you don't understand, but I needed to do this today." I took in a deep breath, hoping this wouldn't be the last time her wildflower scent tickled my senses. "I told you so many times that there was no girl worth giving up my future for. No one who could make me walk away from football. I was wrong. There is someone. You."

I leaned over to kiss her on the forehead, aware of all the stares, some incredulous, some furious, but this was goodbye for now. When I got my life back on track, I would find her and fix this.

Nobody followed me off the field, and I heard Coach yell, "Let's go! We have practice. Do you need to run laps until you remember? Move it!"

Coach Oakley was not a yeller. He must have been really upset.

I changed back into my street clothes and left all my football gear behind. I hoped they would win their game against SMJC. These guys deserved it.

From the information I'd uncovered this morning, I knew I had to go to the registrar's office to get a copy of their withdrawal procedures and the actual paperwork to withdraw. I'd also have to meet with my academic adviser and visit the financial aid office to get everything officially done.

But outside of the registrar's office, I ran into Keilani.

"What are you doing here?" I asked.

"I'm your academic adviser, in case you forgot." She gestured toward a wooden bench. "Can we sit?"

Now that I was on my new path, I wanted everything done as quickly as possible. It felt like she was slowing me down. But I was going to have to talk to her at some point.

We sat and I waited for her to speak, curious about what she had to say.

"I'm sorry about your mother."

"Thank you. And thanks to the athletic department for buying me that plane ticket. I might not have made it in time if I'd gone by bus."

"It wasn't the athletic department. Coach Oakley paid for that ticket himself."

I wasn't sure how to take this news. Was it another kindness he'd showed me that I'd betrayed? Or did it mean that he cared more about me than he'd let on? Had I been important to him?

None of it mattered now, I guessed. That was all over and done with.

"So about this withdrawal thing," Keilani said. "If you quit now, you will have wasted half a semester. You'll have to start over."

"It wasn't wasted. I got to be with Jess." Time with Jess was anything but wasted.

Her eyes softened. "Regardless, what you did today was really brave."

"I didn't feel very brave."

"The opposite of brave isn't being afraid. The opposite of brave is staying quiet. And you didn't stay quiet. Even when it cost you everything. You really changed my opinion of you today."

"Are you saying I haven't charmed you?" I meant it to be playful, but it came out sardonic.

"I thought I had your number and I was wrong. And I'm glad that I was. Because I'm about to solve all your problems."

That made me straighten up. "How?"

"Finance is not my area of expertise, but ever since Jess mentioned what might happen if you two got caught, I've been working on resources. Talking to the financial aid office."

There was no help there. "My credit is ruined. I won't qualify for anything."

"When you got kicked off the team at F&T, did anybody offer to help you to finish out your senior year?"

"No." They'd just shown me the door.

"That's a shame. But I'm going to help you. Yes, you won't qualify for any traditional student loans because of your poor credit score. But there are some high-interest loans that you could take out. I spoke with a local credit union, and they're excited to work with you. And then next semester? We're getting you a bunch of federal grants, because you are very poor, my friend, and need the help. I mean, you're going to qualify for so much money."

It was hard to know how to respond. "Serious?"

"So serious. And I know the loan situation isn't great, but the tuition at EOL is much lower than at other schools. And I figure, better a high-interest loan than to be a semester and a half away from graduating and give up."

"I was planning to come back. When I'd saved enough."

"Well, now you don't have to worry about that, do you?"

Relief like I'd never known filled me up. All my worry, all my fear just dissipated into the atmosphere. She was saving my life. And my relationship. I had never felt so grateful to anyone for anything. "You're like a fairy godmother."

"Just a really good friend. I love Jess, and I expect you to treat her well. And for you to keep up your GPA. You've been doing so great, and I'd hate to see that come to an end. Which means you need to go back to your classes."

"I will. Starting tomorrow."

She stood up, and so did I. "Let's go to my office. I have the paper-work ready to go, and once you sign it, we'll get you a nice fat cashier's check. Do you need a ride to the bank?"

This was like when Coach first walked into my life and offered me a scholarship to play ball again. It felt too good to be true, but after all the crappy things I'd had to endure, I knew I could use a little goodness. "Yeah, I'd love a ride. Thanks."

"You're welcome."

"No." I came to a standstill, and so did she. "Seriously, thank you. You don't know what this means to me."

"Thanks to Jess, I think I have a pretty good idea. Just promise me you'll be good to her. Don't break her heart."

"I promise." I meant those words so fervently. I'd do whatever I needed to in order to keep her safe and happy and loved.

"Then let's go and get you your money."

I'd known my new life was going to start today. I'd just had no idea it would look so much like my old one.

Or it would, as soon as I convinced Jess that we should be together. Despite what she'd said, I knew she loved me. That we belonged to each other.

Keilani wasn't the only one who loved Jess.

CHAPTER TWENTY-FOUR

JESS

At some point soon there was going to be an ugly confrontation with my father. I left practice after Logan did and came home to think about what I wanted to say to my dad. It was not a conversation I'd wanted to have. I'd tried to live my life so that I wouldn't disappoint him. I'd said it was to protect him.

Maybe it had been to protect me. It had made it so that I didn't have to deal with serious emotions where he was concerned. Talk about my mother's death or the night of the attack. We just went on, as if those things had never happened.

But I didn't know if I'd done that for him or for me.

I loved him. He was my father. I'd done my best to take care of him and be the perfect daughter.

Only I wasn't perfect, which he'd found out. There were so many things to tell him, so much that I had to explain. I ran it through my mind over and over again. I didn't want to leave anything out.

I considered grabbing a piece of paper and writing out my talking points, but I figured that might be a step too far. I didn't want to come across as scheming. I needed to speak from my heart.

Because I knew how mad he was going to be. I soon realized that I had seriously miscalculated his anger level.

I'd seen that side of him so rarely that it surprised me when he slammed the front door. I took in a deep breath. Time to have one of those conversations I'd secretly always feared. I would convince my dad to see reason. To keep Logan on the team.

I would make the kind of sacrifice for him that Logan had made for me.

"Jessica Gail Oakley!" Uh-oh. My full name. My dad had gone biblical. He came into the living room and stopped short when he saw me on the couch. "Do you care to explain?"

"Have a seat, Dad."

For one angry moment it looked like he was going to refuse, but then he dropped into his favorite chair.

"I'm leaving EOL. I'm going to transfer to another school."

His eyes went wide. "You can't leave in the middle of the semester. You'll have to start over."

"I can and I will. Then when I'm at another school, Logan won't be breaking any of your precious rules and you can put him back on the team. You need him for the SMJC game. They have one of the best defensive games in the whole country. Your offense has to be perfect. Logan's the only one who can win this game for you. I can show you the numbers, if you'd like."

I could see my father's anger deflating, as if he were a leaky balloon. "You get free tuition here."

"Then I'll go into debt someplace else."

He grasped hard for those straws. "But you're supposed to be starting graduate school in the fall."

"Then I'll go spring and summer semesters to make it up. He's worth making this sacrifice for. I only wish I could do more."

"But . . . I don't want you to go."

"I don't want to go, either."

He sat quietly, staring at his hands. Then it was like he tried to rally his anger, to remember why it was he was so upset in the first place. "You broke my rules."

"I'm not on your team. Those rules don't apply to me." It was one of the reasons why I'd never spoken to him about them before. I hadn't needed to. They hadn't affected me. Now they did, in the worst way possible.

My dad wasn't deterred by my logic. "You also lied to me."

"I'm not trying to split hairs, but I don't think I lied. I did keep something from you. And I've been thinking about that a lot lately. I never used to keep secrets from you. It's why when I knew I was in trouble, you were the first phone call I made. I didn't think about the fact that I'd been drinking and it might make you mad. I just knew I could rely on you. But after that? So much of what happened between us was a lie. I couldn't let you know how I was really feeling. The guilt I had for your losing your job. The pain of what had happened to me, how it intrinsically changed who I was. How every time I said I was fine, every time I smiled like I was okay, when I hid bloodshot eyes and puffy eyelids behind sunglasses? I lied to you. Eventually I was fine. But it took a lot longer than you realize. So this thing with Logan? I don't know. It was one more secret to add to the pile of secrets. But I'm done with that now. I want to be open with you. And the truth is that even though I'm your daughter, you need him more right now. I'm asking you to choose him. My future's not in danger. Don't ruin his whole life because you're overprotective."

"Overprotective?" he repeated.

"Yes. Dad, you already protected me. You kept me safe. You don't have to keep trying. That's the reason for this 'no women, no relationships' rule, isn't it? You've asked your team to be honest, but almost every single one of them is lying to you. That rule is a step too far. Especially since you're not obeying it, either."

His face turned pale. "What?"

"I know about the woman you've been seeing. I know you're dating her and that it seems to be serious. And I'm happy for you. I am. I want you to find love again. Mom always said the entire point of being on this planet was to love other people. Don't you think it's a little hypocritical that you get to date but your players don't?"

"That's completely . . ." He got to his feet and started pacing. Something I hadn't seen him do in a very long time. "That's totally different!"

I blinked slowly, taking in a deep breath. I would stay completely calm. "It's not any different. You're telling people they can't love and you're wrong to do it. You were wrong to do it to me."

He halted midstride. "You love Logan?"

"So much!"

"But he said at practice that you didn't feel the same way about him."

"Because I lied to him. I was trying to protect him. I told him I didn't have feelings for him so that he could stay on the team and graduate. I would do anything to help him. I hoped it would keep him from telling you, but you can see how well that turned out. Now we're not together, and I feel like I've lost a limb."

He put his hands on his hips. "How long has this been going on?"

"You should know that we did everything in our power to not fall in love. We had all these rules in place to keep ourselves safe. I even tried to date someone else! But it happened. As for how long? I don't know. Part of me thinks I've loved him since I first saw him at that bus station. But do you know that I've never even told him? He practically announced it to the entire world today, and I haven't said it to him." The tears started forming, the lump in my throat growing by the minute. I would stay in control. For a little while longer. "I should have had the chance to enjoy falling in love with him. Instead I felt guilty and worried the whole time because of you and your stupid rules. You took that experience away from me, and it's something that I can't get back."

I shouldn't have been blaming him. The choices I'd made with Logan weren't my dad's fault. It was easier to put all the blame on him, but I had to own my decisions. As Keilani had pointed out, I was the one who had pushed Logan away by making a stupid choice. I'd been trying to protect myself just as much as my father had been trying to protect me.

I saw a look of regret on his face. "That was never my intention. I was only trying—"

"You were trying to keep me safe. I know. I'm not a little girl anymore. And I probably should have come to you sooner and talked to you about it. But I was afraid to because I knew how stubborn you'd be about it. Your way or the highway, right? Your rules are meant to protect people from getting hurt. But this situation has hurt me worse than Logan ever could have. Being apart from him is destroying me."

"Jess . . ."

I couldn't take any more. The throat lump was making it so I couldn't breathe; my tears were waiting to fall. "Put him back on the team, Dad. Don't make my sacrifice meaningless. And you better hurry before he leaves school. Logan's not the kind of guy who waits around."

Then I fled, my tears blinding me as I ran up the stairs.

Out of habit, I slammed my bedroom door shut, hard. Like I used to when I was younger.

Only this time it had consequences. One of the shelves near my closet, the one with my mom's fairy houses, fell off the wall, and there was a sickening cracking sound as the houses landed on the floor.

"No, no, no . . ." I ran over, picking up the houses.

Most of them were fine. But there were three, three that had broken. Three that I couldn't replace or get back. I sat on that floor, surrounded by the fairy houses, and cried my heart out. For my mom, for my dad.

For Logan.

I didn't know how much time had passed. It felt like hours. I cried until my head hurt, until my lungs ached, until my throat throbbed. Eventually I heard my dad calling my name. I turned to see him crouched down next to me, looking concerned.

I held up the broken houses. "They're broken. Mom's houses. This happened because I was upset and acting like an idiot."

He took the houses from me. "It's okay. We can fix them. Glue them back together."

"But it won't be the same." Now there'd be scars. People would be able to see where the houses had been glued.

"It will be different, but that doesn't make them any less beautiful. It doesn't change what they mean to you." He took the broken houses and put them on my windowsill and then gathered up all the others and deposited them on top of my dresser. He offered me his hand once he'd cleaned up and had me sit down on my bed. He sat in my desk chair, looking very serious.

"I've failed you as a father. You never should have felt like you couldn't talk to me. That's what I'm here for. We should be able to talk to each other."

I nodded, my throat feeling thick. "I know. We should."

"So I'm going to start." He took in a deep breath before letting it out. "Her name is Sharon. The woman I've been seeing. She's a sales rep for a major sportswear company, which is how we met. She travels a lot for business, and when our schedules sync up we try to spend time together. It's not serious yet, but it could be. I think maybe I've been holding back a little. I'd never try to replace your mom . . ."

His voice caught, causing my heart to hurt for him. "I know that, Dad. But you deserve to be happy. And, as has been repeatedly pointed out to me, to have your own life. So do I."

He nodded. "You're right. After . . . what happened I just wanted to keep you close. So that I could watch over you. Despite what you think, you'll always be my little girl. I've had a hard time letting go."

"Me too. I felt like I owed you. Your life got upended because of the attack and I felt responsible. If I hadn't been there, if I hadn't been drinking, all those kinds of things kept running through my head. You had to give up so much for me, and I wanted to, I don't know, repay you. Stay with you so you wouldn't be alone."

"That's not your job. Your job is to go out and spread your wings and live the life you want. And if that includes Logan Hunt, well . . ."

What was that supposed to mean? "Well, what?"

"Well, I'll probably have to find a way to deal with it. If you love each other and he makes you happy, that's all that matters to me. And you should tell him. You should never put off telling someone that you love them because you never know how much time you'll have."

"Oh, Dad!" I leaned over to hug him tightly.

"But before you do"—his voice sounded slightly muffled—"I need to have a talk with him. There're some things we have to get straightened out. Some changes that have to be made."

I nodded, releasing him. "Does this mean you're going to keep him on the team? Because he deserves that. He deserves to be seen. He doesn't think he's good enough to play professionally, but, Dad, you've coached him. You know how good he is. He should have every opportunity, every chance."

"We'll see. And don't go running off to any other schools yet. Let me see what I can figure out. I've got some phone calls to make."

Then he left my room, and for the first time in a long time, I felt hope.

CHAPTER TWENTY-FIVE

LOGAN

"Dude. Wake up. We gotta go."

I slowly opened one eye to find my roommate staring down at me with a grim expression. "Go where?" I asked. I'd intended to spend tonight at a motel, but with Keilani's check, I'd be able to not only pay tuition but room and board. I could stay put and pay my own way. I just had to ignore that double-digit interest rate that made me feel sick to my stomach every time I thought about it.

"Emergency team meeting. Let's go." He threw my blanket off me, grabbed me by the shoulders, and forced me into an upright position.

"I'm not on the team anymore," I reminded him. "Which means I don't have to go to meetings, emergency or otherwise."

Bash went into my closet and grabbed a hoodie, throwing it to me. "You're still on this team. Nobody's officially kicked you off anything yet."

"Just because it's not official doesn't mean it isn't going to happen. Don't you remember how I broke the biggest rule ever? Don't date Jess?"

"Until somebody says, 'Logan, you're done here, get off my team,' you're still a member. Heck, you're still the mother-father-captain. You have to be there."

I threw my hoodie onto my bed. "You have fun, but I'm going back to sleep."

"Nope. I didn't want to have to play this card, but shuffle, shuffle."

What was he talking about? "What does that mean?"

"You know, the reason you had the time to fall in love with Jess was that I didn't tell anyone about you two. Namely, her father. If I'd told him at the beginning, you guys would have been separated and not even been friends. So you owe me. Now you're going to do this thing for me because I'm your friend and I'm emotionally blackmailing you and friends show up for each other."

I grabbed my hoodie off my bed and yanked it on. "Fine. If it'll make you shut up, I'll go. But don't be surprised when Coach manhandles me out of the locker room. What's this meeting about, anyways?"

Bash shrugged. "No idea. It can't be anything as extravagant as the show you put on today, but I'm sure old Coach has some tricks up his sleeve."

Grumbling, I followed him out into the cold autumn air. I didn't understand why there was a meeting and why Bash thought I needed to be involved. Maybe I'd just sit near the back and sneak out when my roommate wasn't looking.

We arrived at the team's meeting room. It was the same place where we'd had our first Owls meeting. When Coach had told us his rules. And I realized that even if I'd known then how it would all turn out, I wouldn't have changed a thing.

I tried to ignore the stares of the other players, who were probably wondering, as I had, what I was doing there.

The coaching staff stood near the front of the room, involved in a serious conversation. They also looked like they had no idea what was happening.

Coach Oakley entered the room. "Thank you all for coming. I'm going to get right to the point. It's been brought to my attention, rather forcefully, that I have been unfair to you as a team."

Murmurs broke out in the crowd, and I shifted in my chair. What was he trying to say?

He went on. "That some of my rules, especially the one that prohibits you from dating, are wrong. So I'm going to change that."

Now there were full-on conversations, some yelps.

Coach held up both of his hands. "There are some rules that will stay in place and that I will be serious about. Like no alcohol or drugs. I will kick you off the team the first time you fail a drug test. You also need to maintain your GPA and be respectful. But I'm going to meet with my staff about what should be a rule and what should be a guideline."

"You're saying we can date?" Colnetti called out.

"I'm saying you can date."

The entire room erupted in cheers, high fives, and fist bumps.

So now the team could date. I wished he'd made this decision a week ago, when I was still actually part of the team.

Or did this just apply to the guys not dating Coach's daughter?

Bash grinned at me. "See? Aren't you glad you came? You should trust me. Always. That should be one of the rules. 'Bash is always right.'"

"That's it!" Coach yelled. "Everyone have a good night! I'll see you at practice tomorrow. Logan, can I speak with you?"

My roommate slapped me on the shoulder before taking off, and I worried for the women of EOL who were about to be blatantly hit on as the football team left the room en masse.

I made my way down the stairs to where Coach waited for me.

"Logan, I want you to stay on the team. You've done everything I've asked of you, without complaint. You're an exceptional football player, and you deserve to play."

"I . . ." I was so relieved and happy, but I was still confused. "I guess I don't understand what happened."

"Jess happened. She was willing to leave EOL so that you could stay and play. Give up everything for you."

I put my hand over my chest because my heart had started to hurt. "She said that?"

He nodded. "She also pointed out how unfair I'd been, and that I should stay out of my players' love lives."

"So, does this mean that it's okay for me and Jess to date?" I wanted to be very, very clear on this subject. "I can still play for you and go to the national championship and keep my scholarship and date Jess?"

Coach folded his arms and gave me one of his infamous stare-downs. "That's not up to me. That's up to you and Jess. You're a good man, and whatever's between you two, I'm staying out of it. You don't need my permission or my blessing. You two can make your own decisions. I only ask that you treat my daughter with—"

"Respect?" I supplied.

There was a smile at the corners of his lips. "Yes, respect. Be at practice tomorrow. We're going to beat SMJC."

I offered him my hand, and after a moment's hesitation he shook it. That's when I knew we were going to be okay.

Now I just had to find Jess.

I pulled out my cell phone as I headed outside. It was a little late and I should probably wait, but I couldn't. Even though I didn't believe her, it was okay if she didn't love me. Eventually she would. Especially now that there were no more obstacles between us.

My notifications must have been turned off, because I had text messages from Jess. A lot of them.

Where are you?

What did my dad say?

I'm in the parking lot at your dorm.

Where are you? Where are you? Where are you?

I replied.

I'm on my way to you.

It was true. All these obstacles, all these things in our way, they'd been leading us to each other. The path hadn't been easy, but I knew it had all been worth it. I ran the whole way there, back to Jess. I spotted her car right away, and she saw me at the same time. My heart raced with excitement, anticipation, and all the love I felt for her. She got out of her car and ran toward me, launching herself into my arms. I needed this. I needed to feel her pressed against me, her heart beating fast like mine. To fuse ourselves together so that no one could ever tear us apart. I held on tight.

I was never letting her go again.

That lasted for about a minute until she released me, stepping back so that she could look me in the eye. She left her arms around my neck. "My dad texted me to say that he was meeting with the team and that I could come down after to talk to you. I didn't know when after was, so I've been waiting and waiting. What did my dad say? Why did you have a meeting?"

"He said we could date."

"What?" she exclaimed. "Are you serious?"

I nodded. "And I want to date you. I want that more than anything else. I want you to be part of my life. I've wanted that for a while. Like when my mom was dying. I wanted you to come with me to see her. I shouldn't have made that decision without talking it through with you. I just thought I could . . . I don't know. Compartmentalize my life. Protect you from something hard. I was wrong and I shouldn't have done it."

She sighed and I felt her fingers stroking the nape of my neck, sending heated chills through me. "It wasn't like you were the only one who made a unilateral decision about our relationship. I did the same thing when I told you we were only friends. I'm so sorry I did that. I think I put us both through a lot of unnecessary pain."

"We were both making unilateral decisions when we should have been working together. Maybe to protect ourselves. I don't know. But I don't want to do that going forward. I want us to decide things as a couple."

"Agreed," she said. "We'll be adults and figure it out."

"Speaking of, were you really going to leave EOL for me? So that I could keep my scholarship?"

"Of course I was."

I shook my head. "I think no more of that martyr-y stuff, either. We shouldn't push each other away thinking that we're protecting each other. We're stronger together."

Her arms squeezed me tight. "You're right. So let's promise that we'll always talk things out."

"I promise," I told her. Then I kissed her briefly, gently. There were things to say, and now was not the time to get caught up in another soul-searing kiss. There'd be time for it later. "I know how much it would have cost you to change schools." Part of me knew the reason why, but I needed to hear her say it. "Why were you willing to do it?"

That adorable smile I loved made the corners of her mouth quirk up. "Why? Because I love you. I'd do anything for you."

"You love me?" Even though I'd anticipated and hoped for her answer, it was much different hearing the words coming out of her gorgeous mouth. It filled me with warmth, with her sunshine. Jess loved me.

"You know that I love you. Even when I denied it, I loved you."

"Well, yeah, but it's nice hearing you say it."

We both laughed, and I nuzzled her nose. She was mine and I was hers and we loved each other.

I couldn't believe this was my life.

"So if you love me," I teased, "I'm guessing that means you probably want to date me."

The smile slid off her face and the trusting, intense look I loved so much was back. "I'm committed to this. To us. Do you remember what you told me about trying to go out with Ben?"

Way to put a damper on things. "How about we don't talk about What Might Have Ben right now?"

"No, listen. You told me that anything was possible. That it was first and ten. You're right. It is first and ten, Logan. I want to go down that field with you. I want to get another first down and another until we reach the other end and score a touchdown."

That light feeling was back, the one that made me feel like I could conquer the entire world. "You know I don't need your help to score a touchdown, but I get what you're saying. I suppose the real test would be . . . will you go see a French movie with me?"

She laughed and shoved my arm. "This is how much I love you. I would go see a million French movies with you."

"That is true love," I agreed, kissing her. I could kiss her now. Whenever I wanted. I could spend all day kissing her. Other than when I had those dumb class and football obligations.

My phone rang, as if it existed solely to interrupt me kissing my girl. "What now?" There was a number I didn't recognize.

It just said "Portland." My heart beat a bit faster. Was it possible? It had to be a wrong number. But what if it wasn't? "Hello?"

"Hello, is this Logan Hunt?"

"Yes."

"Great. This is Rick Hammerston. From the Portland Jacks. I'm sorry I missed you last week, but I heard you had a family emergency."

"Er, yes." I didn't want to go into detail about what had happened; I was much more curious about why he was calling me. I mouthed his name to Jess, and her eyes got comically big.

"I've reviewed all your tapes and I've made some calls. I'd like you to declare your eligibility this year for the NFL draft."

I almost dropped my phone. "What?"

"What's he saying?" Jess whispered, trying to get my attention.

"I can't make you any promises, but I think your prospects are excellent. We'll be in touch. And tell your coach he only needs to leave one message next time." Rick said the words good-humoredly, but I knew that Coach had stepped up for me again.

This was more than I had ever dreamed possible. I had the woman I loved, and now I had the possibility of playing professional ball. Life could not get any better. I grinned. "Okay. I will. Bye!"

"Well?" Jess demanded when I hung up.

"Rick Hammerston thinks I should declare my eligibility for the draft. He thinks I have a shot at getting chosen."

She started jumping up and down. "I knew it, I knew it, I knew it!" She kissed me fiercely, with so much joy and love that I wasn't sure if my heart could take it.

"We should celebrate!" she said.

Technically nothing had happened yet, but I was in the mood to celebrate, too. "Do you want to go to Gino's and grab a pizza?"

"I do."

I had a flash of Jess saying that to me as we stood in front of a minister, getting married. And the thought didn't terrify me. If anything, it felt . . . right.

"You should practice saying that."

"Saying what?"

"'I do.' Not now. Someday."

She grinned at me. "Someday sounds perfect."

I put my arm around her and we started walking toward her car. "We should try it out. Do you think we'll win our game against SMJC?"

She kissed me again. "I do. But then where will I be when you're a big national champion and NFL superstar?"

"Right next to me. Because none of that means anything without you."

I opened her car door to let her get in, and she smiled. "That probably means you should make sure you guys win that game. Sounds like a lot's riding on it."

"The outcome of the game doesn't matter. I have you. Which means I've already won."

EPILOGUE

JESS

Five months later

"Hurry up!" I called out. He was going to miss everything. The official NFL draft was starting.

Logan came running into the living room, jumping over the back of the couch to sit next to me. My dad hated it when he did that. Which was why he only did it when my dad was gone. Which I still couldn't believe. It was draft day, and my dad was out? Not here, watching? It was very unlike him.

"Don't you think it's strange that my father's not here to see if you get chosen?"

"Not really." He had a weird edge to his voice, like he knew something I didn't. I figured he was nervous about the draft. He kissed me briefly. "And don't worry about it starting. This takes a long time. I haven't missed anything yet."

"It's okay. I don't want you to get snapped up right away."

My fear, even though I hadn't admitted it to him yet, was that he'd be drafted by a team halfway across the country. Once the Draft

Advisory Board had predicted he'd be chosen in the first round, I knew how unlikely it was that he could stay on the West Coast. It's what we'd hoped for, but it would be better for him professionally to be playing in Kansas City than hanging around here in Seattle (or Portland—I hadn't decided which school to attend yet) with me. Truth be told, I was waiting to see where he ended up. As Keilani had told me, there were plenty of great graduate programs all over the country.

We had discussed the long-distance thing; I just wasn't sure I wanted it. He'd been gone for a week at the invitation-only NFL Scouting Combine, and it had killed me to be apart from him that long. I didn't know how I could do months at a time.

My phone buzzed with a text from my father.

> Any news yet?

> No Dad, it just started.

He was out on a date with Sharon, whom I had met and had dinner with several times. I liked her. That seal of approval had helped speed their relationship up a little, and now my father called her his girlfriend.

Which was taking some getting used to, along with the dopey grin he sported whenever he talked about her.

But if she made him happy, then I was all for it.

Plus, he'd seemed a lot more relaxed. It had started when he'd changed some of his rules to guidelines and allowed the players to date whomever they wanted. My dad had confided in me that his fear was that the boys would run crazy without those restrictions in place, but they'd stepped up. If anything, the effect was that the team was able to focus better because they weren't so caught up in hiding their secret lives. The tenor of their practices changed, and they'd won the national championship against SMJC easily. By twenty-eight points.

The draft was set up so that the worst teams got to choose first. That way they could presumably improve their team by getting some of the best players in the country. Or they were planning on grabbing up a player and then trading him to another team for a large cash payout.

The NFL teams were all set up at their tables, and runners took their choices to the various NFL officials.

The team from Cleveland picked the first round. "Anthony Andersen!"

We hadn't thought that Logan would be the number one pick, but I'd still held my breath until the name was read because there had been a chance.

"Now that we know I'm not the number one pick, I should probably go study for finals. I'd really like to graduate in a couple of weeks."

He was ready for his finals. He just wanted to make sure he still graduated with that 4.0. "I have the power to prevent you from graduating. By means of distraction." I started nuzzling his neck.

"You do. Nobody can distract me the way that you can."

"Good." I sat straight up. "Then stay here and watch this live, because it's very important and you can study later. I'll even help you with your math."

"Fine." He let out an exaggerated sigh.

The teams kept choosing and names kept being announced. But not Logan's.

The Seahawks chose somebody else. So did the Raiders. And the 49ers. The Chargers. The Rams. We were running out of West Coast options.

"Just remember that Tom Brady didn't get chosen until the sixth round." Logan had repeated this fact, along with naming other famous players who didn't get chosen until much later, over and over before the draft had even started in an attempt to calm me. But we would have to wait until tomorrow if he got chosen in the second round, and until the day after that if he wasn't picked until the fourth round.

I did not have that much patience.

The doorbell rang, and Logan jumped up. "I'll get it."

"Doesn't anybody need a quarterback?" Besides me?

There were voices at the front door and then Logan was doing something in the kitchen. The first round was coming to a close. Until all that was left was the Portland Jacks.

I crossed all my fingers and started to pray. *Please let it be Logan; please let it be Logan.* It would be so perfect. I could go to the University of Portland, a school where I'd been accepted. I'd decided to focus my graduate degree on education with an emphasis in mathematics. Logan had inspired me. Not only because of how much I had enjoyed tutoring him, but because I wanted to help students see that math wasn't so scary.

The team had ten minutes to make their decision, but the runners were already moving with their note cards. I had to close my eyes.

And then they announced, "Logan Hunt!"

Was I hallucinating? I rewound the live broadcast, just to be sure.

"Logan Hunt!"

I started jumping up and down and screaming. He had missed it. "Logan! Logan! It's the Portland Jacks! You're playing for the Jacks! You're going to get a Super Bowl ring!"

"What about this ring?"

I turned around and initially couldn't process what I was seeing. My heart jumped up into my throat while my knees felt woozy. Logan was down on one knee, holding up a ring box and a glass of milk. He handed me the glass first.

"Emotional-support milk. Just in case you need it."

I kind of did. I took a big drink and then set it down on the coffee table, wiping away any potential milk mustache. Next, he handed me a slice of pizza. I wasn't hungry. I could barely breathe. I set that down, too. At least now I knew why my father was mysteriously absent.

"What are you doing?" I finally asked.

"I'm proposing to you. With accessories."

"You really only need the one accessory," I whispered, afraid to look at the ring. Like if I made direct eye contact, it would disappear. "Did somebody just deliver that?"

He smiled. "No, it's been in my pocket the whole time. The guy at the door delivered your Gino's pizza. Half sausage, ham, and black olives, the other half pepperoni."

"Oh." I sighed. "The first pizza we ever shared. That is so sweet." I waited for him to say something more, my heart still thundering in my chest. "So, were you going to propose today or . . ."

"I've been trying for a while now to find the right words. The ones that would tell you how much you mean to me and how much I love you. I kind of hoped that when we got here, they'd magically appear. And, uh, they haven't."

How could I love this man more than I already did? "You don't need the perfect words. Just the asking ones."

"Jessica Gail Oakley, I love you. Don't tell Bash, but you are my best friend. I want to spend my life with you, laughing with you, having children with you. You are my family and my whole world. I want you to be my wife. Do you want to come to Portland with me? Marry me?"

It was a good thing I'd practiced. "I do."

ACKNOWLEDGMENTS

For everyone who is reading this—thank you. Thank you for your support, for your kind words, and for loving my characters as much as I do!

Thank you to Alison Dasho, my new editor, for your thoughts and insights. I'm excited at the opportunity to get to work with you, and I hope we will be a team for many books to come! Thank you to Megan Mulder for getting me the contract for this book. Thanks to the entire Montlake team for all that you do for me and my books! And a special thank-you this go-round to Charlotte Herscher—for your skill and talent, your patience and understanding, and for helping me to find the heart of the story I wanted to tell. You make everything I do better!

Thank you to the various copyeditors and proofreaders who have worked on this story. Thanks to Erin Dameron Hill for her fantastic cover. Thank you to Sarah Younger just for being awesome and for totally getting my snark. Thanks to Nancy Berland for helping me get this book out into the world.

For my children—I know there have been some rough times lately, but never forget how proud I am of you and how loved you are.

And Kevin, who's built like a linebacker but has the heart of a teddy bear—I will love you for time and all eternity.

AUTHOR'S NOTE

Thank you for coming along on this journey with me! I hope you enjoyed Logan and Jess's story. If you'd like to find out when I've written something new, make sure you sign up for my newsletter at www.sariahwilson.com, where I most definitely will not spam you. (I'm happy when I send out a newsletter once a month!)

And if you feel so inclined, I'd love for you to leave a review on Amazon, Goodreads, the bathroom wall at your local watering hole, the back of your electric bill, any place you want. I would be so grateful. Thanks!

ABOUT THE AUTHOR

Bestselling author Sariah Wilson has never jumped out of an airplane or climbed Mount Everest, and she is not a former CIA operative. She has, however, been madly, passionately in love with her soul mate and is a fervent believer in happily ever afters—which is why she writes romance series like The Royals of Monterra and #Lovestruck. After growing up in Southern California as the oldest of nine (yes, nine) children, she graduated from Brigham Young University with a semi-useless degree in history. She currently lives with the aforementioned soul mate and their four children in Utah, along with three tiger barb fish, a cat named Tiger, and a recently departed hamster who is buried in the backyard (and has nothing at all to do with tigers). For more information, visit her website at www.SariahWilson.com.